"Dylan doesn't bother me, and I didn't ask you to stay in the car so you could thank me."

At last Cade could get his mind back on track to the most important question he'd ever ask.

"Right." Brijette brushed a stray wisp of hair off her face. "Which patient did you want to discuss?"

"I don't want to talk about a patient. I wanted to speak to you in private."

She squirmed in her seat and he imagined she knew what was coming.

"I want you to tell me who in hell is the father of that child."

Dear Reader,

Sometimes we all have secrets we want to keep and preconceived ideas that are hard to let go. In this story, Brijette Dupre has to deal with both. But she'll learn that occasionally when the truth comes out and we let go of our preconceptions, life can be all the richer for it.

I hope you enjoy Brijette and Cade's story as I revisit Cypress Landing, Louisiana, and their volunteer search and rescue team. I love to hear from readers. You can send me a note at Suzanne Cox, 107 Walter Payton Dr., # 271, Columbia, MS 39429 or by e-mail to suzannecox@suzannecoxbooks.com. Be sure to visit me on the Web at suzannecoxbooks.com or superauthors.com.

Sincerely,

Suzanne Cox

UNEXPECTED DAUGHTER

Suzanne Cox

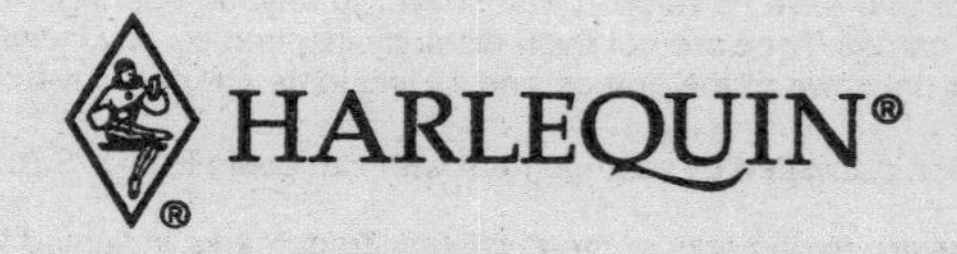

TORONTO • NEW YORK • LONDON
AMSTERDAM • PARIS • SYDNEY • HAMBURG
STOCKHOLM • ATHENS • TOKYO • MILAN • MADRID
PRAGUE • WARSAW • BUDAPEST • AUCKLAND

ISBN-13: 978-0-373-78134-8
ISBN-10: 0-373-78134-2

UNEXPECTED DAUGHTER

This edition published by arrangement with Harlequin Books S.A.

www.eHarlequin.com

Printed in U.S.A.

ABOUT THE AUTHOR

Suzanne remembers writing her first stories when she was about nine or ten years old, and she's been writing ever since. In February of 2002 she decided to try to get her writing published. On February 14, 2005, she sold her first book, *A Different Kind of Man,* to the Harlequin Superromance line.

While trying to decide what she wanted to be when she grew up–besides a writer–she worked a variety of jobs. She has a bachelor of arts in English with a minor in secondary education, a bachelor of science in nursing and a master of science in career and technical education with an emphasis in adult education. She's also a National Board Certified Teacher in career and technical education. Along the way she's worked as a high school English teacher, an elementary school teacher, a registered nurse on a cardiac unit, brain injury rehab unit and several different medical-surgical units. She's also done stints as a home health nurse and a community health educator at a hospital. These days, when she's not writing, she's at her day job as an allied health instructor at a high school career and technology center.

In her spare time, when she can find some, Suzanne enjoys reading, painting, biking and fishing. She's presently "livin' her dream" in south Mississippi with her own personal hero husband, Justin, and her boy in puppy dog clothes, Toby, who masquerades as a miniature pinscher.

Books by Suzanne Cox

HARLEQUIN SUPERROMANCE

1319–A DIFFERENT KIND OF MAN

To my husband, Justin, for being perfect
even when it's hard, like when
I've misplaced my checkbook, again.

To my friends at CLCC–Jan, Steph, Lisa,
Cathy and the guys, who are more like family than
anything else.

To my in-laws for just keeping me in the family
amid all this insanity.

CHAPTER ONE

SWEAT TRICKLED DOWN the side of Brijette Dupre's brow and a few loose strands of jet-black hair stuck to her damp chin. The ancient air conditioner in the other room did little good, especially in this heat. Brijette wiped her face with a paper towel as she counted sample packs of an antibiotic.

"He needs to take these three times a day with food and try to keep those stitches dry and clean. I'll be here next Thursday all day and I'll want to see that cut."

The bony woman moved her head in agreement, her stringy hair falling into her eyes. She held on to the barefoot eight-year-old boy. Brijette made a last swipe with a sterile towel in an attempt to remove one more spot of dirt from the child's skin. She wanted to tell the woman to take the kid home and give him a bath, or at least toss him in the creek. But you didn't tell these people what to do or expect them to live by any other standards than the ones to which they were accustomed. She should know. She'd been one of them for the first seventeen years of her life.

Brijette helped the boy off the portable exam table and led mother and son to the door. The breath of cooler air made her wish she could leave the door open, but she couldn't treat patients in front of the customers who came and went in the run-down store. Anton Guidreaux, who owned the place, had been good enough to let them use an empty storeroom attached to one side of his building as an exam room. As a nurse practitioner, Brijette worked under the license of the doctor in town. She normally practiced in the clinic with him, helping him see patients. But on Thursdays she came to the small community of Willow Point and offered medical care to those not likely to get it otherwise.

More than a few of the people in Cypress Landing wondered why she came here. They figured if those people wanted to see a doctor, they could come to town. *Those people.* Other folks in town made it sound as if she jetted off to another country every week. As though the simple people who still chose the life of the backwater and swamps were of a different species. This was Louisiana, not some Third

World country. How would the woman who'd just left feel, sitting dirty with worn shoes in the pristine waiting room at the clinic in Cypress Landing? No, Brijette was doing what she had to, for them and for herself, or at least for the girl she used to be.

"Brij, I see trouble coming."

Brijette left the storeroom, to see what Alicia was talking about. Alicia Ray was the nurse who assisted her at the weekly clinics in this rural community off the Mississippi River. Brijette joined her on the porch steps and unconsciously gripped the other nurse's shoulder.

"Oh, no!" she whispered.

Ten feet away, a young girl staggered toward them with the help of a boy who looked as if he might faint or run at any minute. The girl struggled with her very large and very obviously pregnant stomach.

The two women jumped to the ground, grabbing the girl. With the young man's help they managed to haul her into the exam room and hoist her up on the table, which was definitely not intended for delivering babies. Unfortunately, Brijette figured transforming the space into a delivery room wasn't an option.

"Go see if you can fine a land-line phone—there's no reception here on your cell. Call the clinic and have them get in touch with the helicopter rescue service. We'll need it. Let them know what kind of situation we've got."

Alicia hurried from the room and the boy followed her.

"You can stay if you want," Brijette called to him, but he didn't respond, shutting the door behind him instead.

"He's scared," the young girl on the table mumbled.

"What about you?"

She started to reply, then gritted her teeth and tossed her head from side to side in pain.

"What's your name?" Brijette tried to hold the girl's hand and dig into her supply box at the same time.

"Regina." The word exploded on a whoosh of air from the girl's mouth.

Brijette let go of Regina as the girl relaxed a bit, and moved to open another box. They didn't stock delivery supplies. But unless the paramedics could materialize on the spot, she might have to deliver this baby with whatever equipment she could find.

"Yeah, I'm scared."

Brijette glanced at the girl who watched her with wide, watery eyes. She'd almost forgotten she'd asked that question.

"Regina, have you seen a doctor during your pregnancy?"

The girl shook her head. Brijette didn't bother to ask why not. At this point her lack of medical care couldn't be helped. She piled the items she might need to use onto the tray by the table.

"How old are you?"

Regina stared at the wall, giving no answer.

"Don't worry. Nothing's going to happen to you or your boyfriend if you tell me."

"I'm seventeen."

"And your boyfriend?"

"He's twenty-two, but he's my husband. We've been married more than a year."

"That's good." Brijette tried not to sigh out loud. What else could she say? She thought of her own daughter, Dylan, who still hadn't reached her teenage years. Kids occasionally had to grow up fast and, like herself, Regina seemed to be one of them.

"Do you have family—mother, father, grandmother—we need to contact?"

"No. My mama and daddy moved a year ago. I didn't want to leave my boyfriend, so they let me stay and get married."

Brijette heard sad stories nearly every time she came here. This was simply another one to add to the list. What kind of parent dumped their teenage daughter off on her boyfriend because she didn't want to move? In the middle of searching for a box of gauze, she paused. How could she be thinking like that? She knew exactly what kind of parent would do such a thing, one less mouth to feed and no kid hanging around your neck. Without her grandmother, that could very well have been her about to have a baby with no family to help.

Brijette pulled more supplies from a box. "Is it time for the baby to come?"

Regina's brows knitted into a confused expression. "What do you mean?"

"I mean, how many months have you been pregnant? Is this your ninth month or is this baby early?"

The girl fisted the sheet covering her and didn't answer.

"Regina, I really need to know if I'm going to deliver a premature infant."

"I think it's eight or nine months. I'm not real sure."

If they ended up with a two-pound preemie Brijette would really be in a mess. Her mind raced to the few times she'd had to help Doc Arthur with emergency deliveries at the small local hospital in Cypress Landing.

She heard the door open as she finished tying a sterile towel to the metal rods on the side of the table, fashioning stirrups as best she could. As Brijette finished preparing the supplies, Alicia entered the room with Regina's husband behind her.

"T.J." The girl reached toward the young man. He looked as if he might keel over.

Brijette smiled at him. "I'm glad you decided to come in."

Alicia began to help Regina remove her clothes and put on the hospital gown Brijette had unearthed from the bottom of a box.

With the girl positioned on the table, she moved the sheet to check her. Brijette sucked her breath in between her teeth and Alicia looked to see what was wrong. The nurse gasped. Brijette reached for sterile cloths, piling them at the end of the table.

"What's the matter?" the girl asked as she groaned with a contraction.

"Nothing. Everything's fine," Brijette responded, which was true in a sense. She couldn't see a thing wrong and the vital signs Alicia called out were good. But there was no way to monitor the baby, who didn't plan to wait for the paramedics. The top of the head was already visible.

"Regina, on the next contraction, I need you to bear down and push."

"Is the baby coming now?" Regina started to cry. Alicia wiped the girl's face with a moist cloth. The temperature in the room had soared and sweat rolled from the four of them.

"I'm sorry, Regina, but this baby is coming now and I need you to work with me."

WHEN BRIJETTE COULD finally step away from the table, she sighed at the sight of her blood-stained scrubs. After throwing her gloves in the garbage, she dumped plenty of antiseptic gel in her palm, rubbing it lightly on her hands and arms before wiping with a paper towel. Not exactly prescribed usage for the stuff but the sink was in another part of the store and this would have to do for now.

There was a banging sound outside and loud voices broke the silence that had finally settled in the small room. With only a brief knock beforehand, two paramedics rushed in with a gurney.

They stopped short at the sight of the healthy baby.

"Guess you don't need us after all, Brij."

She snorted at Michael, the lanky medic. "Well, it wasn't by choice, I promise. At least you can give Regina and her daughter a quick ride to the hospital. I didn't even hear the chopper come in."

"I'm not surprised." He paused as he and his partner eased mother and child onto the gurney. Alicia helped roll the bed to the door, while Michael stayed behind. "The chopper's across the river. We'll have to go back to it by boat. That's where the nearest clearing is."

"I guess if the two of them have made it this far, they can survive a boat ride."

He didn't respond but glanced around the room instead. "So, this is your clinic."

"Yep." Brijette grinned, realizing that most of the medical people in town knew she came here, but few had actually seen her exam room.

Michael took a deep breath. "Stinks like a pigpen, and it's hot as hell."

If she hadn't been friends with the guy for years she might have been offended. "Thanks a lot. We did just deliver a baby in here. Besides, we don't all have the luxury of an air-conditioned ambulance or helicopter."

"Relax, I didn't say you stink, which of course you do."

She laughed and threw the near-empty bottle of antiseptic gel at him. He caught it with a grin. "I better go before your nurse and my partner drop our patient on the stairs."

Brijette followed him out front. From there she watched as Michael trotted down the dirt road after Alicia and the other paramedic, who were rolling the gurney toward a waiting boat. The breath she'd been partially holding since she'd seen the girl struggling to the clinic slipped from her lungs and she leaned against the wall of the store.

"Whoowee, *chère.* Never 'spected *that* when you set up shop here."

Brijette turned to see Anton Guidreaux sitting in a rocking chair several feet away. She hadn't noticed him before.

"Neither did I, A.G." Brijette pushed sweat-soaked hair off her neck. Anton Guidreux was too formal a name for him, so it had been shortened to A.G. long before she remembered making the trek to this place to buy flour, sugar and whatever else her grandmother needed.

A.G. got up to go back inside and paused to pat the top of her head as if she were still five. "Glad you were here, girl. Don't never think folks ain't proud to have you. Might not say it, but you know how that is."

Her head bumped the wall as she nodded. "I didn't come here expecting thank-yous."

"Know that, *chère.* Don't mean I can't tell you thanks here and there."

She bobbed her head again, staring at the floor as A.G. left her standing alone. After one more deep breath she went back to the exam room. Fanning the door, she tried to encourage a bit of cool air to come inside. She wrinkled her nose. Michael hadn't been joking. The scent of sweat and blood hung in the room, making it positively reek. *And me, too,* she admitted with a wry smile. Disinfectant spray bottles sat on top of a box and she took one, squeezing the trigger, shooting generous amounts on the exam table.

"Are we done for the day?"

Brijette continued cleaning the table as Alicia rejoined her. "Unless it's an emergency, we're going to pack and go home. I'm exhausted. Besides, it's going to take an hour to clean up and get the supplies loaded on the boat."

With a shove, Alicia moved a box against the wall and began to mop the floor. In minutes, they were both dripping sweat again.

BRIJETTE SET the last plastic storage container onto the deck of the twenty-eight-foot fishing boat. She could get to her field clinic by car, but it would take hours, beginning with a ferry ride across the river. Traveling by boat made more sense. Alicia untied the vessel from the old dock and Brijette started the engine.

As she steered the boat away, she caught a final glimpse of the wooden store on the slight rise above the water. Past the store sat the small community church with white paint peeling off the walls. A couple of wooden houses on stilts were visible in the distance. They were a ten-minute ride from the river and another ten minutes to Cypress Landing. A trip she knew well. She'd made it more times than she could count, and the summer after her senior year in high school she'd made it every day to work at the tire factory in Cypress Landing and, frequently, the coffee shop on Main Street. But that was another life.

The Mississippi loomed in front of them and Alicia grabbed a handhold as the boat lurched into the faster-moving water. Brijette slowed the engine.

"Can you believe what we did?" Alicia shouted above the hum of the motor.

Brijette stared at the river in front of her. The thought of all the things that could have gone wrong with the delivery hadn't actually hit her until now. Her legs turned to jelly and she leaned against the seat behind her. She and Alicia had brought a life into the world. What would've happened if they hadn't been there? What if the girl had delivered at home or in the back seat of a car? Or even worse, on the bottom of a rusty aluminum fishing boat as she tried to get to a hospital?

"I'm glad you were there with me," she shouted back at Alicia. To her dismay, her throat clogged and her eyes filled with tears. Getting all weepy wasn't her style, but she'd never delivered a baby by herself before.

A hand touched her arm. "Don't worry, me, too." Alicia pointed to her own cheeks, wet with tears, and started to smile. They were both laughing with tears trickling down their faces as the boat bumped toward Cypress Landing.

"I HEAR YOU HAD an adventure today."

Brijette chuckled, stacking the last container in the storage room at the clinic. "It was more of a nightmare than an adventure, Emma."

"Well, the baby and mama were both fine, so you must've done a great job."

"Nature did the work, I just…caught the package." She glanced at her soiled clothes and shook her head at the clinic's longtime receptionist. "I need to go home and clean up."

"Doc Arthur wants to see you before you go."

"I'm on my way."

Located a block off Main Street, the clinic

was actually an antebellum home that Doc Arthur had refurbished to use as his business nearly thirty years ago when he'd first arrived in Cypress Landing. Brijette crossed the lobby and went down the hall to his office. Tapping on his half-open door twice, she pushed into the room.

"Emma said you wanted to see me."

"Brijette, come in. Good work you did today."

"Like I told Emma, I didn't do much. The baby came without much help from me." She didn't bother to say how petrified she'd been that something would go wrong or that the baby would be premature.

"Still, you were there. You do good work in that community."

She shrugged. "I hope so."

The older man tapped his fingers on the armrest of his chair. "You do, and don't ever forget it."

"What did you need me for?" She didn't want to sound as though she was rushing him, but she was beginning to smell herself, which wasn't a good thing.

He sat back in his chair, shoving papers across his desktop. "You know I've been having problems with that valve in my heart. They say I can't put off the surgery much longer."

Brijette rubbed her hands together in her lap. Doc Arthur had been like a father to her since she'd lost both parents when she was young. He needed the surgery, but she wasn't sure how they'd make it at the clinic without him. She sat a little straighter in her chair. Wait, as a nurse practitioner, if there was no doctor here then she couldn't work.

"Don't panic, I'm not going to close and make you find a new job."

"I'm sorry. Was I that transparent? You know I'm worried about you, but I have to admit I really love my job and all the people I work with, especially you. I'd hate things to change."

"Unfortunately, I will have to make a change. I'm bringing in another physician."

"But, that's great. We've been so busy." She couldn't stop smiling, not just because she'd get to keep working here, but because they'd needed help more than she was willing to admit to Doc Arthur.

"I hope he'll want to stay, but in all honesty he's only coming to help out while I'm at home recuperating. He's planning to open his own clinic in Dallas later on."

"We'll have to make him fall in love with Cypress Landing." Brijette couldn't imagine that would be too hard.

The older man studied the far side of the room and she wondered if they were finished. She leaned forward to get to her feet and Doc Arthur suddenly started speaking again. "He's been here before. You know him. That's why I wanted to see you."

Brijette narrowed her eyes. "What do you mean?"

"It's my nephew, Cade Wheeler. You remember him, don't you? The two of you were friends that summer he visited, before he started medical school and you and your grandmother left to live with your aunt."

Despite the air-conditioning, a droplet of cold sweat formed at the base of Brijette's neck and began a slow trickle down the middle of her back. She'd come a long way since that summer and could happily live the rest of her life without seeing Cade Wheeler again. For a brief second, she thought she might get a new job elsewhere—possibly, New Orleans. But she loved her life in Cypress Landing, and she couldn't imagine trying to raise her daughter in the city. The mention of his name made her insides gel with fear. She'd prepared for this possibility, had tried to tie up the loose ends, but her plan had never really been tested. That was about to change.

"Yes, I remember him."

"Good, I know you two will be able to work together."

She could only move her head slightly in agreement. Beneath her feet, the floor seemed to tilt.

CHAPTER TWO

THROUGH THE WINDOW, the silvery water of the creek rippled beyond the edges of the white sand banks. Cade Wheeler leaned against the kitchen counter as he set his glass in the sink. A ham sandwich and iced tea were the extent of his lunch—not exactly like dining at one of his many lunch haunts in Dallas. But he definitely wasn't in Dallas now. When he'd first begun working at the busy family practice in the city, life had been idyllic. Or at least that was what his mother kept telling him. His clients had been the wealthy and often self-absorbed. When he wasn't seeing them in his office, he tried to avoid them. Occasionally, when his mother insisted, he'd attend the same functions as they did on the weekends—extravagant parties or golf outings. Life had taken on a surreal facade as he worked diligently to build his image as family physician to the upper crust. It should've been easy, should've felt right—after all, he'd been part of the upper crust his whole life.

From his office window in Dallas he'd had a view of the designer shopping village across the street, and he'd occasionally wondered if somewhere along the way he'd made a career mistake, perhaps even a life mistake. He had. He should never have imagined he could work there when his heart wasn't in it. One ugly incident at the clinic had exposed the truth about who his friends really were. Most of his colleagues had turned their backs on him when he'd needed their support. Even his mother had been damaged in the fallout. He might not have agreed with her ideals, but he'd never wanted to see her treated badly. Their idyllic life had been forever changed. Where exactly that change would take them remained to be seen.

Empty boxes surrounded him. The wood floors in the kitchen glowed with a new unscuffed coat of varnish. Cade recalled the owner's reluctance to rent the expensively renovated old home. The man had been hoping to sell the place, but after a year on the market and not even one offer, he'd finally acquiesced to the inevitable. A little money each month was better than none.

"It's too much house for you," his mother

had griped when she'd seen it, for the five minutes she visited. He gazed across the yard once again. Sure, the rambling two-story contained more rooms than he'd ever use, but the huge master suite with its luxury bathroom had been like an oasis in the desert of this town. The final draw had been the very scene in front of him. Nowhere in Dallas did you get a house or apartment with a view like this from your kitchen window. Willow trees bent toward the gurgling water of the creek, surrounded by grainy sand. Green grass dotted with oak, hickory and pine trees took up the space in between the water and his house. He'd signed a lease for six months; after that he'd leave Cypress Landing and open his own clinic in Dallas. It was the only life he really knew and he'd promised his father just before he died to make sure his mother's life remained as unchanged as possible, which meant Cade needed to be in Dallas, where his mother was happiest. For now, he'd enjoy the view.

A tree limb flopped at the edge of his yard and he thought he saw something moving near the water. An object appeared to fly through the air and land with hardly a splash in the middle of the stream. It was a fishing cork. Another soon appeared a few feet away from the first.

Trespassers already. Whoever had tossed the cork in the water might not know the house was occupied now. The idea of a couple of old men shouting, drinking beer and generally interrupting his quiet afternoons on the patio made him decide to go down there to make sure the fishermen knew he had taken up residence.

Cade let the screen door slam behind him intentionally, but neither cork moved. Still invisible behind the edge of the trees, the fishermen either hadn't heard him or just didn't care. People had different ideas about property and propriety. If they wanted to call him an ass from the city for asking them to leave, that would be okay.

You don't belong in that town. Never will. His mother's words from years ago echoed in his ears. But that wasn't true. He had fit in and would have gladly stayed forever. That was before he'd learned that even simple country people had hidden agendas. Coming back now had been a matter of obligation, a show of respect for his uncle and nothing else. Starting his own clinic in Dallas wouldn't be easy, but at least he knew what to expect from the people there.

Cade nearly walked on top of the fisherman before he realized it. One lone fisherman with two homemade cane poles—or should he say fisherwoman…or fishergirl. Ragged, cut-off blue-jean shorts revealed a pair of spindly legs connected to dirty bare feet. Muddy tennis shoes sat beside the trespasser. The girl pulled at her blond ponytail, then wiped a gritty hand across her forehead.

"Hi. You're the guy that's renting that house."

"How do you know that?" His eyes narrowed. Was she psychic? And weren't kids taught not to talk to strangers?

"I was in the car yesterday when my babysitter, Norma, brought you that cake. You're a doctor and you work at Doctor Wheeler's clinic. She said you were a nice young man, so I figured you wouldn't mind if I fished at your house."

What was he supposed to say to that? If he sent her packing, would she go and tell the whole town what a mean guy the new doctor was? Finally, he sighed and stuck out his hand. "I'm Cade Wheeler. You seem to know everything else about me."

She giggled as she laid the poles on the ground and scrambled to her feet, placing her damp, grimy hand in his. Huge green eyes fringed with thick lashes studied him briefly before she sat down again.

"Wanna fish? I got two poles."

The moment had arrived when he could let her know, in no uncertain terms, that he didn't want people fishing in his yard. What if she fell in the water, drowned and the parents decided to sue him? Or worse, what if someone came along and suspected he was some kind of child molester, hanging out with a young girl he didn't even know. He knew what he'd do in the city: run back to the safety of his house. But the country was different. People knew their neighbors and took care of each other and their kids. Overhead, the sun fought its way through the leaves and flickered in the emerald eyes shining up at him. Well, hell, he couldn't resist that, could he? He couldn't be mean to the kid.

He sat on the bank and held out his hand. She grinned, passing him the extra pole. "I'll fish with you for a minute, but then we probably need to let whoever's in charge of you know where you are."

She nodded. "I'm Dylan. That's a big ole house just for you, or do you have some kids coming later?"

"No, it's only me." The girl sighed and he hated having to dash her hopes of future playmates. "You live around here, Dylan?"

"Not too close. A few miles that way on the other side of the road." She waved her hand in the general direction. "I stay with Mrs. Norma during the day when my mom works. Mrs. Norma lives right there."

She pointed up the creek to a clearing a few hundred yards away, where the creek disappeared around a bend. The frame house had probably once been part of the same property as the house he now rented. But over time, as with many things around here, the property had likely been sold for cash.

"Your mom and dad work in Cypress Landing?"

She didn't reply immediately, watching him instead, as though trying to deciding how much information she should give a stranger. He wondered how old she might be. He'd seen kids in his clinic but guessing their ages hadn't been one of his strong points. This one could be anywhere between eight and thirteen.

"My mom works in town." She didn't supply more, but gripped her pole when she noticed that her cork had disappeared. Pulling her line in with no fish attached, she dug into a plastic cup sitting next to her, producing a soggy piece of liver to put on her empty hook. "Mrs. Norma keeps this for me in the freezer for bait."

"She doesn't care if you're fishing here by yourself?"

"I probably shouldn't go this far, but there aren't any fish behind her house. I can swim and this creek isn't more than waist-deep. Besides, she'll come look for me in a few minutes."

As if on cue, a figure appeared at the clearing. Dylan waved and the woman moved out of sight.

"She's probably coming."

Within minutes Dylan's babysitter had negotiated the path to where they were sitting. Cade handed his pole to Dylan and got to his feet.

"Dylan, you shouldn't be this far from the house by yourself."

"I know, but I wasn't catching a thing there, haven't in days. This is Cade. You brought the cake to him yesterday, remember?"

Norma relaxed. She obviously hadn't recognized him immediately. He offered his hand.

"It's good to see you again. I really enjoyed the cake."

She frowned at the child, who chose to ignore both of them to focus on the corks bobbing in the current. "I hope she's not bothering you."

He glanced at the skinny blond girl, feeling the tug of what he was missing as a single man with no kids. Something he'd been feeling a lot lately. "No, she can stay. I've got to finish unpacking." He was such a pushover.

"As long as you don't mind, she can stay for one more hour. Your mom will be by to get you soon."

Dylan nodded.

"I've got to get back to the house. I left a roast cooking."

"Nice to see you," Cade called as Norma hurried down the path.

"You, too."

He stood for a minute, watching Dylan toss the line of each pole into the water.

"She seems like a nice lady."

The girl studied him between her long lashes. "She is. I've been staying with her since we moved here three years ago, after my grandmother died. We'd been living with her and my aunt in Layfayette, but my mom wanted to come here." She stopped abruptly, as though she had decided she'd shared too much.

He waited for another minute, then remembered he needed to be emptying boxes. He had to go to the clinic in the morning to start learning the office routine before his uncle left. Doc Wheeler had tried to get him to wait until Monday, but he figured he'd need as much time as possible with the old man there, so going in on a Thursday made sense to him. What else would he be doing other than shuffling boxes around?

"I don't have a dad."

He jerked his attention to the girl, wondering where that statement came from.

She must have realized his confusion. "You asked if my mom and dad worked in town. I told you my mom did, but I don't have a dad. I mean, I do have one—I guess everybody does—but I don't know him. He didn't want kids, so he left before I was born."

Cade couldn't be sure what had brought on that outburst but Dylan had returned to eyeing her cork, anxiously waiting for a fish to take it under.

"I'd say that was his loss."

She gave a soft smile. "Why don't you have children?"

He decided he definitely should have stayed in the house. Kids asked too many questions. "I don't know. I guess I'm waiting for the right woman to have them with."

Dylan rubbed her thumb against her pole and seemed to ponder that for a moment. "You mean, you've never met a woman who could be the right one? Not once?"

It took him a second to answer. When he did, the words were much more wistful than he had intended. “I did once. But she didn’t feel the same way.”

“And I’d say that’s her loss.”

He laughed at the silly grin she sported. He saw the end of one pole bob and noticed her cork had gone under the water. Swinging the pole in the air, she brought the silvery catfish to the bank.

“I knew there were fish here, Mr. Wheeler,” Dylan shouted and grabbed the fish to remove it from the hook.

Cade smiled as she grappled with the slippery thing. “I better get back to unpacking. And you can call me Cade. None of that mister stuff.”

The girl nodded, busy sliding the fish into a bucket of water she’d brought. Cade had always liked the fact that having fun in Cypress Landing often didn’t include a party, a golf course or a group of people you didn’t care anything about. Maybe spending time here wouldn’t be so bad.

DYLAN HELD HER POLES as she watched Cade walk back to his house. Tossing the lines into the water again, she looked at her watch and decided she might as well go. She pulled the lines in and wound them around the poles, then dumped the single fish back into the water.

"I'll be back for you another time," she whispered.

She started down the path to Mrs. Norma's house. Her friends would say Cade was cute, and he was. But he was older too, maybe even older than her mom. He was fun like a dad might have been if she'd had one. She twisted around to get one last look at him before he went inside and decided she wouldn't tell her mom she'd met Cade right away. She might not like Dylan being friendly with a stranger. Her mom and Cade would be working together, and soon enough, he wouldn't be a stranger. If she ran and jumped in the car when her mother came to pick her up, Mrs. Norma wouldn't have time to tell her. She smiled at her neat plan and hurried on to the house. Maybe this wouldn't be such a boring summer after all.

THE SMELL OF HAIR SPRAY in the nurse's thickly teased gray hair had become noticeable. At least, it had Cade crinkling his nose. For the fifteenth time this morning, she frowned and gritted her teeth at him because he had to ask her where to find something, bandages this time. Either Mary Carson was mad about his being there or else she was generally in a bad mood. He wasn't sure which. Today he'd run nonstop from patient to patient, often dressing wounds and giving a shot while Mary was busy helping his uncle. They'd had to eat their lunch of take-out po' boys in the little kitchen at the back of the clinic in between seeing patients. Cade knew one thing was certain: the nurse practitioner would not be going off on Thursdays anymore with the clinic's only other nurse in tow to see patients for free somewhere in the backwoods. When Uncle Arthur left, she'd have to stay and help him here. No wonder his uncle's heart was bad, if he had to work with this little help. Sighing, Cade pushed open the door to one of the examination rooms, prepared to dress another wound.

"I'M GOING TO CALL and have the receptionist make you an appointment to get hyperbaric treatments for the sore on your calf." Cade took a final look before pressing the last piece of tape on top of the dressing. He still had another patient waiting and the hands of the clock were already approaching half-past five.

He noticed that both the older man on the table and his wife standing next to him looked perplexed, which told him he'd forgotten to use people speak instead of doctor talk.

"You need to go to Baton Rouge and have

special treatments to help your leg get better. You're diabetic, which means you don't heal as easily as most."

The woman fidgeted with her threadbare handbag. "What's a hyperbark treatment?"

Cade made a mental note to be clearer in the future. He'd been accustomed to his patients often having as much knowledge as he did concerning their diseases and potential treatments.

"It's nothing to be worried about. They'll put you in a special machine that puts you under pressure. It makes your body heal faster."

"How often I gotta go?" the man asked, wiping at the last few wisps of oily gray hair on his head.

"I don't know. It could take several treatments."

"I ain't got the time or transportation to get to Baton Rouge several times. I need to work, and my old truck can't take long trips."

"It's less than an hour."

"That's a far enough piece for some folks."

"Your leg might never get well if you don't go."

The man glared at him, and Cade tried to maintain his most professional demeanor and not show his ever-shortening temper.

"Where's little Brij? She always fixes me up fine without any trips out of town."

"I don't know Brij. But I know you need to go to Baton Rouge." Cade's voice modulated an octave or two louder than he'd intended.

"I wanna see Brij and see what she thinks!" the old geezer responded in a voice that rattled the walls. Behind Cade the door to the room swished open and he dreaded the sight of the scowling Mary Carson.

"What's the problem?"

He didn't look up immediately, but he noted that this wasn't Mary's voice.

"I'm trying to talk with a patient, if you don't mind," he barked, turning angrily toward the door. He'd really had enough of people second-guessing his opinion. He was the damned doctor, after all.

"Brij, I got another sore on my leg."

The old man sat quietly waiting as doctor and intruder stared at each other. Cade knew shock registered on his face, but he couldn't control it. Brij was obviously short for Brijette, a name he would've shot to the moon and back to keep from hearing again. Now the woman had materialized in front of him.

"What are you doing here?" He tried not to wad the patient's chart in his hand.

She stepped into the room, shutting the door behind her. Green scrubs skimmed over more curves than he remembered, but her silky hair remained jet-black. He wondered, when she let it loose from the tight knot, if it would flow halfway to her waist like it used to. The skin on his chest tingled at the memory of the midnight strands washing across his body, and his hand rubbed the tingling spot automatically, as if the silken pieces had actually touched him.

"I work here." She passed in front of him to stand next to the patient while he tried to drag his mind to the present, to remember the truth about her.

"You can't."

She glanced at him, then began pulling at the tape on the dressing he'd applied only minutes ago. "I can and I do. But don't you think we should discuss this later?"

Cade hated to admit she made good sense. He stood by while she examined the wound, wanting to tell her she had no business coming in here undermining his authority. She'd likely recommend a hoodoo magic mud potion for the guy and in a few weeks they'd be sending him to a surgeon to have the leg removed.

"I recommended hyperbaric treatments. I believe they have the equipment for that in Baton Rouge." He waited patiently for her to argue and possibly offer to say a few words over the leg. She'd always had a way with what she called swamp medicine. He called it mumbo jumbo.

"I'm afraid Dr. Wheeler is right."

"But why can't I use that red stuff you gave me before?"

"I don't think that will work. This is much worse than what you had before. I'll see that Emma schedules transportation for you when she makes the appointment."

The old man and his wife nodded while Brijette taped the dressing in place. Cade followed her so closely he nearly bumped into her when she stopped in the hall.

"I appreciate you not offering some other treatment to my patient."

She shrugged. "You ordered what was appropriate."

"Well, thank you very much, considering that I am the doctor here."

"And I'm the nurse practitioner. I happened to have seen that patient several times before. He doesn't take care of himself like he should. But I guess you didn't see much of that where you came from."

He frowned. "So what was the red stuff you gave him before? A potion you whipped up from the eye of a lizard and some swamp root?"

A cool mask settled on her face. He didn't make a habit of belittling people's backgrounds, but she had made him this way, showed him what really mattered to her. So what did he care if he hurt her feelings?

"Actually, it was a new wound medication we've just gotten in. I've used it occasionally with good results."

He hadn't expected her to answer, and when she did he realized not only did he sound like a complete ass, but they'd drawn a crowd. Two patients from other rooms waited in the hall, watching them. Emma, the receptionist, peered around the corner and a blond girl he'd never seen before appeared near the back door with a plastic box in her arms. She was wearing scrubs, so maybe she worked here, too.

Rather than respond, especially since there wasn't much he could say, he strode to Emma's desk and dropped the man's chart on the counter.

"Schedule hyperbaric treatments for him—it's in the chart." He glanced toward Brijette. "And transportation."

Whatever "transportation" meant. He hoped Emma knew what to do. He didn't wait for an answer, but left the desk and stomped to his uncle's office. On the way, he pulled the prescription pad from his pocket. How he'd overlooked her name on it all morning, he'd never know. Maybe his brain had been selectively blocking everything about Brijette Dupre from his mind, including her name printed right in front of him.

CHAPTER THREE

"WHY DIDN'T YOU TELL me Brijette Dupre worked in this clinic?"

His uncle leaned away from his desk. "Why don't you sit down, Cade?"

Cade walked across the small office and dropped into a chair.

The older man sighed. "Honestly, I wasn't sure what existed between the two of you all those years ago. I knew you didn't part...' happily. I figured you might not come if you knew she worked here. I hoped once the two of you met again, you could get past your differences."

Realizing his lungs might burst from holding his breath, Cade let the air slip between his teeth in a soft hiss. He'd made an idiot of himself in front of his uncle. Uncle Arthur knew he and Brijette had been more than friends, but if Cade acted like a scorned lover, everyone would think he still had feelings for her.

"I'm concerned she'll practice her brand of medicine in this clinic on patients I'm responsible for."

"What brand of medicine do you mean?"

"You know exactly what I mean—all those voodoo, hoodoo remedies. I know her grandmother taught her that stuff."

"She does know the old customs, but she's a licensed nurse practitioner and that's what she does here." Doc paused for a moment, his brows knitting together. "Brijette's completely ethical and would never jeopardize a patient's health."

Cade twisted in his seat. "Well...I'm not sure if I trust her."

His uncle smiled. "You'll see she's completely trustworthy. Remember she was only seventeen when you were here before. Whatever happened, just keep that in mind. You've both done some maturing since then."

He nodded, unwilling to say what he was really thinking, which was that certain people never changed. Instead he moved on to another topic of concern.

"If I'm going to run this clinic, she's not going to be off on Thursdays. I'll need her here."

Doc sat forward, crossing his arms on the

desktop. "No, she won't go for that. Besides, she's not off on Thursday. She has a makeshift clinic in one of the small communities near the river, taking care of patients who can't make the trip here to see a doctor."

"She'll have to postpone it until you're able to work again."

His uncle straightened, his features hardening. "No, Cade. I've worked this clinic by myself and you can, too. If it's too much for you, I'll postpone my surgery until I find another doctor to help while I'm away."

If he'd wanted a reason to leave, he had one now. He could say it was too much work and take off to Dallas immediately. He studied the slightly pasty complexion of the man in front of him. He actually owed his uncle more than a few months' work at his clinic. The man had taught him about life, and not the high-society life his mother had so wanted him to adhere to.

Cade had spent his first twenty or so years learning how to live with the country-club set from his mother and father. When he'd come to Cypress Landing, he'd seen how much his uncle cared for his patients and the community in general. People truly respected the man, and not because he had money. Uncle Arthur didn't have a multi-million dollar business. Cade had never known another doctor who really helped people like his uncle did, and it had inspired him. He'd begun to see a different kind of life than what he'd always known with his parents.

After everything had gotten so ugly, he'd decided he'd been mistaken about what life in Cypress Landing would be. So he'd gone to work in Dallas at the ritzy clinic and found that unreliable and untrustworthy people weren't confined to one geographical location. He'd been happy here, at least for a while. He could do this. Besides, half his boxes were unpacked and he'd made one friend already, if you could call the little blond trespasser his friend. He needed more time away from Dallas, to get that nasty taste out of his mouth. No, he'd stay here and deal with Brijette Dupre. How hard could it be?

ANYONE WHO PASSED HER in the aisle of the small pharmacy would have thought she was in the throes of debating what type of lotion best suited her. She hadn't really looked at the bottles lined meticulously on the shelf, even though she did intend to buy one. Instead she kept seeing the image of Cade unwavering in her mind. His blond hair still hung long across his forehead, shoved slightly to one side to show off his green eyes. On the outside Cade hadn't changed much at all; she wondered if he was still the same on the inside.

Anger and shock, that's what she'd seen on Cade's face. Doc Arthur hadn't told him she'd be in the clinic even though he'd told her a few weeks ago his nephew was coming. Had he been afraid Cade would be a no-show if he knew she'd be around? Did the old man know everything that had happened years ago? She hoped not. He didn't act as if he knew a thing, but he could know the whole story and be faking it for her benefit. He might have even realized the truth. That idea made the cold sweat pop up on the nape of her neck again. Doc was like family to her. He wouldn't betray her, even though Cade was his real family, would he?

"Brijette." The voice of the pharmacist at the back counter brought her mind into the present.

Thankful to be able to stop herself from that line of thinking, she grabbed the nearest bottle of lotion and hurried to the rear of the store where Elliot Arneaux, the pharmacist and owner, bagged several bottles of pills for the elderly Mrs. White. The lady waved at Brijette when she left, and Elliot motioned for her to come behind the counter.

"What's wrong, Elliot?" She leaned her hip against the cabinet.

"I won't keep you long, but I wanted to show you this." He held a piece of paper in front of her.

It was a prescription written from one of the clinic's pads with her signature at the bottom. On closer inspection, however, she saw that it wasn't her signature but a fair likeness. A sick feeling started to grow in the pit of her stomach.

"Elliot, this is for OxyContin. You know I don't write scripts for narcotics like that. Doc Wheeler writes those."

The pharmacist frowned. "I thought so, but I figured with Doc Arthur sick, you might have done it without thinking. I didn't know the guy who brought it in. I told him I'd have to check with the clinic before I could fill it. He wandered around the store, like he was waiting for me to call, and the next thing I knew he was gone."

Brijette passed him the prescription, trying to keep her fingers from shaking. "You'll have to report this."

"I'm going to. I wanted to talk to you first."

"Thanks. This could get me in trouble if it's happening in other towns. You guys do monitor these narcotic scripts, right?"

"Yeah, we report excessive narcotic prescriptions from individual doctors. But we're small, and I know most of the people who come in here. In some other town this would've been filled without a question."

The sick feeling in her stomach began to spread. She didn't need another problem to add to her list. A prescription with her name on it that she didn't write definitely fell in the territory of trouble, especially when it was for a narcotic with a very nice street value. Brijette decided she'd have to talk with Matthew Wright as soon as possible. If this had been happening in other pharmacies, the sheriff of Cypress Landing would know, and if he didn't, he'd check with the city police. Noticing the time on her watch, she hurried to the front to make her purchases. It was late and she still had to pick up Dylan.

GRAVEL CRUNCHED under her tires as Brijette began the quarter mile trip off the highway to her house. The small white clapboard was like a hundred others in the area. Most had been part of a larger plantation at one time or another. She and Dylan had lived in different phases of remodeling for the past three years, while they turned the once ragged place into a comfortable home for the two of them. The blue Tahoe bumped hard in a rut in the drive and Brijette made a mental note to borrow the neighbor's tractor and box blade to grade the road this week.

"Isn't that Mr. Robert's truck?"

Brijette glanced toward Dylan, who she'd just picked up from Norma's, then she spotted the dual-wheeled truck parked in front of her house. That was convenient. She wouldn't have to go to Robert Hathorn's house to ask permission to borrow his tractor, she could ask him now—although the reason he was here would likely cause her to go to his house anyway, or at least to his barn.

Shoving the SUV into Park, she lowered the window. Dylan hadn't even bothered to undo her seat belt. "That crazy horse of yours get loose again?"

The older man stuck his upper body through the window of his truck and banged his hand on the door. "I don't know how he did it. Jumped the fence this time, I guess. Think you could help me find him?"

"Sure, I can help you. How long has he been gone?"

"Maybe two hours. I put him in the field and went to town. When I came home, he was gone."

Brijette waved to him before raising her

window to follow the man to his house, not far from Norma's.

Beside her, Dylan sat straighter. "He should get rid of that horse. He runs away all the time."

She could see the light in her daughter's eyes. Despite her complaining, Dylan was obviously excited to have a change in what must have been a boring day for her. The girl reminded Brijette of herself when she was younger. When her grandmother used to take her into the woods to trail an animal, or frequently a person, her senses would be firing, trying to decipher every nuance of her surroundings.

Brijette had learned more about the woods and the land when she was young than many people would ever know. Some people said she had a special gift, or "the sight," because she could follow a trail so easily and so well. Brijette considered her ability more akin to having very good intuition—at least, that's what she liked to label the feeling she got when she was on a hard track. She'd moved away from here to go to college where she'd discovered organized search-and-rescue groups and she'd begun adding professional training to her home-taught knowledge. Now she was a member of Cypress Landing's volunteer search and rescue team, which often meant local people came calling for her help when they needed to find lost pets—and high-dollar horses, of course. But the lessons she'd learned from her grandmother were important ones that she wanted her own daughter to appreciate, lessons that couldn't be bought with money.

When they came to a stop at Robert Hathorn's house, Dylan leaped from the truck and bounced on her toes.

"Ready?"

She nearly laughed at the girl, who took off toward the wooden fence. "Don't step in front of the gate, Dylan. There'll be enough tracks there already. We don't need to add more."

Dylan paused to glance at her. Brijette didn't have to be close enough to see her to know that she was rolling her eyes. "I know that, Mom."

All three of them stopped at the edge of the gate. Robert waited behind them while she and Dylan squatted to get a closer look at the ground. Over time the grass had been worn away, leaving only dirt, which was helpful for her.

She tapped Dylan's shoulder. "Let's take a walk around."

Dylan straightened and they started a slow

march along the perimeter of the fence that surrounded the pasture. Brijette knelt several times to study the grass or a weed that was bent at an unnatural angle. When they'd made it all the way around, they checked inside the pasture area and finally returned to where Robert waited patiently. Dylan stuck her hands into her pockets. Brijette knew her daughter was glad she didn't have to tell Robert the bad news.

"That stallion is worth a lot of money, isn't he?"

Robert frowned at her, pushing back his red hat to scratch his forehead. "Of course he is. He's one of the top quarter horses around here. I get several thousand dollars stud fee and I could easily sell him for four or five times that. Why?"

"The horse didn't jump the fence, and he certainly didn't open this gate and close it by himself. He was stolen. See this—" Brijette motioned for him to come closer, then pointed "—these aren't your boot tracks. Someone came here, went in the pasture and got the horse. They circled him around and shut the gate, which was really stupid, because if they'd left it open you'd have been more likely to think he'd gotten away on his own." She took a breath, caught a glimpse of Robert's wide eyes and stopped. He must have been more attached to that horse than she'd thought.

She put a hand on his arm. "Why don't you go call the sheriff? Dylan and I will follow the trail to see where it goes. They probably put him in a trailer, farther away from here. I'll take my cell phone and call you when I find where."

Robert started toward his truck. He stumbled once and Brijette wondered if she should check on him. But he righted himself.

Turning toward the field, she saw Dylan nearly at the woods. "Come on, Mom. They went this way. That's Mr. Robert's favorite horse and he paid a whole bunch of money for him."

Whoever had taken the horse had also taken the path of least resistance in their escape. The trail led straight to a worn path that followed the creek along Robert's property. In a few minutes they passed Norma's yard. Dylan raced ahead of her, and she was satisfied to let the girl lead the hunt herself. However, Dylan picked up the pace considerably and, before she realized it, her daughter was out of sight. Brijette increased her speed. She wasn't afraid Dylan would get hurt in these woods, but she didn't want her to stumble onto a horse thief.

Farther ahead, she heard Dylan's voice

shouting. The words brought her to a dead stop. Pure fear sent her into an instant run, ignoring the thin tree limbs that slapped her face and body. Her daughter was saying the name "Cade" and another voice answered—a deeper one.

Brijette broke through the last of the bushes onto the thick carpeted grass of Cade's yard. Or at least she guessed it was Cade's. Robert Hathorn had been trying to sell the house, a piece of the family property his great-great-grandfather had built. It had been on the market for months since he'd had it remodeled. She'd never imagined Cade would be living here, but he could certainly afford such an extravagance. Lord knows he had the money.

On the patio, Cade Wheeler stood next to a smoking grill watching Dylan gesture wildly. Even from here Brijette could hear the rumbling of his laughter at her daughter's antics. Dylan could be quite dramatic in a hilarious kind of way when she embarked on sharing a story, especially one that involved tracking. Brijette hurried toward them. She had to be careful now, for Dylan's sake as well as her own.

She was almost on top of them when she heard Dylan say, "It's my mom." Cade turned toward her, and for the second time today the color drained from his face. She wondered how many of these shocks his heart could take.

Dylan was pulling at her, dragging her closer to him.

"Mom, this is Mr. Cade. I met him when I was fishing. He's going to work with you. Have you met him yet?"

"What are you doing here?" The words came out with far more force and heat than Cade had intended, effectively stopping Dylan's chatter. From the corner of his eye he could see that she had gotten very still. The little trespasser, his fishing partner, was Brijette Dupre's daughter?

"I guess you did meet her at the clinic." Dylan ground her toe against the patio concrete and Cade cringed slightly. It wasn't the kid's fault her mom was...well, what she was. A word that would adequately describe Brijette defied him.

"That's right, Dylan, I work with Dr. Wheeler at the clinic. Now come on, we've got to finish tracking Mr. Robert's horse."

The girl tossed her mother a look that Cade wouldn't have thought kids learned until they reached at least seventeen and believed they knew everything.

"Get real, Mom. You don't think I dumped the trail like *that,* do you?" The girl snapped her fingers when she said the word "that" and Cade had to fight to keep from smiling. She pointed to the yard behind his garage. "The trail ended right there. A truck and trailer were parked where you couldn't see them. Maybe Mr. Cade stole the horse." She winked at him.

This time he couldn't stop the smile. "Dylan, I told you it's Cade, no 'mister,' all right? And no, I haven't stolen a horse or even seen one."

Brijette moved to the grassy area Dylan had pointed to. The young girl hurried over to her and motioned for Cade to follow. He obeyed without a second thought.

"See, Cade." Dylan pointed to the grass, which he could now see had been flattened.

"Mr. Wheeler or Dr. Wheeler, Dylan," Brijette interrupted, and Cade reminded himself to be angry, though with Brijette's daughter around it was difficult. Oh, well, that was all it took. The fact that she was Brijette's daughter immediately made him fume again.

"He told me to call him Cade."

Brijette glared at him. "You haven't seen anyone around today?"

He shook his head. "No, but I was at the clinic at eight this morning and didn't get home until six."

"Your house okay? Nothing missing, nobody broke in?"

"Everything's exactly as I left it."

"Probably thought the house was still empty." This she mumbled more to herself than to him. She retrieved a small cell phone from the chest pocket of her scrubs and dialed a number while walking away from them. Cade hurried to the patio, remembering that he hadn't even put his steak on the grill yet.

"I'll tell my mom we're eating supper with you as soon as she gets off the phone."

Damn, he'd completely forgotten he'd given the invitation.

"Mom, Cade invited us to eat with him, okay?"

Brijette dropped the phone into her pocket, and at last he got to see her look shocked. "I'm sure you misunderstood Dr. Wheeler, Dylan."

Dylan's lips curved into a pout. "No, I didn't. He said me and my mom should stay for supper. He said it right before you got here."

"Hmm. I really don't think we should impose on Dr. Wheeler. Come on, let's go." She focused her attention on him. "The sheriff will be around to check the area."

Brijette began to stride across the yard toward the creek.

"But, Mom, he invited us and he's new here. He needs to have company so he won't have to eat all by himself."

"Dylan, I told you once and I'm not going to say it again. And since when did you start whining?"

Dylan didn't move from where she'd positioned herself next to him. Brijette frowned at her from across the yard. Were those tears he saw in the girl's eyes? He sighed and shuffled like a prisoner until he was in front of Brijette.

"I did invite Dylan and her mom for supper. It won't take long to get two more steaks ready, so stay. Seeing as we're going to be around each other a lot the next few months, we might as well get used to it."

Brijette glanced past him to where Dylan awaited the verdict on the patio.

"You didn't know I was her mother when you gave that invitation or you wouldn't have done it. I don't want her to think she can start whining and get her way."

"You're right. I wouldn't have given the invitation if I'd known who her mother was. But I did give it, because I like Dylan. And I still do, despite who her mother is. She seems to be a good kid. Wonders never cease, do they?"

He spun on his heel. This round went to him.

Brijette's tight jawline and partially opened mouth gave him a slight feeling of satisfaction. He chose to ignore the other feelings seeing her again caused.

Stopping on the stairs to the patio, he looked back. One more thing he had to get straight. "Oh, and Brijette, my name is Cade, not Mr. Wheeler, not Mr. Cade and damn sure not Dr. Wheeler. People who know each other as intimately as you and I don't usually use that kind of formality."

THE THREE OF THEM finished their meal much faster than Dylan would probably have liked. When Cade offered them a ride to Mr. Robert's to get their car, Dylan was thrilled, but Brijette would rather have crawled through the woods on her hands and knees than spend more time with him. He'd acted as though she'd said they were going to wade off into the swamp when Brijette told him they'd go through the woods back to their car. In the end it had been easier to agree than to try and explain her reluctance to Dylan.

Dylan wanted to sit up front by him, but he held open the back door and motioned for her to get in, forcing Brijette to take the passenger seat. Dylan asked him questions from the back seat during the ride. He didn't seem to mind and Brijette was just thankful that she didn't need to join in. When they stopped at Robert's, the house was dark and his truck was gone.

"Do you think Mr. Robert is trying to find who took his horse, Mom?"

"He's probably at the sheriff's office. Now, thank Cade for the supper so we can go. It's late." She was desperate to extricate herself from this situation.

Dylan already had her seat belt off and she pushed herself between the front seats. "Thanks for the supper, Cade. We'll have to do it again soon. Maybe you can come eat with us one night."

Brijette pushed her into the back. "Dylan, good grief."

Her daughter wasn't the least perturbed by the reprimand. She was grinning herself silly in the back seat while Brijette was trying to decide if she could take a leave of absence from work. But there'd be no avoiding Cade. She had to work with him, but she didn't want her daughter to be so awestruck by him. That could only lead to trouble. Brijette reached for the door, but Cade caught her arm. "Wait, Brijette. Dylan, go wait in the car. I need to talk to your mom about a patient and we have to do that in private."

Dylan nodded and slid from her seat, kicking gravel all the way to their SUV. At least he'd made her mad in the end. She hoped Dylan would stay miffed at Cade for, oh, the next six months.

The lights from the dash glowed on Brijette's skin and Cade had to tell himself twice to take his hand off her arm. Some things never changed and that shotgun-blast feeling he got from touching Brijette Dupre was one of them. He didn't want to remember how her skin felt under his fingers, but he did. She faced him and he could feel his body leaning toward her, something about those dark eyes… He forced himself to straighten and put more distance between them. Thankfully, she spoke and that bewitching spell broke.

"Thanks for being so nice to Dylan. I'll try to make sure she doesn't worry you at your house."

"Dylan doesn't worry me, and I didn't ask you to stay in this car so you could thank me." At last he could get his brain on track and onto the most important question he'd ever asked.

"Right. Which patient did you want to discuss?"

"I don't want to talk about a patient. I wanted to speak to you in private."

She squirmed in her seat and he imagined she knew what was coming. "I want you to tell me who in the hell is the father of that child."

CHAPTER FOUR

THE QUESTION she'd dreaded most, and it was coming from the last person she'd ever expected to say those words. Brijette didn't try to answer right away. Nothing good could come of this. But, if she could keep Cade from learning the truth, then he'd leave and her life would be normal again, maybe. But how normal would it be for Dylan? In just a minute she would deny her child her father. A man who could buy her things, take her places Brijette never could. But would he teach her to love and care for other people, to give back to the community that raised her? Probably not. He hadn't wanted a child with her years ago and she couldn't imagine that he or his stiff-and-proper mother would want one now.

"She's not yours, that's for sure."

His features seemed to crinkle in the dim light.

"How old is she?"

His words were softer than she expected. She might have described them as sad if she hadn't known better.

"She's almost ten."

His eyes slammed on her with a force she could feel and she dug her back into the seat.

"So she could be mine. Unless you jumped into bed with someone else as soon as you got rid of me."

"I think you know where I spent the three months after you left."

He had the decency to stop glaring at her after that. She opened her mouth to ask him why he was so concerned about a child he'd never wanted in the first place—a child he'd been more than happy to get rid of. But she froze with her lips barely parted. What if he'd never known she was pregnant? Doubt had entered her mind when Cade's mother told her of his decision, but she'd tossed the suspicions aside. Mrs. Wheeler was his mother and a seventeen-year-old Brijette had no reason to think the woman would lie. He'd probably decided to pretend it never happened. That he'd never had a part in anything so ugly as paying her off to have an abortion—not him, not Cade Wheeler. If he wanted to feign ignorance, she'd be more than happy to go along. It served her purpose to ignore the whole incident.

She'd been presented with money for an abortion, then left to spend three months in a youth correction facility. Brijette wouldn't allow Cade to show up now and start making waves in hers and Dylan's lives. From the moment she'd had her daughter she'd been planning for the possibility of Wheeler interference, though she hadn't expected it. Thank goodness she'd made the effort anyway, because she was about to put those plans into action.

"Dylan was born twelve months after you left here, and I have the birth certificate to prove it. Unless I'm a human oddity, that's a couple months too late for her to be yours. I'll show you the birth certificate if you're that concerned."

The steering wheel creaked under the pressure of his hands. "Left that place and jumped into bed with the first guy who came along, huh?"

Brijette thought she wouldn't care what Cade said, how he saw her. She was wrong. It hurt to know he thought she had no morals. But then he'd believed her guilty of a lot things before now. He was staring at the front windshield and she was amazed that looking at him like this could still make her heart skip. Maybe it was just fear affecting her rather than the glint in his eyes or his slightly full lower lip that she recalled kissing indiscriminately. She'd kissed a few men since, but no one like him. Cade had been in a class by himself.

She didn't respond and he continued. "Where's her father? Does he visit, send money?"

She eyed the green light on the radio's digital display and shook her head.

"Are you telling me he doesn't know he has a child?"

Her breath caught deep in her lungs then came out in a gust. "I'm telling you he wasn't interested in having a child. He took off and hasn't had a thing to do with us since." That statement was the most honest one of the evening. "I need to go now. I can't leave Dylan sitting in the car by herself." She fumbled with the door, but he caught her arm before she could get away.

"Bring that birth certificate to work tomorrow. I am that concerned."

She stumbled from his truck to her vehicle, thoroughly confused. Cade continued to drill her with questions about Dylan's father and the more he asked, the less she wanted to tell him. Maybe he regretted the decision he made then. If so, she didn't care about his change of heart. But why didn't he mention her pregnancy, their child, the abortion he thought he paid for? Her uncertainty multiplied and she rammed the heel of her hand against her forehead to stop her panicked speculation. With any luck his questions ended here. Now she needed to keep Cade and Dylan apart and hope no one else noticed the uncanny resemblance of the two.

THE CAR DOOR slammed, the engine hummed to life and the red taillights of the SUV disappeared. Gone again and good riddance.

Cade put his own vehicle in motion and tried to beat down the feeling in the pit of his stomach. He was *not* disappointed. At least, that's what he kept telling himself. But for an instant, just a moment in time, he'd thought the cute little blonde could be his, his own daughter. Then that witch had ruined it, like she'd ruined everything between them. Sharing a child with her would have been pure hell. His child couldn't be raised by a woman like Brijette, untrustworthy, a liar. A host of even worse descriptive words butted into his brain but he swept them aside. It didn't matter, the kid didn't belong to him. Brijette had gone to bed with a lowlife who got her pregnant and took off.

How quickly things could change. At one time Cade had expected to spend the rest of his life, after medical school, right here in Cypress Landing, with Brijette. Then in an instant his plans had come apart. Brijette had been arrested while they were together and she'd been carrying a large package of prescription narcotics in her backpack. Enough to get her sent to that youth correctional facility a few hours away. Before she was sentenced, she'd told his mother she'd take money to stay away from him. He'd wondered what had happened to the girl he'd fallen in love with. But his mother had convinced him Brijette had just made a fool of him, acting as if she cared. So he'd left without another word to her. He hadn't seen or spoken to her again, until now.

His gut twisted slightly at the thought. Had that been the right thing to do? He shook his head. Of course he'd done the right thing—no need to second-guess a decision he'd made that long ago. He pulled into his drive only to be hit with blaring lights from three sheriff's vehicles. He recognized Matthew Wright, who was only a few years older than himself and had been with the sheriff's department when Cade was here before.

Cade climbed out of his car and gripped Matt's hand. "Hey, how are you? It's been a long time."

Matt nodded. "Yeah, it has."

Cade stuffed his hands into his pockets and leaned against the truck door. "I think you were the investigator when I was last here."

"I took over as sheriff a few years after you left."

The ever so slight pause between "you" and "left" didn't get lost on Cade. More than one person in this town likely thought he'd been as guilty as Brijette. He hadn't been, which is why he'd gone home before things had gotten worse.

"You're going to be the new doctor in town." The sheriff seemed to be sizing him up.

"Only until my uncle recovers from his surgery, then I'll go back to Dallas."

"City boy, huh?"

Cade shrugged. "I guess. My mother likes Dallas and doesn't want to leave. She's getting older and I need to be nearby."

Matt accepted the answer without a response. It was one that would make sense around here—a son doing his duty by seeing to his aging mother, the honorable thing to do. Cade didn't know how honorable his intentions were when part of him resisted it so much. But he'd made promises to his father and, being an only child, he felt the need to keep them.

"Don't think we'll get much here."

Cade swung his attention back to the sheriff. "No idea what happened to the horse?"

"Not yet. I wouldn't even have noticed those tire tracks if Brijette hadn't told me where to find them."

Cade smiled against his will. He didn't want the image of Brijette kneeling, studying the grass in his backyard to make him smile, but it did. It was what had drawn him to her when they were younger, the way she would get completely engrossed in something and forget everything else. These were not the memories he wanted to think of right now. Actually, he should eliminate them from his mind permanently.

"Her daughter's the one who found the marks first."

Sheriff Wright rubbed his chin. "That figures. The kid's part bloodhound, same as her mother."

"What was her father like?"

The man's lips thinned. "I don't know the girl's father. Maybe you should ask Brijette. Or better yet, let things like that lie."

What a quick freeze—the sheriff's friendly attitude had shifted so abruptly. But a part of Cade couldn't let the subject go. "I thought he must be from here and you'd know him."

"Like I said, I don't know the guy." Sheriff

Wright turned away from him. "We've done what we can for now. We'll be going."

Matt Wright waved to the other men and they climbed in their respective cars, leaving Cade standing in the damp grass. He walked to the door of the kitchen still feeling the tension that had hung in the air this evening. After flipping off the light, he made his way to bed, trying to decide if he was sorry he'd come to Cypress Landing or not.

THE WHOLE HOUSE seemed to shift as Dylan's bedroom door slammed shut. The girl hadn't said a word since Brijette had gotten in the car and driven them home. The child had been around Cade one evening and already Brijette's life was changing—and not for the better. She took off her shoes and counted to ten before padding down the hall to stand in front of the closed door.

She tapped lightly. "Dylan, I'm coming in."

A muffled *no* penetrated the wood, but Brijette ignored it. She was the adult around here.

"What's going on? Why are you so mad?"

"You don't even like Cade. Why did I have to sit in our car while you got to stay there and talk to him?"

That set her back and she had to struggle to

get her thoughts together. She hadn't expected her spending time alone with Cade would make Dylan angry. "He told you we had to discuss a patient, and we can't do that in front of you."

"I can keep a secret."

Brijette's muscles tightened. "I'm sure you can, but you'd better not keep secrets from me."

"Why? You and Cade kept whatever you talked about in the car a secret."

From nowhere, tears pricked behind Brijette's eyes. She hadn't planned to keep secrets from her daughter, but in reality she had. Protection, she reminded herself. I'm protecting her from the family who would never really accept her because she's part of me. Focus. She had to focus to get this problem solved.

"Discussing patient care is not keeping a secret. And don't go to his house bothering him when you're supposed to be staying with Norma. He's a busy person."

"I'm not bothering Cade. He said so. And I only went in his backyard to fish. He's the one who sat down and fished with me."

Brijette sighed. "You fish behind Norma's house where she can see you. That creek can be dangerous."

"It's shallow."

Brijette fought the urge to stomp her foot. “Dylan, you heard me. It’s dangerous. Don’t do it.”

The girl hugged a pillow to her and faced the wall.

“I’m going to take a bath and go to bed. Do you need anything?” Dylan didn’t move or answer, and Brijette leaned over to kiss the top of her head. “I’ll see you in the morning.”

She pulled the door closed behind her and went to the bathroom that adjoined her bedroom. She could afford the small two-bedroom house, which was all that mattered, even though at times she longed for one of those huge tubs with the jets to wash away the aches and pains of a long day.

Dropping her clothes onto the floor, she stepped under the spray of the shower and leaned her head against the wall. Hopefully, this trouble with Dylan wasn’t a premonition of things to come. They’d had their spats during the years as parents and children do, but they were closer than most because they depended so much on each other. In a way, they’d grown up together. She had imagined that one day she’d find a man to marry, to help raise Dylan and be the father the child never knew, but life hadn’t worked out that way.

They had to get through this summer. Doc Wheeler would come back from his surgery and Cade would be gone. All those things he'd said years ago, about living in a small town and helping people the way his uncle did, had been a lot of words that had meant nothing. Thank goodness for that, because the sooner he left, the sooner her life and Dylan's could get back to normal.

AT SIX in the morning Cade nosed his vehicle into a spot on the edge of Main Street in front of the Main Street Coffee Shop. Cypress Landing didn't seem to find a need for originality in names. What else would one name an eatery on the town's main street? He'd been hungry the minute his feet hit the floor, and he remembered the diner opened early.

He found a stool at the breakfast counter, avoiding the tables, several already occupied by brooding gray-haired men. They either gathered up here or at the old store on the highway that led outside of town.

An older woman stopped across the counter from him. "You want the same breakfast as usual?"

He hadn't been in Cypress Landing long, but he'd already been in the Main Street Coffee Shop enough that Alice Berteau, the waitress and owner, knew what he wanted. "That'll be good."

She poured him a cup of coffee and disappeared into the kitchen.

A man took a seat beside him and waved to a waitress, who smiled and motioned that she'd be right there.

"Mr. Mills, right? Jody Mills's dad."

The man gave him a confused look.

"I'm Cade Wheeler, Dr. Wheeler's nephew." Mr. Mills had lost weight since Cade had last seen him, but he'd spent a lot of time with his son, who'd been one of his best friends during his first visit here. Maybe he and Jody could get together again, go fishing like when they were younger.

Recognition finally passed across the man's face and he nodded. "I almost didn't recognize you, you've grown some. Heard you were coming to help your uncle while he was laid up. That's good of you."

Cade wished people would quit telling him he was being nice to come and help his uncle. They made it sound as if he'd left a lot behind to come here, when in truth his uncle's plea for help had filled a blank hole that had appeared in his life.

"What's Jody doing? I'd like to see him."

Mr. Mills's jaw tightened and he wadded a

paper napkin in his hand. "I thought Dr. Wheeler would have told you. Jody died close to a year ago. Got mixed in with the wrong people and started messing around with drugs. Ended up gettin' shot."

"I'm sorry. I didn't know. Did they ever catch who did it?"

The man grasped the plastic container the waitress had brought for him and shook his head. "Ask that Brijette at the clinic. She can tell you more. She's the one who found him. They took to being friends when she moved back here." He paused as if he realized his voice had gotten louder. "I'll be seeing you, son. You stay out of trouble, you hear?"

Cade could only watch as the man hurried from the diner.

"He's changed since Jody died."

A plate slid across the counter in front of him and Alice propped her arm on the counter. "They never did find who killed the boy and it's made the man bitter. Wants to blame everyone."

"Whose fault was it?"

She frowned. "It was Jody's fault for gettin' involved in all that. Can't really blame no one else. Mr. Mills thinks the sheriff isn't trying hard enough, but there's only so much that can be done. I don't know. Maybe I'd feel the same if it happened to my child." She moved on as a customer at the other end of the counter asked for a coffee refill.

He couldn't imagine why his uncle hadn't told him Jody had been killed. Of course, his uncle hadn't been too pleased that summer when his parents had shown up and carted him back to Dallas. At the time, Cade had just wanted to escape. He'd had very little contact with his uncle after that. Even at his father's funeral, the man hadn't mentioned Cypress Landing or the events of that summer. That was why he'd been surprised when his uncle had called and asked for his help. Now that Cade was back in Cypress Landing, his life seemed to be getting tangled in ways he hadn't expected. All he wanted was a simple medical practice, a wonderful wife and two or three beautiful children. Was that asking too much? He forked a piece of omelet, letting the cheese ooze and wondering if those things would ever happen for him.

BRIJETTE TRIED TO control the jump in her chest, tried to tell herself it wasn't her heart racing the minute she saw Cade stroll in the door. The same locks of hair slipped over one eyebrow, framing emerald eyes that could draw you in deeper and deeper. His shoulders strained beneath the fabric of his lab coat, making him appear much larger than she remembered. The young man had gone. This Cade seemed to fill the hallway. His blond good looks were what had attracted her to him in the beginning; his warm caring heart was what had made her stay. The chart she held dropped to the floor, scattering loose pieces of paper. That heart had transformed into an iceberg the minute their little sea of love started having a few waves. She'd been crazy in love with him and she hadn't wanted to believe he'd left. Then his mother came. She took a deep breath and stretched to get the last paper, but her head made a thumping sound as it rammed into Cade's. He'd crouched to help her get the papers and she hadn't seen him. Why did he do that? She didn't need his help, not now, not ever.

"Sorry." She snapped the file shut, gritting the word between her teeth like a nasty piece of candy.

"Are you all right?"

"I'm fine." She turned to leave, but her foot wobbled in her open-backed clogs. The chart went flying and her shoulder bumped the wall at the same time a hand grabbed her upper arm. Cade steadied her.

"Don't move."

He let go and gathered the chart while she stood there, unsure why she kept following his directions but unable to get her muscles in gear. When he had the chart together he caught her arm and pulled her into an empty room, shutting the door behind them.

"I'm sorry about last night."

If she'd been holding the stupid chart she'd have dropped it again. "What do you mean, you're sorry?"

"It's not a riddle. I'm sorry. I said a lot of nasty things to you. We have a past, but it's just that, past. If we're going to be working together, we have to get along. Neither one of us may be comfortable with it, but this is the way things are going to be."

Brijette couldn't do much more than stare at him. This was how it was going to be? How could they possibly work together with all the resentment between them? What had old Dr. Wheeler been thinking?

Cade caught her hand and squeezed her fingers. "We can do it." And there he was, the old Cade she'd fallen in love with. The you-and-me-against-the-world Cade, the even-if-the-world-kicks-our-butts Cade. But the world had come to kick their butts, and there hadn't been a you and me.

"It'll be fine." She heard herself say the words but didn't feel as though they came from her.

He dropped her hand, disappearing through the door, only to reappear seconds later. "Oh, and no swamp medicine."

Blood rushed to her head and she opened her mouth to reply, but he cut her off, laughing. "Hey, I was joking, okay? We'll do what works." He paused, as if contemplating his next words carefully. "I'd still like to see that birth certificate."

She nodded. Damn Cade Wheeler. She didn't need this confusion in her life. She fiddled with the exam-room supplies on the small desk. She'd have to find a way to deal with him until he left. Suddenly there was a shout and a thud from the direction of the lobby. Then Cade's voice seemed to rattle the window in the small room.

"Brijette, get in here now."

CHAPTER FIVE

A BODY SPLAYED prone on the office floor first thing in the morning did not spell good news. Cade rolled the young man over.

"What's his name?" he shouted at the bony girl with him.

"Ray," she cried. "Is he gonna be all right?"

Cade ignored her. "Ray, can you hear me?"

Ray didn't move. He made a wheezing sound, then went quiet. Leaning close to the man's face, Cade couldn't feel air on his cheek. "He's not breathing."

An ambu bag appeared over his shoulder and he fit the plastic piece over Ray's mouth and nose, holding it in place, squeezing the attached bag to give the man air. Brijette knelt on the floor and stripped Ray's shirt off, slapping on the pads for the automated external defibrillator.

"Tell me we have a crash cart."

Brijette gave a quick shake of her head, then pointed to a large red tackle box.

"How am I supposed to know his heart rhythms or what meds to give? Do we even have the equipment here to intubate?" Surely his uncle kept supplies here in case of breathing emergencies, so he could put a tube into the lungs and get air to a patient who couldn't breathe.

"We've got the AED here to administer a shock if needed, and the ambulance is on the way. We can unhook the big monitor from the cardiac exam room and roll it up here, but…" She paused as sirens shrieked outside. "But the ambulance will probably be here before we get it."

The medics rushed in and Cade moved back, letting the two men take over. In seconds they had the man called Ray on the stretcher, racing to the ambulance.

Ray's distraught girlfriend or wife waited in the doorway. "Is he going to be all right?"

Brijette crossed the room and stood in front of her. "We don't know, but it doesn't look good."

Well, she didn't sugarcoat that.

"It would help if we knew what kind of drugs he's been taking. He did take something, didn't he?"

"It… I think it might have been OxyContin. But he had a prescription."

"Why did you bring him here instead of the emergency room?" Brijette asked.

The slender girl hugged her purse to her body. "He didn't seem that sick. He walked in here. He was real weak and not breathing too good. This was the first place we passed, so we stopped."

Cade groaned, watching Brijette head back to the desk. He stared at the girl.

"It wasn't like he was doing illegal drugs, you know. I tell you, he had a prescription."

The girl hurried through the door and Cade reached the reception desk in time to hear Brijette finish her report to the hospital's emergency-room doctor. She leaned back in her chair and sighed. "Sorry we didn't have the equipment you wanted. I've talked to your uncle, but he says we're so close to the hospital that we don't need it."

"Sounds like him."

She smiled and Cade realized he was glad she'd been here. He'd worked in a clinic for such a long time that he'd forgotten what it was like to try to save a life in the immediate sense rather than the long term.

"You don't seem surprised about the OxyContin."

She snorted. "Not a bit. Some people tend to forget that drugs aren't candy."

"And the fact that he had a prescription?"

"Plenty of doctors will write prescriptions for anything. And then there are always stolen prescription pads."

"Get much of that around here?"

She shrugged and glanced away. "A pharmacist in town had one on me yesterday."

He hadn't expected that. "How'd they get the pad?"

"Stole it when they had a visit here, or tore a sheet off when I laid it down. I try to keep up with mine, but your uncle leaves his where he drops it."

"I'll keep that in mind when I'm writing prescriptions."

She nodded and got to her feet. For an instant he imagined how nice it would be to forget the mess that was their past and pick up anew. He'd like to smile at her, maybe throw his arm over her shoulder. But he couldn't. He couldn't trust her for more reasons than one. He followed her into the hall to see the first patient he had waiting.

THE SUN HUNG LOW in the sky as Brijette turned the key to crank the boat. If Norma wasn't such a good person she'd have quit being Dylan's sitter long ago. Brijette ran late at least once every week, usually on Thursday when she went to Willow Point. She hated missing time with Dylan, but she hoped her daughter would learn from her example to help people who didn't have the opportunities she'd had. She wished now she'd brought Dylan with her to the field clinic today, something she often did during school vacations. Her daughter enjoyed helping A.G. at the store or fishing at the dock with the local kids. She and Dylan didn't have a lot, but it was important for her to learn that many people had even less, and they were still good people, happy people. Things she'd never learn if Cade's family had their claws in her life. She'd worried more about Dylan lately. They'd had such a close relationship, until recently…until Cade came back. Her lip hurt as she chewed on it, trying to remind herself that her problems with Dylan really had nothing to do with Cade. The girl was growing up and disagreements were a natural part of that. Twice lately she'd mentioned her father, and both times Brijette had supplied the story that he'd left them because he'd been afraid to try to raise a child. That particular lie made her stomach lurch every time. She hated lying like this to her daughter but it was a necessity, to protect her, to protect both of them. Lately, however, it felt like a merry-go-round that was spinning so fast they couldn't jump off.

She looked at Alicia. "When summer's over we can't stay this late. I don't want to go back in the dark."

Alicia glanced at her watch. "Yeah, we still have daylight left, but not much. It's nearly seven."

Brijette nosed the boat away from the dock. "Seven o'clock already. Norma's going to kill me."

"Oh, I forgot." Alicia grabbed onto the seat, leaning closer to her. "When I called Norma to tell her we'd be late, she said she needed to go to her sister's this evening, but Cade offered to watch Dylan until you got home. Wasn't that sweet of him?"

Brijette's hand dropped from the throttle and the boat idled along. "What? Why didn't you tell me this before? We'd have left early and told the patients to come back."

"Those patients couldn't wait until next week. Besides, why did I need to tell you? Norma said he offered, and it's not like he's a criminal or a child molester, unless you know something I don't."

"No, it's not that. But… I mean… How did he know I'd be late? Was he at Norma's house?"

"Yeah, he was. She had made a cake for him

and he stopped by to pick it up. What's wrong with you? The guy's only trying to help."

"You don't understand."

"Well, you're right about that. He's practically a god with that blond hair and those killer eyes. He has money and he obviously likes your kid. You could do worse, you know."

Brijette gripped the wheel tightly. "What do you mean?"

"I'm thinking you and him together might be a good thing. Rumor has it you two were an item at one time."

Brijette grabbed the throttle, giving it a shove. Alicia gripped the seat harder as the boat shot forward.

"You seem to have only heard part of the rumor." Brijette spoke loudly above the engine.

"Are you going to tell me the rest?"

"No, I'm going to get us home." She pushed to a faster speed, putting off further conversations, as Alicia hung on. Brijette wondered what she would be able to tell Alicia to pacify her. Part of the story might do it. The part everyone else in town knew. Dancing around all these lies and half-truths was beginning to make her feel worse than bad, but right now she needed to get home and get her daughter away from Cade.

CAR LIGHTS FLASHED in the window as darkness had begun to settle in. Eight-thirty was pretty late for Brijette to be coming home.

"Does your mom get home this late very often?"

Dylan swallowed the last bite of her chocolate-chip cookie. "No, she's hardly ever this late. I go with her to the clinic sometimes."

"Do you like it?"

The girl grinned. "Yeah, it's fun, but my mom says it's hot right now and I might not want to go. Besides, I'd rather stay here and fish with you if you get home in time."

A knock sounded on the door and he yelled for Brijette to come in. He heard her shoes slapping on the floor before she blew into the kitchen. Her scrubs were stained and strands of hair had come loose from her ponytail. She looked windblown, understandably, since she traveled to and from the clinic on a boat. And she'd never been more beautiful. He crushed the thought immediately, along with the napkin he wadded in his hand.

"I'm sorry, Cade. This won't happen again. Let's go, Dylan." Her words were clipped.

"Hey, it's okay. I offered to let Dylan stay here so Norma could go to her sister's. Do you want to eat?"

"Yeah, Mom, Cade made crawfish pasta and it's awesome. You've got to try it."

"I'm not hungry." She turned to him. "I hope this didn't inconvenience you."

"Mom, how rude. You could at least try the pasta."

Cade went to the cabinet and found a plastic container, filling it with leftovers from his and Dylan's meal. The air in the room was thick with tension and he hated it, but it was partly his fault. He gave the container to Dylan.

"Your mom may want this later when she's feeling better."

She glared at him over Dylan's head and he frowned. "I don't feel bad now. I just don't want you saddled with my daughter."

"And for the fiftieth time, I offered to let her stay."

"I imagine you couldn't have had much choice. Besides, I told her not to come here and bother you."

"But, Mom…"

"Don't 'but mom' me. Go get in the car. It's late."

He thought they'd settled on a truce the other day, but Brijette obviously thought it didn't extend beyond the walls of the clinic. "I went by Norma's to pick up a cake. Dylan didn't come here."

The girl crossed her arms in front of her with the kind of smug expression only a nine-year-old can get away with. "See, Mom, I tried to tell you."

"Dylan, wait in the car."

The girl slid off the barstool, muttering about her mom going whacko, and Cade nearly grinned. But Brijette's expression stopped him. She didn't seem angry, but completely panicked. He waited until Dylan left the room to try to reason with her.

"I don't know why my keeping Dylan is making you nuts, but I won't offer again. Although, I don't know what you expect your babysitter to do, when you're late and she has plans."

"She can tell me she has plans and I'll stop what I'm doing and come home."

"It didn't make sense for you to come home. Besides, by the time you would've gotten here she'd have been late going to her sister's."

"It's not your responsibility."

Her sharp voice hit a sore spot in him. "You're right. It's your responsibility, but I guess you should've thought of that before you got pregnant, right?"

It was a harsh thing to say, but he was feeling a little harsh at the moment. He could see he'd taken her breath and he nearly apologized, but then she was the one who'd gotten in trouble and taken money to end their relationship.

She opened her mouth but snapped it shut before she spoke. "I was a kid."

He imagined she'd wanted to scream those words; instead, they were a barely audible whisper. Under her olive skin she had gone pale and Cade sighed. This wasn't what he wanted to happen.

"I shouldn't have said that. We all make bad decisions when we're young. Really bad."

He crossed the room and put his hands on her shoulders, but she wouldn't meet his eyes.

"I don't want her to get attached to you."

"What?" He caught her chin and tilted her face upward.

"She doesn't have a father around and I don't want her to get attached to you when you'll be leaving soon. It's not fair to her."

"A lot of things aren't fair. But I do see your point. I'll try not to spend too much time with her if that's what you want."

Under his palms, her shoulders drooped with relief. "It's for the best."

And then he did the unthinkable. His hands

slid around her back and pulled her to his chest, where he'd always felt she belonged. She felt it, too, had to. He could tell by the way she snuggled in closely, her own arms circling his waist. He thought he might want to keep her next to him like this forever, but she pulled away.

Cade let his arms drop to his sides, as did Brijette.

She studied the floor intently. "Thanks." Her voice wasn't much more than a whisper.

"For what?"

She cleared her throat and looked up at him. Her eyes were shiny with unshed tears, but her voice was strong. "For understanding about me trying to protect Dylan…and for the hug."

He caught her hand and squeezed it. Then she smiled and he couldn't believe how the blood rushed through every part of his body, leaving him a bit dizzy.

"I guess you weren't expecting me to thank you."

He shook his head and she pulled her hand away to press it against her eyes, though she was smiling. "Sorry, I don't mean to get weepy and hormonal on you."

"Are you having problems with your hormones?"

She glanced at him, and he realized he had

taken on a much more serious expression than he'd intended.

She started laughing. "That's such a doctor question."

"Well, I am a doctor."

"It was just an expression. My hormones are fine. I appreciate you letting me have a 'moment.'"

"Do you mean a weak moment?"

Her smile softened. "Yeah, I do."

"Everybody has them and they can certainly use a hug from a friend when they do."

"Even the calm and steady Cade Wheeler?"

"Especially me."

"I guess I'll owe you one, then."

"I definitely plan to collect." He hadn't meant to lose his smile or to let the heat that had suffused his body become evident in his voice, but he had.

Brijette fidgeted with the hem of her scrub top. "I'd better go."

He didn't move until he heard the door slam, and then it was only to go to the window to watch them leave. Dylan was a well-adjusted kid and Brijette seemed to be doing a fine job as a single mom, but if tonight was any evidence, she needed a little help. The thought of trying to help Brijette should have been the last one to enter his head. But maybe she'd changed. He certainly had.

If he could go back in time he'd likely do things different. He now knew what it felt like for everyone to believe you'd done wrong when you hadn't. What if Brijette hadn't been in the wrong but had been an innocent victim, as she'd said? What if he loved it here in Cypress Landing this time as much as he had when he'd first come? He might even want to stay. He shoved himself away from the window. Promises. He'd made his father a big one before the man died and Cade couldn't go back on that.

HER MOTHER had officially gone nuts. She'd come in blasting Cade for no reason. He'd only been trying to help. Couldn't she see that? Then her mom had sent her to the car like a three-year-old.

From the corner of her eye, Dylan watched her mother steer the car onto the highway. She was acting really weird.

"I thought I asked you not to bother Cade."

"He told you he came to Mrs. Norma's to get something."

"Don't get smart, Dylan."

She pulled at the seat belt strap across her chest. "I'm not getting smart. It's true."

"I'll be sure not to be late from now on. I don't want this to happen again."

Dylan held on to the side of the seat as the SUV bumped up their drive. "Yeah, right."

She could feel her mother's eyes on her for an instant. "What is that supposed to mean?"

"It means you're always going to be late because you're always working."

The car came to a stop and they both unhooked their seat belts. Her mother leaned toward her. "I have to make a living, you know."

"And you get paid how much for what you do at the *free* clinic?"

"That's not fair, Dylan. You've been there and seen how little those people have, and how much they need medical attention."

"I didn't say they didn't need it. I just said you weren't going to just up and stop being late, so you need to quit freaking out because Cade let me stay at his house."

"I'm not freaking out. You need to remember that Cade's not going to stay here. When his uncle is better, he'll go back to the city."

Dylan flung the door open. She didn't want to think about Cade leaving. She intended to do everything she could to get him to stay. "If you'd be nicer to him he might not leave."

She jumped from the car and ran up the steps, her mother right behind her. The grip on her shoulder kept her from escaping to her bedroom.

"What's gotten into you lately? You never used to act like this."

"Like what? How am I acting, Mom? Because you never used to act like you are."

"You are being rude and downright hostile. I don't want you hanging around Cade so much. He's a grown man and you're a little girl. I'm sure he needs his time off to rest."

Dylan jerked her shoulder away from her mother's grip. "You're just mad because Cade likes me and not you. I heard someone at the store say Cade was your boyfriend a long time ago when you were young." The look on her mother's face was enough to tell her that what she'd heard was true. "Well, I won't stay away from him, and I'm going to try to get him to stay here."

She spun around and ran, making the whole house shake when she slammed her bedroom door. With the stereo blasting, she didn't have to listen to her mother move around the house. She was actually surprised her mom hadn't come in and thrown a cat fit over what she'd said. It only proved that she was right. Her mom was mad because she wasn't still Cade's girlfriend or even his wife. Things had gotten really mixed up lately. She loved her mother more than anything, but she had some niggling doubts about some of the things her mom told her. Plus, she heard stuff around town, when people thought she was out of earshot or just didn't care. No one ever said a name, but they speculated about who her father was. She tried to ignore them, but, darn it, she really wanted to hit them in the head. Glancing at the clock, she decided to wait another hour, then if the house was quiet she'd go take a bath. Cade had to stay in Cypress Landing. Somehow she'd find a way to make him.

CHAPTER SIX

ACROSS THE DESK, Sheriff Matt Wright shuffled papers that he'd pulled from a file. "You know, Brijette, we did a bust last year on the edge of the parish and found prescription drugs in large quantities. Those prescriptions had been written by doctors in several towns an hour or more away. This is the first I've heard of anything involving your clinic. I can check with the city police, but they usually let us know when they have an investigation going."

She shifted in the hard wooden seat. Even though she visited the sheriff's office frequently as part of the search-and-rescue team, she never really got past that uncomfortable feeling that hung low in her middle. "It's probably just an odd occurrence, but I wanted to know if you'd heard of more. I don't need that kind of trouble."

"Don't worry. I know you'll work with us, and if I have a problem, I'll ask you. I don't think anyone around here thinks that you're writing illegal prescriptions."

She raised an eyebrow and he frowned. "I meant what I said, Brijette. No one's digging up the past."

"People are always digging into other people's pasts."

"Around here we go on the evidence, not rumor and speculation. Jackson Cooper's in charge of investigating drug trafficking, the prescription kind in particular. I'll have him keep you updated on any new findings."

"Thanks, Matt." She stood to leave and he followed her to the door of the office.

"How's Doc Wheeler's nephew doing at the clinic?"

"All right, I guess. He's actually a little faster than his uncle is."

"I imagine. You know, I met him the other night at his place when we went to check on Robert's horse. He asked me if I knew Dylan's dad or if the guy was from here."

She stopped with her hand halfway to the doorknob. Angry, shock riveted her in place. "He did what?"

"Yeah, that's how I thought you'd feel. I told him the truth, though. Said I didn't know a thing and he needed to ask you."

"Good."

"I was a single parent for a while before I remarried. I remember not needing extra problems. That job has plenty of problems on its own."

She raked her fingers through her hair trying to get a grip on her anger. "You're right, and I definitely don't need extras."

The rest of the hallway that led from the sheriff's office passed in a blur. Cade had nerve trying to mine the locals for dirt on her. Thank goodness he'd leveled his first questions at Matt, who hadn't been willing to share a bunch of gossip. Why did Doc Wheeler have to ask Cade to come here and why didn't he hurry and recover so Cade could go home? She almost laughed at herself. Now she was blaming poor Doc Wheeler for her problems, like he planned to have a faulty heart valve. Her difficulties were rooted in decisions she'd made years ago, as a young and stupid girl.

No, she wouldn't confront Cade yet. Right now she was angry and she didn't really want to say things to him in anger, not anymore. But since she'd placed undeserved blame on the old doctor, the least she could do was go by to check on him. Dylan had gone off with Norma and she didn't have to pick her up first, though

Doc Wheeler would be disappointed that the girl didn't come. He didn't have any children and counted Dylan as his only grandchild—at least until Cade married and had children... She caught herself in mid-thought. Boy, how did things in her life ever get this confusing?

BRIJETTE KNOCKED on the older man's door and waited. In a moment, Doc opened the door himself.

"Aren't you in perfect health?"

He stepped back to let her in, motioning for her to follow him. "I'm feeling good today." He entered the spacious kitchen and sat at the table. "I'm having supper—and where's my little girl?"

"She went with Norma to visit her sister, but I don't want to interrupt your meal."

"You're not interrupting, and there's plenty of food. Jeanine baked enough chicken for five people. Now, tell me how things are running at the clinic."

"Things are fine. It's really busy, though. Dr. Hershing finally closed his office the other day and we've gotten his patients."

Doc Wheeler nodded. "He's wanted to go help his son in his practice in Boston for a long time. But you and Cade are handling the extra load?"

Brijette bit into a piece of baked chicken and chewed for a minute before answering. "We're doing okay." She couldn't very well tell him how inundated they were with new patients. Before, they hadn't had time to go for lunch and had had to eat it in the clinic; now they seldom had time to even eat, and were running at least an hour or two later since Dr. Hershing had closed his office. If he knew, Doc Arthur would only worry and try to come back to work before he'd had time to recuperate. She especially didn't want him trying to convince Cade to stay. With any luck, this first influx after Dr. Hershing's move wouldn't last long and soon their schedule would be back to normal.

"Cade says you had an overdose victim collapse in the lobby the other day. He says we need to update our equipment to respond to that kind of emergency. Not the first time I've heard that."

She grinned and shrugged, downing the last bite of her squash casserole.

"Are they seeing a lot of OD victims in the ER?"

Brijette wiped her mouth on a napkin. "I don't know—I could check. But I did want to let you know that Elliot at the drugstore caught an illegal narcotic prescription with my name on it a few weeks ago. I went by the sheriff's office today and he said they hadn't found anything from our clinic at their drug busts, but they had found find scripts from other clinics."

Arthur Wheeler's brows drew together. "Did the sheriff think the prescriptions were written by the drug dealers or by the doctors?"

"I think it was a bit of both."

"I don't know why that kind of thing happens. The law will take care of these people, don't you worry. I've had folks write illegal prescriptions on script paper they stole from my office. You and Cade just keep your pads on you."

She snorted. "You're one to talk, Mister Where-in-the-world-is-my-prescription-pad-now."

He laughed. "I didn't say do what I do."

Brijette smiled and finished the last of her tea, then sat toying with her napkin.

"What else is on your mind?"

Frowning, she tried to decide how to word what she wanted to ask without steering herself into a discussion she'd rather avoid.

"Usually best to spit out what you want to say and worry about the cleanup later."

"I just wondered why you didn't tell Cade he'd be working with me at the clinic before he came. You let me know weeks in advance, but he was shocked when he saw me."

Doc Wheeler grinned. "Yeah, I'd have loved to see that myself."

"You intended for him to be surprised?"

"I didn't imagine he'd come if he knew you were working here."

"Why in the world would you ask him to work for you if you knew he'd be miserable working with me?"

Doc Arthur pushed a chicken bone around on his plate. "He's not miserable. The boy has no idea what he wants or needs in his life. Those parents of his have pulled his strings for as long as I can remember. As an only son, he feels he has a duty to respect his parents' wishes. But what they wanted for him and what he wants has always been different."

"I can't imagine that he'd want to work with me. I surely don't want to work with him. Couldn't you have found someone else?" She dropped the fork she'd been holding onto her empty plate and the clinking sound echoed in the kitchen. "That was a rotten thing for me to say. I'm sorry."

"Is it that bad? I didn't do it to make things hard for you. I wanted to help Cade, and he needed a change of scenery right now. Besides,

I thought..." He stopped to take a drink of his iced tea. Setting the glass on the table, he wiped at the condensation with his finger.

"You thought what?"

"That the two of you would work on things, maybe get together again. You were such a happy couple before."

"I was seventeen. And I hate to say it because Cade's your nephew, but he showed me years ago what kind of man he'd be in a pinch, and he didn't impress me."

"A lot of things were going on that summer and, like you said yourself, you were both young. He's solid, dependable and he'd be the perfect father for Dylan."

Her eyes met his. She searched their depths for a hidden meaning. Had he guessed the truth? She could tell nothing from watching him, and she could only pray that if he knew anything he'd keep quiet. "I don't want my child to grow up thinking she can do whatever she wants and pay her way clear of trouble because her father has money. And I certainly don't want her to look down her nose at people because they don't have the advantages or opportunities she has, because then she'd be looking down her nose at me."

"It wouldn't be like that."

"I think it would."

He shrugged. "Have you talked to Robert about his horse?"

She nearly laughed out loud at his abrupt change of subject. As if he knew he wouldn't be changing her mind today. "No, I haven't."

"He came by this morning and brought me some books and magazines. When I asked about his horse getting stolen, he said he asked the sheriff to discontinue the investigation because he thinks his nephew might be involved."

"What? I didn't even know he had a nephew."

"Well, apparently he does. He has a much younger sister who lives out of state. It's her son, and the boy's been in trouble with drugs. His parents cut him off financially, so Robert thinks the boy took the horse to sell."

She shook her head and stood to go. "How awful for Robert."

Doc only nodded as she left the room. Poor Robert, she thought, families with money had their problems. Maybe if Cade's mother had realized that, all their lives would be different now.

THE SCENT OF GARLIC in the steam flavored the air and Cade stirred the sauce a few times, then poured it over the shrimp in the heavy black skillet. It was too much food for one person but he'd put it in the fridge for tomorrow. A loud ring made him drop the potholder to the floor.

He went to the living room and on the other side of the leaded-glass door, he could see Brijette on the porch, shifting from one foot to the other. She'd been especially short with him the last day or two, which bothered him even though he wished it didn't. He'd finally had to admit he enjoyed working with her at the clinic. The Cypress Landing clinic demanded more from him than the clinic in Dallas, but he enjoyed the work more. A fact that didn't really surprise him, nor did it change anything. He'd always wanted a practice like this, but he hadn't been able to voice that wish to anyone in a long time. Brijette was quick, efficient and good with the patients. She'd even offered him a few pointers on dealing with the locals, which had helped him tremendously and earned him a homemade chocolate cake from one elderly lady.

This evening, she didn't appear too friendly when he opened the door. "Brijette, what's up?"

"I need to talk to you if you have a minute."

He glanced toward the kitchen and his dinner.

"If you have company I can come back another time. I don't want to bother you if you're entertaining."

He snorted. "I don't have a soul in this town to entertain except my uncle, and you know it. I'm in the middle of making dinner, but if you'll come into the kitchen you can talk and I'll finish what I'm doing.

"Where's Dylan?" he asked as he shoved the shrimp into the oven.

"She's staying overnight with a friend, but she's why I'm here."

"If it's because I've been fishing with her, it was only for a few minutes."

"I've been thinking about this since I heard it a few days ago. It's not the fishing. It's you questioning the sheriff to find out who her father is that bothers me. Her father is none of your business."

He grimaced but tried not to let it show. Small-town rule number one: things get back to people. "I wanted to know if he'd ever lived here or if I knew him."

"Why do you care who it is?"

"I don't know. I don't care." He threw the dish towel he'd been holding onto the counter. "That's not true. I do care, but I'm not sure why."

Shock molded her features into a mask. His

words surprised him, too. Thoughts like that had been flitting around in his mind for days, but he hadn't meant to share them with her or with anyone else. He watched her try to control her emotions. He couldn't read them, not the way he once could. Her long black hair was pulled back, as usual, and her black eyes were impenetrable. His gut tightened, followed by other parts of his body. She had that effect, always had. He wondered how she kept her skin so smooth that the sight of it made him clench his fists to keep from touching her. Her charcoal gaze didn't leave him. Were his emotions more visible than hers? He felt compelled to explain himself.

"I hate what happened when I left here before… I wish I could change it but I can't." He realized now he should have talked to Brijette himself when his mother told him she'd asked for money to stay away from him. He could have believed in her enough to hear her side. But he hadn't. He'd been hurt, and he'd let his mother convince him he should walk away and not look back.

"It was your choice."

Her anger made her jaw tight, and he knew she wanted to blame it all on him, but she'd played a part in the events that had led them here. He wasn't going to let her pretend she hadn't.

"You could have agreed to see me."

Her eyes narrowed. "Don't be ridiculous. I made every effort to contact you. I even called your house. I was told you wouldn't speak to me ever again."

Cade rubbed his forehead. He should have known. "I was told *you* wouldn't see *me*. When they told me about the money I still wanted to hear it from you."

"Who said you couldn't?"

"My mother," he sighed. "I guess I shouldn't have believed her, but she had seen you and she'd never lied to me. But she'd never interfered in any relationship I'd had before either."

"I'm sure you were careful to stick to acceptable country-club girls prior to me."

He leaned closer to her and he imagined he could feel her breath against his skin. "I'd never truly loved anyone before you, so she didn't have a reason to get involved."

He knew those were tears glistening in her eyes. Hell, admitting how much he'd loved her made him swallow hard to maintain his composure.

"But you left as soon as I got into trouble and you never looked back," she whispered.

"I know I made a choice to leave, but you chose to ask my mother for money to stay away from me."

"Your mother gave me money to stay away from you."

He wasn't quite sure if she was asking a question or repeating his statement. She still had that odd expression on her face, as if she'd rather not discuss this. Maybe they shouldn't delve into it. Maybe the past was better left lying right where it was. But one thing was certain. He had to touch her. His hand closed around hers and tightened, feeling the strength he'd always admired and the vulnerability he'd hoped to protect. The temperature in the room went up a notch, but she didn't pull away. She needed to feel the connection between them, too, though she pretended she didn't. It nearly took his breath, but he was determined to stay in control.

"I realize now why you asked for the money. I mean, I had just abandoned you when things were at their worst. You needed the money to start a new life, to go to school."

"Yes, I did. I..." She paused, her head tilting slightly to one side. "What did you think when she told you I asked for the money?"

He raked his free hand over his face and

decided to be straight with her. "It hurt like hell. When I realized you were going to that youth correctional center and I had gotten off completely free, I was surprised. I mean, the drugs were in your backpack, but we were together and we both denied knowing anything about the package. Part of me was relieved even though I felt bad for you. When my mother told me you'd had the court-appointed lawyer contact her and that you'd offered to stay out of my life for good if she'd give you money, I was crushed. At first I felt like you were a person I didn't even know."

"And what do you think now?"

"I realize your wanting the money probably didn't have a lot to do with our relationship, but more to do with your own survival. You were able to go to school and get a degree, take care of yourself. It was worth it." In that breath he realized his words were true. The hurt, the betrayal, was actually worth seeing Brijette be able to get to where she was today. Even if he'd imagined other ways they could have done it together. Maybe she'd needed to make it on her own, without depending on anyone. The revelation was a lot for him to swallow and obviously for her, too, because she didn't say anything else, just stared past him.

What to do now? He could usher her to the door, but he didn't want that. The rush of heat to his skin when he saw her only proved his enormous attraction to her. But had she really not known that package was in her backpack all those years ago? His words and mind said he understood her taking a payoff to end their relationship for good, but his heart nearly froze at the thought. There had been a time when he'd believed they were perfect together. The fact that they came from such different worlds hadn't bothered him. He'd never even considered it. Brijette had always said the wealthy would do anything for money, but in the end he'd seen her live by the same code.

"You're welcome to stay and eat. I've got plenty." The words tripped past his lips.

She shook her head, but still appeared to be preoccupied.

"It's my best barbecue shrimp. Besides, we're working together now. Surely we can put the past behind us."

"Maybe."

"Come on, we'll talk shop." He could tell the scent of his cooking enticed her. He wished the idea of spending the evening with him would make her want to stay. But since he doubted that was the case, he let go of her hand and found his pot holder, pulling the skillet from the oven, waving it near her.

"Talk shop?"

"You know, about the clinic, medical stuff." Maybe she had a headache. Her expression was pained and a little bit lost.

"I guess I could stay and eat."

"Good." He pulled an extra plate from the cabinet and loaded it with spicy shrimp and French bread he'd heated earlier. After filling his own plate, he joined her at the kitchen table.

"Okay, we're talking shop. Now here's what I think." He peeled a shrimp and chewed, watching her.

"Mmm..." She bobbed the shrimp in her hand over her plate. "This is really good."

"Thanks. But back to my plan. I know a guy in Dallas and he wants to leave the city to open a practice in a smaller town. I think he'd be perfect to help at the clinic."

Her eyes widened. "You're kidding. How long would he stay? Until you leave?"

"Not at all, he wants a permanent position. I know you and Uncle Arthur will need help when I'm gone. Lord knows, you and I need it now."

"And you think you can sell Arthur Wheeler on this, and you really believe your city friend will be happy here in the country? There was a time when this was what *you* wanted, but now you're more than ready to take off when you're done."

He tapped his fork on the side of his glass. "That's not how I feel, but yes, my friend will want to stay here."

She wiped her hands on the wet towel beside her plate. "How *do* you feel?"

"I'm doing what I need to do." He hadn't meant to give her such a short answer, but he didn't want to discuss his reasons for not staying. "It would make it easier for you on Thursdays when you go to your field clinic. You won't have to worry about what's going on at the clinic in town."

She rested her chin on her fist and he was reminded of the much younger Brijette who had been in love with him. "You don't have to convince me we need another doctor. Your uncle's the one who's so resistant to change."

He leaned toward her. "But you're willing for me to tell him you agree to it?"

She smiled. "He knows I'd agree. I've been on him to get more help for a long time."

"Good. Now, tell me what's been happening in Cypress Landing the past few years."

She snorted and gave a low laugh that made him remember all the good things about being with her. Things he thought he'd forgotten.

CHAPTER SEVEN

HE DIDN'T know.

Brijette rinsed a glass Dylan had left in the sink after breakfast. Since that first night Cade had asked her about Dylan, she'd had a nagging suspicion that he didn't know about her pregnancy. It was the reason she'd held her tongue instead of lashing out at him over his quick and callous choice to abort their child without discussing it with her. She wasn't sure what kind of game Cade's mother had been playing, but she'd dealt them both a handful of lies. Cade had no idea she'd been pregnant, that his mother had offered her money on the condition that she have an abortion and never speak to Cade again.

Mrs. Wheeler was a liar. She'd told Brijette that Cade felt they were too young to have a child. Stunned that her sweet and perfect Cade hadn't been the man she'd thought, Brijette had taken the money with no intention of ever having an abortion. Mrs. Wheeler had the money put in an account in Brijette's name in Lafayette, where she'd planned to go to school. They'd both left Brijette to serve her three months in youth prison. The people there knew she was pregnant and she could have gone through with her promise to Mrs. Wheeler, but it had been a promise she never once considered keeping.

She closed the dishwasher and lingered at the kitchen window, watching a raccoon in the shadows of the trees. The air conditioner hummed, but she could still hear the noise of frogs and crickets filling the humid night. Mrs. Wheeler had told Cade that Brijette had asked for money to stay away from him. She'd always wondered why he hadn't come himself, if she'd misread him so completely. At least now she knew what she'd seen in him hadn't been all wrong. She roamed around the house, picking up a pair of Dylan's shoes she'd left near the front door, straightening magazines on the end table. After Brijette was arrested and charged for possession of narcotics, her asking for money to end their relationship must have made Cade feel as betrayed by her as she'd felt when his mother said he wanted her to have an abortion and disappear.

Dropping Dylan's shoes in her room, she flung herself across the child's bed. She could tell him. She could tell Cade that his mother had offered her money for an abortion. Maybe he'd stop thinking she'd been a poor back-woods money-grubber. But in some ways she had been like that, because she could have refused the money completely. She hadn't. The easier road to her education had been offered and Brijette had taken it.

Telling him Dylan was his daughter wasn't an option. She knew the Wheelers. Cade's father might have died but his mother remained capable of wreaking havoc in Brijette's life without her husband. She'd proved that years ago. Being steamrolled by the Wheelers once was enough for her. To them she was a poor girl from the swamp who lived in a shack. Her real estate might have changed but they wouldn't believe that she had changed, too. Even though she'd enjoyed tonight, Cade couldn't be in her life again.

The image of him leaning across the corner of the table flickered in her mind. She'd had to stop herself from sliding her palm across his chest to see if it would still feel incredible, as she remembered it had. But she held no illusions when it came to rekindling a relationship with Cade. She didn't know him now, and he didn't know her, either. She needed to keep it that way.

In her mind, huge question marks surrounded him. Brijette couldn't risk going up against the Wheelers to keep Dylan. They had more connections than she could imagine, and she hadn't raised her daughter alone this long to lose her. Pulling a quilt from the bottom of Dylan's bed, she covered herself and closed her eyes, praying she wouldn't dream.

THE PLASTIC BOX landed on the floor of the storeroom with a thud and Dylan groaned. She hated carrying boxes back and forth to Willow Point. In the morning you took them out, in the evening they went back in. It was so stupid.

"Dylan, that box is not heavy. Why are you making such a ruckus?"

"It *is* heavy and I need to go to the bathroom."

Her mother placed her container against the wall. "Well go, then. Alicia and I will finish putting everything away."

Dylan didn't bother to glance back at her mother or Mrs. Alicia. She raced to the bathroom, slamming the door behind her. She didn't really need to go, but she did need to wash her face. She'd spent the whole day at Willow Point where her mom ran the free clinic in the store. One of the local kids had a pirogue and they'd spent the day paddling around the creeks and backwaters. She knew her mom was from there. She'd once taken Dylan to see the rotting shack that had belonged to Dylan's great-grandmother. Dylan was glad Willow Point wasn't her home. She'd seen how the mean kids in Cypress Landing made fun of people who lived in the backwaters and didn't have much. She often wondered if other kids had been mean to her mom.

Right now, though, she couldn't have dirt on her face and wild hair. She didn't want to look like a swamp rat when Cade saw her. He probably dumped her mom years ago 'cause she wasn't from a good part of town. Of course, if she thought about it long enough, that would make Cade kind of a bad person. She didn't normally like people who turned their noses up at others because they were poor. But Cade wouldn't do that, even if he did have money. She'd heard Mrs. Norma and her husband talking, and they said Cade was filthy rich, the kind of rich where you drove fancy cars and had more than one house. But Cade didn't drive a fancy car. That kind of talk confused her.

Dylan only knew she liked Cade. What else mattered?

She didn't see a soul in the hall when she left the bathroom, so she went to the small kitchen and pulled a soda from the refrigerator. From the window in the kitchen she could see old Mrs. Carson, the nurse, get into her car. Thank goodness she was gone. The woman always looked like she wanted to gripe at her about something. A figure trotted across the street to enter the small lot. No wonder the woman had such a frown on her face—there was her outlaw son. The young man got in the car with his mother and the two drove away.

Her mom said Mrs. Carson's son had a drug problem and that was why she seemed worried all the time. Her mom had had to explain to her exactly what a drug problem was since she hadn't had a clue. Even after the explanation, she still thought it sounded strange that anybody could do the things he'd done because of some pills. She was just glad no one she knew was mixed up in it. The most important thing was that Cade's car was in the staff parking lot. Thank goodness he hadn't gone yet. Following the sound of voices, she skipped toward the front lobby. It was time to go home and she was trying to think of ways she could get Cade to invite them to his house or to dinner in town, which would be even better.

In the lobby, her mother and Cade leaned against one side of the reception counter, and across from them stood Mr. Cooper. The big man could be pretty scary, but she knew him from the search-and-rescue team and he wasn't mean. Maybe he was here because of search-and-rescue. She sure hoped no one was in big trouble. Sidling closer to the counter, she heard Mr. Cooper mention prescriptions with Cade's name on them. Was Cade sick? No, it was prescriptions he had written for a patient, like a doctor is supposed to do. Except Cade said he hadn't written them.

"Dylan, go fix yourself a sandwich in the kitchen."

Darn it, she'd been noticed. "I'm not hungry."

"Then go wait in my office and read that new book we got you."

"I don't want to read."

Her mother gave her a stern look. "Dylan, we're talking business here, and I said go."

Dylan took two steps toward the office. Her mom started talking to Mr. Cooper about prescriptions and junk that she had no interest in whatsoever, but Cade was here and here was where she planned to stay. Now that she was out of sight she would…

"Dylan, you heard your mom. Now take off."

Her throat tightened. How could he? How could Cade order her to leave like that? He'd taken sides with her mother, which so wasn't fair because her mother didn't even like him. She blew her breath hard between her teeth as she stomped down the hall.

"And quit huffing and puffing. You're too old for it." His words echoed behind her as she slammed the door on her mother's tiny office. She grabbed the new book and threw it across the room. It bounced off the wall and landed at her feet. She picked it up again. Reading was better than sitting and doing nothing.

CADE DRUMMED his fingers on top of the counter. "I didn't write those prescriptions, which means someone is stealing prescription papers from here and signing my name to them."

Brijette looked up from the computer. "Cade's right, Jackson. We don't have a patient by that name in our records."

The big man nodded. "Well, be careful with your prescriptions."

Cade crossed his arms in front of him. "All they need is one—and a good copying machine—and they could write hundreds of prescriptions."

He'd wanted his time in Cypress Landing to be a break from the problems he'd had in Dallas. But since coming here, there had been nothing but one headache followed by another—first Brijette, now this.

Jackson stuck his folder under his arm. "I'll keep in touch."

When the door shut behind the officer, Cade stared at Brijette.

"What?"

"Why is this happening?" He sat on the desk that jutted below the counter.

"I don't know. Stuff like this happens, it's… Oh, I see what you mean."

He heard the anger in her voice and though he hadn't meant to insinuate she might be at fault, he could see how she'd make that connection.

"You think I was involved before, so naturally I'm in on this. I guess my being part of search-and-rescue is a good cover for all my illegal dealings." She began to shut down the computer.

He pinched the bridge of his nose. "I didn't say that."

"But that's what you were thinking."

"Don't tell me what I'm thinking. We'd both

better start trying to find out how this is happening before it gets worse."

She sighed and twisted in the chair. "You're right, and I wouldn't blame you if you thought I might be part of this."

"I don't think that. You said you didn't know the drugs were in your backpack. I believe you."

She scratched at a spot on her scrub top, refusing to look at him. "You didn't before."

"I didn't know what to think, then."

"Well, if your intuition had been to think I was guilty, you'd better stick with that because you'd have been correct."

He slid into the chair across from her, his legs sagging under his own weight. In his heart he'd believed Brijette had told the truth. And now she sat in front of him telling him she'd been a drug courier.

She knotted her fingers in her lap and finally met his eyes. "A driver at the tire factory where I worked asked me to drop a package off for him at a guy's camp on the river. I said sure, and he gave me cash for doing it, for gas in the boat, he said."

"How much did he give you?"

"A hundred bucks."

Cade gave a low whistle. "Weren't you suspicious? A hundred dollars is a lot for gas."

"I didn't really think it was drugs. To be honest, I tried not to think about what was in there. I figured I'd do it this one time and then never again. I knew it wasn't quite right, but I needed the money for college. I made a mistake, and I learned a hard lesson."

"I'd say it was, Brij. Three months in a juvenile detention center would likely teach anyone a lesson."

She rocked in the chair as though weighing what she was about to say.

"It wasn't the detention center. I could have learned all the best ways to be a criminal if I'd wanted, but I knew that wasn't the person I wanted to be."

His hand went to her knee, without his planning it. He had to touch her as much as he had to take his next breath. "Are you the person you want to be, now?"

Her pink lips curled into a smile. "I think I'm pretty close. Aren't you going to scream and yell at me about lying and doing something I should have known better than to do?"

Why wasn't he furious? Part of his brain told him he should be angry that she'd lied and that she'd let him go with her when she was doing something that could get them both in trouble. But the anger wouldn't come. Not now, not when so much time had passed and they'd both been through more than enough.

"If someone had asked me the other day if this would make me mad, I'm sure I'd have said yes. But hearing you say it, admit it to me..." He shrugged. "I don't feel anger. You paid for what you did in that youth prison and learned from it. I've had to learn from my mistakes, too."

"You went to jail, Mom?" The angry question echoed from the doorway, bouncing off the walls. Brijette drained to a pale ash. Cade had to admit, he'd forgotten Dylan was still in the clinic, supposedly in her mother's office, but obviously not.

Brijette leaped from the chair as Dylan appeared in front of her. "How could you not tell me? Does everybody know? I bet all the kids talk about this behind my back. You said I should tell you if I didn't think you were being a good mother. Well, I'm telling you now. You're awful."

Her blond ponytail swished as she spun and fled, her tennis shoes smacking against the wood floor. Brijette didn't move except to raise her arm, as if she wanted to follow her but couldn't.

"Let me get her. I'll bring her home. You

lock up and go to your house. We'll see you there." He knew she had to be in shock when she didn't argue, only nodded her head. Reaching into his pocket for his keys, he raced after Dylan.

CHAPTER EIGHT

CADE JUMPED INTO his truck and drove in the direction of Brijette's house. He'd only traveled a hundred yards when he saw his intuition was correct. One angry blonde jogged on the side of the road.

He lowered the passenger window as he pulled alongside her. "Get in, Dylan."

"No, I don't want to."

"You can't walk all the way home."

She rubbed the back of her hand across her forehead. "I'm not going home."

He checked his rearview mirror, glad to see no cars behind him. "Where are you going?"

"I don't know."

"Well that sounds like a great plan. Now get in here. Don't make me put you in." She paused in midstride and climbed into his truck—maybe it was the male authority in his voice that she wasn't accustomed to. He was simply glad she hadn't fought him more.

When they passed the driveway to her house, he could feel her eyes boring into him. "Where are we going?"

"I thought you might want to ride awhile and cool off."

"I'm not hot."

He laughed. "I mean, until your temper cools off."

She watched the trees passing them in a blur. "She should have told me, and she shouldn't have done whatever she did."

They rode in silence a few minutes longer before Cade eased the truck onto the side of the road.

"Your mom grew up in a run-down place near where she has her clinic. She didn't have much."

"I know. She took me to see it before. It was horrible."

"Then you should know you can't judge your mother for what she did as a young girl. She had to make a better life for herself, and later on for you. I don't know the whole story, so I'll let her tell you, but you remember that."

Cade couldn't be sure at what point he'd begun to believe in Brijette Dupre again. Maybe he'd never stopped believing in her. He'd never been desperate for money to survive like Brijette had. She'd made choices he couldn't understand. But now that he was older, had seen people not nearly so desperate for money make even more despicable choices, her sins didn't appear nearly so black. He turned the truck around and started toward Dylan and Brijette's house.

The lights glowed in the windows and Brijette waited for them on the porch. The girl jumped from his truck and would have run past her mother except Brijette grabbed her by the shoulder. He'd have liked to stay to see how they worked through this. What did you tell your kid when they realized you were once young and foolish, too? But he didn't stay, because he wasn't part of that family, and he tried to ignore whatever it was inside of him that whispered how much he wanted to be. He drove past the trees that lined the drive and went home, letting mother and daughter try to patch things up.

THE SOUR CREAM made the salsa a pinkish color as Brijette stirred the spoon in the bowl. She dipped a chip into the mixture and pushed it across the bar to Dylan. After three detailed explanations of what had happened that summer, Dylan had finally calmed down. Hearing, by accident no less, that your mom had a criminal past had to be tough to take.

"Cade said you did that thing so you could have a better life."

Brijette tried not to choke on the chip she'd swallowed. She'd been afraid of what Cade might say to Dylan, but at the time she hadn't been able to react fast enough to go after the girl herself. Not that Dylan would have gotten in the car with her.

"When did he say that?"

"In the truck."

Thank goodness for miracles, especially the ones that had Cade Wheeler paint a decent picture of her to her daughter.

"Was that why he dumped you? Because of the drugs?"

"No, that wasn't why he dumped me. Well, it might've been part of it, but we ended our relationship because we were too different."

"What does that mean?" Dylan stuffed a chip into her mouth and watched her expectantly.

Brijette gritted her teeth. How did she explain things she didn't understand herself? "You know where I came from, how I lived. I was poor backwoods trash to people like the Wheelers. Cade and I didn't have a future. His family would never have accepted me."

"Would they accept you now?"

"To the Wheelers, if you're born trash, you're always gonna be trash."

"Does that mean I'm trash, too?"

She wiped up a drop of spilled salsa. "No, Dylan, no one's trash. I'm just saying that's how people occasionally think."

Her daughter straightened on the barstool. "Well, I don't think Cade believes that stuff."

"He didn't used to, a long time ago, but family is important and you usually live the way you were taught. I may have been poor, but my grandmother raised me to have morals and respect for others. I made mistakes, but like she always said, 'you gotta be true to your raisin'."

"What's my 'raisin'?"

She ruffled Dylan's blond hair.

"Same as mine. Be good to other people, do what's right, money isn't everything and take care of your neighbors."

Dylan held her glass of lemonade and swished the liquid around inside. "Is going to the jail place how you learned money isn't everything?"

"Yes, it is. Now I know that if I work hard I'll get the things I need and most of the things I want."

Dylan chewed a chip. "I believe that, too."

"Good, so we're okay."

Dylan nodded as Brijette stood. "I'm going to take a bath. You finish the chips."

In her room, Brijette sat on the edge of the bed. One secret in the open and it hadn't killed her. She hadn't wanted Dylan to know she'd spent time in the detention center, not yet, but she had planned on telling her.

When? She pushed away the accusatory voice in her head. *I was waiting until she was old enough,* she told her nagging subconscious. Obviously the girl could handle it now, but not the other secret. That one had to stay locked tight for good. She'd been careful to say to Dylan, during her explanation, that this happened before she met her father. *How fair is it to Dylan to never let her know her father?* Now Brijette wanted to strangle the voice in her head. Having no father had to be better than having one whose mother had never even wanted the child to be born. How would the Wheelers treat Dylan amid all their high-society friends? They'd either make her feel like a second-class citizen or they'd change her into a rude rich kid. No, Brijette wasn't having that for her daughter. She got to her feet and hurried to the shower, that irritating voice reminding her how wonderful Cade had been with Dylan since he'd been here. How naturally he slipped into the role of Cypress Landing small-town doctor. It was an act, she reminded herself. When the time came for hard decisions, the real Cade Wheeler would appear, the one who ran out on a girl when she got into trouble, who let his mother make his decisions for him. That's the man she had to protect her daughter from, him and his mother.

CHECKING HER WATCH, Brijette couldn't believe they'd finished for the day. Across the small staff parking area, Cade still sat in his truck and she tilted her head, trying to see inside. His door opened and he waved at her.

"My battery is dead, lost charge. Could you let me jump my truck off you? I have jumper cables."

She tried not to be surprised that the rich boy actually had jumper cables in his vehicle. That he drove a truck instead of a Porsche or Jaguar had surprised her even more. She pulled next to his vehicle, popped her hood and waited as he put the cables in place. When he tried to start his truck, the engine remained quiet. He waited and tried again. Still nothing.

"The battery's shot. Could you give me a ride to the store to get a new one?"

She started laughing. "You do realize that

it's after five so we'll have to drive for nearly an hour to get to a store that's open."

"No, I hadn't thought of that."

She shook her head. "Get in. I'll take you home and get you in the morning. Your place is only a couple of miles from mine. You can get a new battery tomorrow."

"You think my truck will be safe here?"

She lifted an eyebrow at his question. "Unless the thief has a new battery or a tow truck, you should be fine."

He smiled, climbing into the passenger seat. "I guess you're right."

As she pulled onto the street Cade asked her about a patient, but before she could answer, her cell phone rang. Expecting Dylan, she groaned when she saw the number.

"Sheriff's office," she said to him as she punched the button to answer the call.

Jackson Cooper's voice boomed in her ear. "Brij, can you get to the old Johnson place on River Road? We need you to track. Now."

She paused. "I kind of need to take Cade home. His truck wouldn't start."

"Bring him. We need you here ten minutes ago."

Pushing the end-call button, she drove her SUV away from the direction of their homes.

"I'm afraid you'll have to come with me, or I'll let you stay here in town and you can try to hitch a ride."

"I'll go with you. Is it a missing kid?"

"I don't know. They didn't say."

She punched the button set to dial Norma's number and told her she'd be late getting Dylan. They drove the next few minutes in silence until Brijette pulled into the driveway of an old weathered house.

"This can't be a missing kid," Cade said.

Brijette contemplated the sheriff's officers in their bulletproof vests, guns slung at their sides. With them were Cypress Landing's city police, which indicated that whatever was going on required more manpower than the sheriff's office alone. "I think you're right."

Jackson met them at the front of her vehicle. He tossed Brijette a vest and she saw Cade's eyes bulge.

"We're after an escaped prisoner from Parchman."

"What's Parchman?" Cade asked, stepping nearer to Brijette.

She grinned at him. "It's a prison in Mississippi." She focused her attention on Jackson as she finished fastening the vest. "What's he in for?"

"Life sentence for multiple murders." She tried not to smile as Jackson ignored Cade, who appeared shocked.

Cade's fingers closed around her shoulder. "You can't go running around in the woods after a killer. Brijette, you have a child at home. What if something happens to you?"

She patted his arm and winked at Jackson. "I'll be fine. This huge cop will be with me. He blocks all bullets that come my way."

Jackson chuckled, but Cade tightened his grip. "Why are you doing this? Are you trying to rectify things you did in the past by being a volunteer hero?"

She couldn't believe Cade could nail her so squarely with a truth she'd never really admitted to herself. Extracting herself from him, she started after Jackson, who strode toward the house. "You don't know what you're saying, Cade Wheeler."

"Yes, I do, and you know it."

They stopped at the rear of the house.

"Officer Cooper, why can't you bring in a dog to track this person?"

Jackson glared at him, but Cade didn't waver, though he hoped he'd never actually have to tangle with the man. He knew Brijette volunteered for the search-and-rescue team, but surely chasing escaped murderers was not part of the job description.

Finally, Jackson sighed and decided to answer. "We've got three people who took off from this house in different directions. Only one of them is the one we want to follow. We know his shoe size and that he got shot in the leg. I can't really explain all that to a dog, now can I? Besides, Brijette's right here and the nearest dog team is hours away."

Cade frowned. "I'm going with you."

Brijette snorted and Jackson actually rolled his eyes, which kind of made the big man a little less intimidating. "No, you're not. No private citizen is going with us. I'll cuff you to the car if I have to."

Sheriff Matt Wright stepped over to them. "Why isn't Brijette on the trail already?"

Jackson poked a finger at Cade's chest. "'Cause this guy is holding us up. He wants to go with us."

Matt stared at Cade, not responding immediately, which he hoped was a good sign. "Throw a vest on him. He's a doctor. If someone gets shot he might come in handy."

Jackson groaned. "But, Matt, what if he's the one who gets shot?"

"It's his choice. We'll automatically induct him into the search-and-rescue team."

"As what?" Brijette asked. Cade could tell she didn't want to have to deal with him a minute longer.

Matt grinned. "Tracker's assistant, I guess."

Cade pulled on his vest while trying to follow Brijette and Jackson. Ahead of him, Jackson stopped as Brijette moved forward. When Cade tried to pass, the big man gripped his arm.

"We wait here until she decides which trail to follow. We don't want to ruin the tracks for her, do we, tracker's assistant?"

"Look, I'm worried about her."

"I know. That's the only reason you're here and not handcuffed to the steering wheel of my car."

Cade crossed his arms and waited, watching Brijette. She moved slowly, staring at the ground. Here and there she stopped, touched the dirt, placed her fingers to the earth and appeared to measure. Then she'd start again, periodically taking strides longer than her natural one. After a few minutes, she waved at them from the edge of the woods and they both hurried toward her.

"You know, Jackson, we'd have saved a lot of time if you guys would've noticed this blood." She pointed to some leaves on the lower part of the trees. “I wouldn’t have spent all this time deciding where to start.”

Cade grinned as the sheriff’s officer had the decency to be embarrassed.

“Come on.” She smiled and winked at Cade. “Let’s get going. This should be quite an adventure for you, city boy.”

“Just so long as no one shoots at me.”

“I’m pretty sure that won’t happen. At least, it never has before.”

“And how many murderers have you tracked before?”

She glanced at Jackson as they pressed deeper into the woods. “We’ve done two, right, Cooper?”

Jackson nodded. Cade kept quiet and followed them. What was Brijette thinking, doing this when she had a child at home?

From that point forward, Cade kept quiet, more because he was in awe of Brijette than because he feared he would attract the escaped prisoner’s attention and get shot, although he didn’t want that to happen, either. He didn’t really see much on the ground or in the tree limbs that would indicate which direction they should go, but Brijette must have had a built-in device in her brain that spotted the trail, because she watched the ground and knew exactly when to turn left or right.

The trees began to thin and they made their way onto what appeared to be a dry creek bed, with the banks on either side rising well above his head. Still in the lead, Brijette started to climb the embankment. Jackson caught her halfway and shook his head. Thankfully, one of the two had a bit of sense. Cade joined them as the officer bobbed his head above the edge for a fraction of a second. Shots split the evening air, spraying dirt in their faces as the bullets tore into the ground. Pushing Brijette, Cade rolled with her to the bottom of the creek bed. Jackson landed in a heap beside them, blood trickling at the side of his temple.

"Jackson, are you okay?" Brijette called out in a low voice.

He sat up, wiping at the blood. "It's a scratch." With a quick call on his radio he notified the sheriff of their location.

"He's in a deer stand, there," Jackson motioned toward the top of the creek bed. In the sky, they heard a helicopter, and in a few minutes officers came running.

"All right, you two, we've got this area blocked off now and he's not coming in this direction, so y'all can head back the way we came."

Cade got to his feet, pulling Brijette with him. They passed through a line of officers.

"Never get shot at, huh?" Cade said as they trudged along.

Brijette shrugged. "First time for everything."

"Only takes one time to get killed, though."

She kicked at a stick. "We can't all live our lives in a safe little vacuum."

"I'm telling you to stay alive so you can raise your child."

"This is important to me. Dylan understands that, and she understands the risks—though to date there haven't been many risky situations."

"Dylan's a child. It's not for her to understand."

She didn't answer him but marched faster through the woods, making him nearly jog to keep her in sight. Occasionally, she let a limb go at the right moment so that it would smack him. He had no choice but to follow her, otherwise she'd have to track his lost butt in these woods. Of course, she'd probably refuse, saying it was much too dangerous.

They got in her car and she started the engine before she finally looked at him.

"I know what you're saying—that I could get hurt. But I could get killed on our way home, too. Cade, I can't live my life always worrying that something might happen to me so I can't take care of Dylan. I grew up afraid of everything, afraid of what people would say, of how we would make ends meet, of where money would come from. It led me to make a few bad choices. I can't do that anymore. I've got a talent—tracking—and I have to use it to help people. What's more dangerous, me helping catch this guy or him being loose to possibly hurt other people, maybe the mother of another child?"

He leaned his head against the seat. At times like this, when she made so much sense, he didn't know whether to argue with her or kiss her. It had always been like that. He made up his mind and reached across the seat, catching her neck beneath her hair, pulling her forward. His lips met hers before she could protest and before he could consider the consequences of his actions. But that one touch flooded him with years of past emotions and all the same wanting he'd known in his early twenties. He hadn't expected to kiss her so long, with so much passion. He'd half expected her to stop him. But she hadn't and he pulled her closer. He slid the fingertips of his other hand lightly across her cheek, down the side of her neck, to feel the pulse hammering at her throat. Her knuckles rubbed his chest as she knotted his shirt in her fist. Outside, a car door slammed and she faltered, her palms flattening against his chest, shoving him away from her. She pressed herself against the door on her side, her lips still parted, and he nearly went to her again, but she held up her palm as if to ward him off.

"What are you doing?" she whispered.

"I don't know." And he didn't. He watched people moving in the dark by the house. Night had fallen and he hadn't noticed.

"We need to go."

He didn't answer, and neither one of them spoke as she drove to his house. When she stopped in his front drive, he reached for the door handle. Something needed to be said.

"Don't do that again."

Not exactly what he'd had in mind, but it would suffice. He opened his mouth to tell her he might not be able to help himself, but instead he got out of the car. From the porch, he watched her taillights disappear down the long winding drive. He should never have left here, should never have deserted Brijette, even if she had been guilty of making a very bad decision and even if she'd asked for money to stay away from him. Most of all, he should never have promised his father he would stay in Dallas. He knew now those mistakes had become obstacles to his happiness. He hadn't come to Cypress Landing to make all these realizations, but that was what had happened. Now, what was he going to do about it?

CHAPTER NINE

WHEN SHE HEARD Alicia call the patient's name, Brijette hurried to finish straightening the room she'd used. The young girl holding a baby, accompanied by her husband, followed the nurse into the exam room across the hall and Brijette entered right behind them.

"Regina, T.J., it's good to see you." She opened her arms and the girl handed the small bundle to her. "She's perfect." Cuddling the infant closer, Brijette decided she'd have to follow this family—her first, and hopefully only, delivery at her free clinic.

"Are you seeing us today?" Regina asked as Brijette gave the child to the girl's husband.

"No, Dr. Wheeler will be seeing you. I just wanted to say hi and to see if y'all are doing okay."

T.J. seemed very comfortable holding the baby, which relieved Brijette. She'd been a little worried that the scared kid she'd seen in the clinic that day might run out on this very big responsibility. "We're doing fine," he said, laughing as Alicia slipped into the room and took the child away from him.

"I want to show her to Emma," she said.

"Regina wants to go to school," T.J. continued. "We're trying to get a place here in town. That way she can take classes toward her General Equivalency Diploma since she didn't ever finish high school."

Regina nodded. "I did good in school. So did T.J. I'm trying to talk him into getting his GED, too. I met with a counselor at the college and she said if we had the GED we could take developmental college classes that wouldn't count toward a degree but would help us pass the real courses later on."

Brijette noticed Cade standing in the doorway, waiting impatiently, since he had a long list of patients to see. But he'd have to wait. This would be an important lesson for Cade in working at a small-town clinic. Here, you didn't run in and see your patients, then shoo them on their way. She and Doc Wheeler took time to talk to everyone, especially people like Regina and Theodore Jerome Broussard. A young couple wanting to get educated to create a better life for their baby deserved their attention and help.

"Do you have an idea what you'd like to study?"

"I'd like to be a nurse." Regina turned to T.J., whose cheeks pinked with a bit of embarrassment at the fact that he had aspirations beyond the backwaters, when he had quite a distance to go.

He shrugged slightly. "I've worked in construction and I think I'd like to maybe be an engineer." He glanced at Cade. "But we got a lot to do first."

"We need to get this checkup done," Cade said from the door, and shouted for Alicia to bring the baby.

Brijette hurried from the room, knowing that she had indeed taken a good bit of Cade's time. "Sorry, I know we're busy," she whispered as she went by him.

He only frowned as she passed him, then shut the door.

REGINA AND T.J. HAD LEFT by the time Brijette had finished seeing the two patients she had waiting. At the front desk, she leaned over Emma's shoulder, scanning the computer screen. Cade stood at the counter, holding a big brown bag that smelled like lunch.

"Sandwiches are here from the Main Street Coffee Shop," he said, but she ignored him.

"Emma, did we bill that young couple?"

The older woman tapped the computer keyboard. "They had a baby checkup and they're getting assistance. They paid their part, which wasn't much."

"Okay, I only want to be sure they don't have a huge medical bill. Can we see if they have a hospital bill?"

"No, we can only get that information from them the next time they come. Do you want me to?"

Brijette chewed her lip. "No, it would embarrass them, I'm sure. We'll see what happens."

"Brijette, come eat your sandwich." Cade took her by the wrist, dragging her down the hall before she could say any more.

In the small kitchen, he set the bag on the counter and rested his hip against the cabinet. "What are you doing?"

"How do you mean?"

"With this couple. What are you doing? Finding their personal information, making sure they don't have a bill here—we're not going to make this a free clinic, you know."

She gritted her teeth. "I'm not trying to make this a free clinic. You'll find that we don't run our patients through here like a bunch of cows. Most of them are our neighbors and friends, and we treat them that way."

"How helpful is it to encourage those two to go to college? Do you know how hard that would be for them? Shouldn't you help find them a good job? Or better yet, stay out of it, because it's their life."

"I know exactly how hard it would be," Brijette said, clenching her fists at her sides.

The anger that came over her made Brijette's face hot. When a difficult situation appeared, the real Cade emerged, the rich kid who had no idea what it took to go to college and build a life for yourself without money from your parents. A niggling voice in her brain questioned if she really knew, either. She had, after all, had help from a chunk of Wheeler money. But that had been different, she told herself. She'd still had plenty of struggles even with the money, not to mention what she'd endured to get it. With a good bit of effort, she quieted the guilty voice that said she really should have found another way, done it on her own, not taken the damn Wheeler money.

"I think you shouldn't expect too much when trying to get them to go to college," Cade continued.

"And I think you're a rich ass, who doesn't know what it means to help people who haven't been born to money and who don't have the advantages that come with it."

She raced past him, bumping into Alicia, who paused at the door with her eyes wide, obviously thinking that, once again, Brijette had ruined her chances with the rich doctor. If she only knew all Brijette's chances with Cade had been ruined with a lie that she kept hiding behind.

THE SOUND OF THE PHONE ringing jolted Brijette from a deep sleep. Disoriented, she struggled to a sitting position in her bed, realizing that closing her eyes for a minute after her bath had turned into good night lady. The clock on the nightstand read nine, early for a summer night. Dylan was still watching television.

"Mom, the phone's for you." The girl pushed the bedroom door open, holding the phone in one hand, a pair of tennis shoes in the other. "It's Mr. Cooper at the sheriff's office," she added, sitting in the middle of the floor to put on her sneakers.

On the other end of the phone, Jackson Cooper's voice cracked amid the rattle of radios and conversation.

"Brijette, we need you at a rental house on Small Ridge Road, right past Joe Canton's place."

"I know where it is. Is it a fresh trail you want me to follow?"

"I'll explain when you get here."

Dylan was waiting by the front door when Brijette got dressed and left her bedroom. "I hate having to drag you along like this, Dylan."

"I want to go. Do you think I can help track?"

"We'll see when we get there."

The hot and humid night air surrounded them, and Brijette flipped the air-conditioning in the vehicle on low. The thick trees hanging near the edge of the road made ghostly images in the receding light. But the shadows and milky reflections washed away when they pulled into the drive of the small brick house. Several patrol cars surrounded the home with their lights glaring, assisted by a few sets of battery-powered spotlights scattered near the edges of the woods.

Parking the car, Brijette killed the engine, but before she could open her door Dylan went bounding across the yard.

"Cade!"

Brijette studied the crowd of people through her window. Sure enough, Cade waited next to Jackson. Maybe this wasn't a regular tracking assignment.

Halfway to where the group had gathered, she met Dylan scuffing her way back to their car, frowning and huffing words under her breath Brijette couldn't understand. Cade and Jackson watched her.

"What's up?"

Dylan put her hands on her hips. "You're my mother. Would you please tell them it's okay for me to be here and that I can help you track?"

"What did they tell you?"

"That I needed to wait in the car."

Brijette gave a half smile. "I guess you should wait in the car."

"But, Mom, I'm big enough to help."

"You are big enough to help in most cases, but if Cade and Jackson feel you don't need to be in the middle of this, I'll have to trust their judgment."

Much more humphing and sighing followed, but Dylan stalked to the vehicle. Brijette hadn't had much to say to Cade since they'd disagreed about her helping the Broussard couple. He'd suggested she and Dylan come for dinner twice, and she'd refused. Now she couldn't avoid him.

"I'm guessing you didn't call me here to follow a trail."

Jackson frowned. "Not exactly, though I

imagine you'll want to give the place a once-over and let me know if you have an idea what's going on here."

"They've found a stash of drugs. Some of them are prescriptions with mine and your names on them." Cade's jaw was tight with anger.

"Your uncle says this happened to him in the past."

"I don't think he's had a problem like this before," Jackson said.

"I don't care if it has happened before. I don't need this right now."

She twisted to confront Cade. "And you think I do?"

"I'm saying I haven't had this problem before I came here." He planted his feet apart as if ready to take her on in an argument.

She didn't even try to keep from sneering at him. "Well, heaven forbid that the little country town's going to tarnish the good city doctor's reputation."

Cade moved in closer to her, his voice dropping an octave. "If you have an idea of what's going on here, you'd better come clean with it."

Her body went stiff. "What does that mean? Why am I the one who might have information?"

Jackson stood back, watching them, until he finally waved his hand to get their attention. "Why don't you both come inside? You can decide whose fault it is later, preferably not on my time."

Brijette followed behind the big officer, embarrassed that she'd let Cade get to her and still angry at what he might be insinuating. It wasn't fair that she'd made one mistake when she was seventeen years old, and now every time an issue with drugs surfaced, she had to be put under a microscope and scrutinized.

Dusty lightbulbs illuminated the house, revealing a filthy mess with trash scattered in the sparsely furnished rooms. In the kitchen, dirty dishes and empty food containers littered the cabinets and table. An acrid smell burned her nose amid the general stench of nastiness.

"This place reeks."

Jackson wiped the back of his forearm across his mouth as if the idea of being sick lurked nearby. "Yeah. Among other things, they were cooking crystal methamphetamine. But that's not why I called you."

In one of the tiny bedrooms sat a rather expensive copy machine and several bottles of prescription medications and blank prescription pads. Bending to look at the bottles,

Brijette saw a few with her name and several with Cade's. A pad from their clinic sat next to the bottles. Right beside them were two more from towns that were at least two hours away. Most of the bottles had been filled in other towns, even though they had hers and Cade's names on them.

"Are these patient names familiar to you, and are these prescription pads originals from your clinic? Also, see these scripts written with your name on them? Is any of that your actual handwriting? If we can locate who might have come to the clinic to get these, or who you wrote one prescription for, we'll have a lead."

Brijette flipped through the papers, reading the names. "How did you find out about this place?"

"I had a report from some folks fishing on the river. They spotted unusual traffic coming this way and when they came to fish on the creek in those woods, a man told them it was private property and they'd have to leave. Of course, the guys fishing were from this area and knew the owner of the real-estate agency that has this house, and he'd never minded them fishing here before. We checked with him, and the person renting the place paid cash and when we investigated further we found the identification he'd used to get the rental was fake."

Brijette stepped away from the evidence that she had to admit could look very bad on her. No one would give Cade a second thought, but she'd immediately fall under suspicion.

"I'd like to check the grounds."

"You think there are tracks to follow?" Cade asked.

"No, but I might get a sense of the comings and goings of the people in this house. It probably won't accomplish a thing, but I'll feel better."

At her vehicle, she pulled a clipboard from a box. In the passenger seat, Dylan sat mutely, not even bothering to acknowledge her mother or Cade, who'd tagged behind Brijette.

He thumbed a finger at the SUV as they walked away. "How long will that last?"

Brijette snorted. "Once I would have said not long, but lately these moods haven't been following patterns from the past."

"My fault, you think?"

"Possibly, or maybe a sign of the teenage years ahead."

Cade groaned. "Teenage years. It even sounds scary."

She laughed, pulling a pen from her pocket and forgetting for a minute his earlier accusations. "Yeah, it does to me, too."

She started circling the house, not really sure what she might find. Her circle enlarged and the number of footprints decreased. She imagined most of what she'd seen near the house had been made tonight. Farther on, she began to notice more patterns and similarities. She took the clipboard and drew the prints on separate sheets of paper. Then she went to the first one again, examining it more closely, making notes on the paper. She ran her finger lightly around the print, feeling the dirt and the indentions.

"What are you doing?"

She put a finger to her lips, telling Cade to be quiet until she finished. After a few more minutes she straightened. "I'm trying to separate these prints. They're not made by the same person, you know. For example, this one is a man, fairly large I'd say, and he goes this way regularly with no meandering around, straight from the house and onto that path, probably to the river. But this one—" she flipped the page to another print and trotted across the yard away from the edge of the woods "—he wanders around quite a bit. Maybe he's watching the area."

She flipped to another sheet. "This set is different." Tapping her finger on the paper, she tried to imagine the guy ambling along. "I only found a few of these."

"Maybe it's one of the police from tonight."

"No, the shoes aren't like what the sheriff's people wear, they're different. And the stride is odd, not like a man walking normally. I'm not sure what it is." She rubbed the nape of her neck. "It doesn't feel right."

He grinned. "That's important, huh? How the track feels?"

"Oh, okay. I know it's weird, but I do get a feeling for a trail on occasion, for who made it."

"Psychic, huh?"

Laughing, she smacked his arm with the clipboard. "Don't be ridiculous. I'm not psychic. It's more like intuition, a gut instinct."

"I've got a gut feeling, myself."

She frowned at him. "Really?"

"I made you mad the other day and I didn't mean to, and I did it again before we went in the house. It sounded like I was accusing you."

"No, you *were* accusing me."

He mumbled words she couldn't understand.

"What did you say?"

"I was wrong, okay?"

She smiled even though she was still aggravated and, to be honest, hurt. "Is it that difficult to say?"

One side of his mouth tweaked upward and for an instant his slightly full lower lip mesmerized her. "Occasionally, it is hard, and I feel like I've needed to say it way too much lately." He hung his head, contemplating the ground. "Honestly, Brijette, this scares me and I went a little nuts. We're under suspicion for writing unnecessary narcotic prescriptions and I really don't need trouble here."

She nearly gaped at him. This wasn't like the strong, unshakeable Cade she knew so well. He was truly worried, which made her even more concerned. Touching his hard bicep, she tried to give a reassuring smile. "Don't worry. It's stressing me, too. We'll have to try to help the sheriff's office take care of it."

His gaze fell to her hand gripping his arm. She started to let it fall to her side but he placed his on top, keeping them connected. "And the other day, with that couple?"

She shook her head. "We're too different, Cade. That's probably why it's good we parted when we were younger. You can't understand what's important to me because of where you've come from. The way you were raised and the things you've learned to value are completely opposite of what's important in my life."

"That's where you're wrong. But I can't convince you because you've already decided who I am, and no matter what I say or do, you only see what you want to see."

"That's not true."

"It is true. The other day, I didn't admit what was really bothering me, but I should have. My main concern that day was that you would get involved in helping the Broussards, and when and if it went badly you'd be hurt."

She froze, unable to hide the shock on her face. She wanted to ask why he cared if she got hurt, but she couldn't get the words to come.

He retreated quickly, as though the expression on her face had made him regret his admission. "Now is not the time to discuss this. It's getting late and I know Dylan's ready to go." She started to leave but he caught her shoulder. "Maybe one day you'll take those blinders off when you're looking at me." His fingers loosed, his hand slipping to his side.

Crushing the clipboard to her chest, she hurried to her car, leaving Cade in the yard behind the house.

When she got in the SUV, Dylan continued to ignore her. As she fastened her seat belt, she noticed Cade talking to Jackson. His words rang with truth. She didn't want him to be anything other than what she had made him in her mind. If he wasn't the horrible person she'd imagined, he might still be the boy she fell in love with, the one who had seemed to share her hopes and dreams. He'd be the man she'd been dreaming of meeting and falling in love with all this time that she'd been unable to meet the "right" guy, the "right" father for Dylan. It was an impossible situation on several different levels. Unfortunately, much of it was her fault.

She peeked at her daughter still sulking in the passenger seat. The child needed a father, but at what cost to the life she'd made for the two of them and the values she'd tried to instill? Could she really trust Cade?

CHAPTER TEN

AN UNCHARACTERISTICALLY quiet afternoon had Brijette sighing with relief. Everyone had hurried home as soon as the last patient had left except for her, Cade and the receptionist. Lately they'd been swamped. The last couple of Thursdays, she'd returned from Willow Point to find Cade still inundated with patients, so she'd stayed late to help him. He'd never asked her to cancel her visits to the field clinic. She was glad, because more people were coming and starting to trust her. If she didn't show up, what would they think? Cade had mentioned getting help, but she'd not heard another word, so she imagined his uncle had vetoed the idea.

The sound of voices from the front of the building caught her attention. She slipped into the hallway and clutched the door frame for support. Her other hand caught her throat, then dropped to her chest to remind herself to breathe. She'd never suffered a panic attack before, but the beginnings of what had to be a monstrous episode started in the middle of her stomach and spread through her body. The thin older woman with a chic bob paused in the middle of a sentence, her hand midair in a gesture. She recognized the echoing look of panic on the woman's face. Brijette used her grip on the door frame to drag herself back into the exam room she'd been tidying. Where was Cade? She prayed he'd stayed in the building, that she wouldn't have to meet this woman alone, not again. Taking a deep breath, she straightened her shoulders. Cade hadn't protected her before and she had no reason to expect him to now. Mrs. Wheeler had no power over her. Brijette wasn't a teenager grappling with her morals to try to survive.

THE DOORKNOB JIGGLED before she'd really convinced herself that she had nothing to fear from Cade's mother. Expensive cologne filled the air when Ellen Wheeler entered the room, every hair in place, makeup perfectly applied. "If you want Cade, he's probably in Doc Wheeler's office."

"I don't need Cade. I'm wondering why you're here and why no one bothered to tell me you and Cade were working together?"

"I work here and have for three years. As far as your being informed of it, well, you'll have to take that up with your son or brother-in-law."

"Don't worry, I plan to. I'm not sure how this affects the little arrangement we made years ago." She glanced away from Brijette, scanning the small exam room and, as if finding it lacking, frowned.

"This has nothing to do with that, since I wasn't the one who reentered Cade's life. Your family made that decision."

"I promise they didn't consult me. I hope you haven't discussed the details of our agreement, even with Cade. He wasn't privy to them, especially the amount of money I gave you."

"Or the fact that I was pregnant."

For a moment, Mrs. Wheeler appeared a little embarrassed and possibly afraid. "You're right, and I'm certain it was for the best that he didn't know that you were more than willing to get rid of his child for money. Hopefully, you haven't been stupid enough to tell him the truth."

"No, I haven't."

She longed to tell the woman how she regretted taking the money. Not because she'd used it for what it had been intended. She only wished she'd found other ways to have her child and rise above the circumstances she'd been born to, ways that didn't include Wheeler money. That whole time in her life had been one wrong decision after another. The only bright light had been Dylan and the building of Brijette's own resolve to never get in that position again.

"Just so long as we understand each other, I plan to do everything I can to get Cade to come back to Dallas with me."

"But what about Doc Arthur and this clinic, how will he keep it open while he's recuperating?"

The older woman wavered. Brijette could see it in her face, but she didn't respond. Instead she spun around, her gray hair swinging slightly, and she was gone, the sound of her classic leather shoes on the wooden floor fading as she returned to the front room.

Brijette dropped the rag she'd been holding, letting it land in the middle of the floor. She didn't finish cleaning but raced to her car. She needed to get her mind around the fact that Mrs. Wheeler had arrived in Cypress Landing ready to cause trouble. Finding a new job wasn't impossible, but it wasn't what she wanted. How did this woman keep discovering ways to come in and send her life spiralling toward a disaster? *Because I let her.* Brijette rested her head on the steering wheel before starting the engine. Not this time. This time she wouldn't let Cade's mother knot the strings of her life.

"I'D SAY WE'RE BOTH in trouble with my mother." Cade stood at the stove in his uncle's house, warming the food prepared earlier by the man's housekeeper. Uncle Arthur had invited Cade and his mother to dinner. She was still at Cade's house getting ready. An event he'd decided not to wait on—she'd been at it since leaving the clinic that evening.

"She'll get over it."

"You don't know my mother."

His uncle set plates on the counter. "Yes, I do."

"She's changed a lot since you knew her well. She wants me to come back to Dallas immediately because Brijette works at the clinic."

Arthur turned to him, resting his hip against the cabinet. "It doesn't matter what your mother wants, this is the way things are at my clinic and she'll have to live with it, unless you choose to go. You and your father have given in to her every whim until she thinks her life is supposed to be that way."

Cade ran his finger along the edge of the counter. "That's how my father wanted it."

Arthur Wheeler shook his head. "Making a person think every nuance of his or her life should be completely within his or her control is unrealistic. That can only lead to trouble, not to mention missing a few of life's best surprises."

Cade had absolutely no idea what his uncle was talking about but it made perfect sense to him. He wanted to live his life like that, not like his father and mother had lived theirs.

"Do you want to leave?"

Cade frowned. "Of course not. I'm not going anywhere."

He felt his uncle's hand on his shoulder. "Why do you do it, son?"

Cade grabbed a spoon and stuck it in the nearest pot on the stove. "Do what?"

"Spend your life doing what your parents think is right for you?"

Cade didn't answer. Instead, he kept stirring the red beans and sausage simmering on the stove. His mother would no doubt have something negative to say about the food. She'd wonder why Arthur hadn't brought in gourmet instead of plain old country food. He checked the cornbread in the oven, reminding himself that his uncle had asked him a question and he'd kept him waiting, longer than was polite. Cade hadn't intended on unearthing the deep, dark secrets that had driven his everyday life until he'd returned here. He should have shrugged his shoulders, but he couldn't. This time he wanted Uncle Arthur to know.

"I disappointed them with so many decisions that I kept trying to find at least one or two that would satisfy them."

"You should be more concerned with making yourself happy."

This time he did shrug, and tried to keep silent, but the words came on their own. "My dad never wanted me to become a doctor. He wanted me to go into business and finance, like he did. When I insisted on medical school he wanted me to be a surgeon, but I didn't do that, either. I finally went to work at the clinic in Dallas because it was the only thing I could live with that he wanted."

His uncle took the spoon from him and placed it on a saucer. "He's gone now. You could stay here and work. I know it's what you want. You can pretend to other folks, but not to me. You've wanted to be here since that summer before med school."

"And my father felt betrayed because of it. I

was his flesh and blood, but he saw me as more your child even though you were miles away. He always said, 'You're just like your uncle Arthur. I don't know how that happened.' He'd sigh and walk away like I had disappointed him."

"It wasn't only about you, Cade."

"Who was it about?"

The man pushed a crumb around with his fingertip. "Me and your mother."

"You're talking about the relationship between you and my mother before she married my father?"

"That's part of it. But the summer you came here your father was really upset that you might want to join me when you finished school. He made a lot of accusations about your mother and me having a relationship while they were married. He thought you might be my son."

"Did he have reason to think that?" Cade tried to keep his hands from knotting and breaking into a sweat. He'd had enough revelations since he'd come to Cypress Landing to last a lifetime.

His uncle gave a wistful smile. "You're the closest I'll ever come to having a son of my own, but you're not mine, and my relationship with your mother ended when she decided to marry your father."

"Did my father believe that?"

"I think he still had his doubts. That's why I didn't have much contact with you or your family after you left here."

"Is that why you didn't bother to tell me Jody Mills died last year?"

Arthur Wheeler rubbed his forehead then sighed. "That was wrong of me and completely selfish. I knew I had to have this surgery soon, and I wanted to get you back here to fill in for me. I was afraid if you came and found Brijette here, I wouldn't be able to get you to come when I needed you."

Cade nodded. "You're right. It was a rotten thing to do, but at least now I know why."

Lights flashed in the window and his uncle shuffled across the room. "We'll have to discuss that another time. That should be your mother, or Brijette and Dylan."

Cade pushed his uncle aside getting to the door. "Please tell me you're kidding. It would be a crazy thing to invite Brijette and my mother to a meal."

"We'll be seeing how crazy shortly."

"Why would you do this, to Brijette and to me?"

"Because it's time."

His uncle opened the door and Dylan raced

into the old man's arms, then over to Cade as though she hadn't seen him in months, when he'd gone fishing with her just the other day.

The two had barely cleared the threshold when another set of lights flashed in the drive.

"What are you doing here?"

Brijette hadn't noticed the other car yet because she'd focused in on him. Cade had been so worried that she'd have to deal with his mother, he hadn't given a thought to the fact that she might not want to have dinner with him. The idea disappointed him, probably because deep in his subconscious he'd imagined the two of them having dinner together, alone, one day very soon.

"Uncle Arthur invited me—" he paused, trying to think of an easy way to say it, but he couldn't find one "—me and my mother to dinner."

She squared off with Doc Wheeler, anger contorting her features. "How could you do this to me?"

"I'm not doing this to you. This is my family and I feel like you and Dylan are my family, too. I wanted everyone together tonight. Is that too much to ask?"

"Yes, it is for me." She reached for Dylan, who'd been standing next to Cade, holding on to his arm. "Come on, Dylan, we're leaving."

Cade felt slim fingers tighten against his skin and knew this fight had only just begun. "No, I want to stay and eat with Cade and Uncle Arthur. Why can't we?"

"Because I said so."

"That's no reason, Mom. Why can't we meet Cade's mother? You act like she's mean or something."

Brijette glared at him as if he'd arranged this. God knows, he never would have inflicted this on them, himself included. His uncle must have lost his mind.

The possibility of leaving without a confrontation had passed. Mrs. Wheeler stood in the open door, confused.

"Are you Cade's mom? That's my mom." Dylan waved a thumb over her shoulder in Brijette's direction and skipped in front of the woman, her hand outstretched. Confusion transformed to pale-faced shock, but Mrs. Wheeler shook the child's hand from pure instinct. Obviously, she had no idea Brijette had ever had a child. Cade frowned at his uncle, who grinned at the whole bunch of them. The guy had kept more secrets than a sleazy politician.

"Brijette and her daughter, Dylan, are having dinner with us," Cade informed her.

At least his mother had the good grace not to protest in front of the child, though Brijette seemed ready to break and run at the first opportunity. His uncle herded them to the kitchen. Mrs. Wheeler sat at the table, and Dylan, always the conversationalist, sat down beside her. Brijette filled glasses with iced tea, while he and his uncle put food on the table. At last they were ready to eat.

Thirty seconds. Cade smiled to himself. That's how long it had taken Dylan to completely wrap his mother around her little finger. The woman laughed at something the girl said, glancing toward him with a smile he couldn't quite put a name on, but he liked it. They might even pull this evening off.

He'd finished his last spoonful of red beans and rice when the peace ended. Thus far, Dylan had kept his mother entertained with the inner workings of small-town life in Cypress Landing, right down to the number of domino games played by the old men at the local country store. He and his uncle had participated in the conversation. Brijette sat stirring her food aimlessly.

"You seem to have a good head on your shoulders, Dylan. I'll never know how your mother did it on her own, as bad a decision-maker as she was." His mother spoke the words and he wondered if she heard how callous they sounded or even if she'd meant to say it, though she didn't seem the least bit regretful.

Brijette's chair skidded on the tile floor, but Dylan only stared at Mrs. Wheeler before responding.

"My mom says it's not nice to say things like that. And she makes good decisions. She's practically a doctor. Well, once when she was younger she wasn't so smar—"

"That's enough, Dylan. We're going."

"But, Mom, we can't eat and leave. We haven't helped with the dishes or had dessert or anything. That's rude."

Brijette caught Dylan's wrist, her mouth in a tight line. "It's my turn." She pulled the protesting child from the room and to the front door. They were gone before the other three could move.

Cade pushed his chair back with a loud groan. "Nice job, Mother." He went to the sink and began rinsing his bowl.

His mother followed him. "Why didn't one of you bother to tell me she had a child?"

At the table, his uncle fiddled with the salt shaker. Cade set his bowl in the bottom of the sink. "What's the difference if she has a child?

She works with me at the clinic. The end. The past is done, now leave it alone."

"Is it? Is it really behind you or have you not bothered to look at that girl?"

"What is that supposed to mean?" Cade watched his uncle slink from the room to safety. He was glad. He had no idea where this conversation was going but he doubted he'd like it.

"She's you, in case you haven't noticed."

"Dylan has blond hair and green eyes, as do lots of other children. So what?"

"That child could be yours."

"Brijette never said she was pregnant and never tried to get me to marry her. If she was willing to take money to stay away from me, don't you think she'd have tried to get more if she'd been pregnant? She'd have told me. I'd have married her and she knew that. She'd have had everything she needed, unless of course you'd have cut me off financially for marrying her."

"I damn well would have." The look on her face told him the words had tumbled across her lips before she'd weighed them.

"Is that how it is? I dance to your music or no money for me? Just so you know, I don't need Wheeler money anymore. I can do fine on my own. And to clear away the doubts you have about Dylan, Brijette has a birth certificate that shows the child was born too long after I left for her to be mine."

"So she's a trashy whore."

Cade threw the dish towel he'd been holding on the counter. "I'm done here." He left the room and his uncle's house feeling a weight on him the likes of which he hadn't felt since he'd left Cypress Landing the first time and left Brijette to shoulder her troubles alone. He'd been an ignorant, scared boy, ruled by his parents' beliefs and judgments and, yes, even by their money. He'd left that boy behind and he never wanted to see him again. He was a better man than that. Brijette needed to know it.

CHAPTER ELEVEN

BRIJETTE SAT on the sofa, staring vacantly at the television. She'd seen Mrs. Wheeler's face. The woman suspected the truth.

After settling Dylan in bed with a vague explanation of why she and Mrs. Wheeler didn't get along, she'd bathed, but couldn't sleep. Hugging a pillow to her middle, she assured herself that the birth certificate would fix everything. Once Mrs. Wheeler saw it, there'd be nothing else for the woman to say. Headlights flickered in the window and she wondered who would be coming to her house at—she consulted the clock on the wall—eleven-thirty at night. She groaned. It was probably the sheriff wanting her to go and track. Occasionally, he was good enough to bring help from his office to stay with Dylan. More often, she had to drag her daughter from her bed and let her sleep in the car while Brijette did her job.

But that wasn't the sheriff's car in front of her house. It was Cade's truck.

She threw open the door and met him on the porch. "What do you want?"

"To apologize."

"So apologize and leave."

He smacked his arm. "The mosquitoes are having a feast on me. Can we please go inside? I'd like to talk to you."

Cade Wheeler was the last person who needed to be in her house, but she moved and let him in, because part of her still wanted him to be her knight in shining armor, however tarnished that armor might be.

She sank into the sofa cushions while he lingered in the middle of the room, swaying from side to side.

"Oh, sit already. You're giving me a headache with that rocking."

He settled in beside her. Closer than she wanted, but she did sort of like it. "Why did you let your uncle invite Dylan and me to dinner with your mother there?"

"You think I knew? I heard what was going on when you drove up."

She shook her head. "I don't know what he was thinking. Maybe since his surgery, his mind's not right. Surely he knew how horrible it would be."

"Actually, it was much better than I imagined,

except for my mother's rudeness at the end, and I apologize for that. What she said was uncalled for, but I think Dylan put her in her place."

Brijette felt herself smiling even though she didn't mean to. "Yes, she did do a good job. You know your mother hates the fact that I'm at the clinic. She wants you to leave, right now."

"I've already told her that's not going to happen. She's used to having her way, because my dad and I have always given in to her. That stops now. I never intended my being here to cause you trouble, and especially not pain."

She tugged the pillow in front of her again. "It hasn't."

"Tonight that wasn't true." His voice hummed in the air and she imagined she could feel the words against her skin.

"It's done now." Her words slipped into a whisper.

Cade continued, leaning closer. Now, not only his words but his very breath touched her. "I know, but we were getting to the point where we could enjoy each other's company without having the past hanging over us, and I liked it. I liked it a lot."

When he stopped, his chest rose and fell as if he'd put much more effort into the statement than would have seemed necessary. Brijette understood. Her head whirled as though she'd been oxygen deprived. She wished Cade hadn't said those things. Hearing, or even thinking about feeling enjoyment in his presence could lead to nothing but more trouble, the unearthing of lies she preferred remain buried. She'd lived with the lie long enough that it had become a security blanket and being uncovered was practically inconceivable.

She tossed the pillow aside and curled her legs under her. "Don't say things like that, Cade. We can't ever go back to how we were."

His hand came to rest above her knee, his thumb moving across her skin. "I'm not thinking of what's behind us. Now is the time I'm concerned with. Right now."

She took a few deep breaths to control the pure hunger building inside her. It really stank that her own body could betray her this way. She'd always thought what she'd felt years ago was so strong because she'd been young and inexperienced. But she felt exactly seventeen again, nearly giddy with passion, and he'd barely touched her. She had to focus or she'd lose control. "Right now may be fine for you, but I have a child and her feelings to consider. What happens two months from now when you're in Dallas? Will you be concerned about you and me, about Dylan, then?" She hated that her words sounded a little bit breathless, but what came next completely took her by surprise.

"I'm thinking of staying here."

The statement sent a chill of both pleasure and fear along her nerves, but she struggled to hide it. "Yeah, right. I can tell by your mother's behavior tonight that she'd be one hundred percent for that."

"I don't live for my mother's happiness."

She dug hard to find a bit of sarcasm to mask her building excitement. She absolutely didn't want Cade to make her feel this unsettled. Not because of his body. Not the thought of his staying in Cypress Landing. Nothing. "Oh, since when did that happen? I thought you answered to her for everything. Although I can't for the life of me understand why, unless inheriting the Wheeler fortune is that important to you."

His fingers tightened on her leg. "I don't need the Wheeler money, and it's not exactly a fortune. I'm an only child and I do have a responsibility to my mother, especially since my father died. I made—" Cade stopped and, releasing her leg, trapped her hand in his, holding it to his lips for a moment before pressing it to his chest. "I made promises to my father, to stay in Dallas and take care of my mother. He wanted her to be able to live there in the same lifestyle she'd always had with him. I've been keeping those promises, but I don't know if I can do it anymore."

"Why?" She clamped her teeth down on her tongue as the word escaped. Hearing Cade's reasoning wouldn't change things. She still felt that pull to be near him, to hold him and be held by him. A weakness she couldn't give in to, could she?

"Because I'd rather do this."

His mouth trapped hers in a kiss that she would have thought she'd want to stop but she didn't. It lingered on, and she wrapped her arms around his neck, drawing him closer. He groaned and she remembered how wonderful the sound always made her feel, and that same fluttering soared into her stomach.

Cade pushed her farther into the sofa and she began to not care why they shouldn't be together. When her back made contact with the cushions, his lips left hers to slide their way to the base of her throat, where he tugged at the V-neck of her T-shirt, revealing the gentle rise of her bare breasts. She fully intended to hold inside the feelings that threatened to crush her, but she couldn't, and they burst free on a fervent moan that ended with Cade's name on her lips.

She wound her fingers in his hair, hauling his mouth to hers again. He struggled to get a better position on the sofa, his foot banging the coffee table and sending the picture of Brijette and Dylan crashing over. She glanced at the table, realizing she desperately needed to take control of this situation. She gripped his shoulders and pushed him away.

"We can't do this."

He scrambled to the edge of the sofa, each breath audible as he raked his hands through his hair. He followed her gaze to the fallen picture.

"Maybe you're right. We should take things slowly." He kissed each of her palms, rubbing one against his cheek, the soft stubble prickling her skin. With her eyes locked on his mossy green ones, he continued, "This will happen, Brijette. You know it as well as I do. We belong together."

She squeezed his fingers. "I thought you hated the things I'd done in the past."

He let his hands drop to his lap, still holding hers. "I may not like everything about your past, but I'm not real pleased with a big chunk of my own. I'm trying to make better decisions now."

"And you think this is one of them?"

"I know it is," he said with a smile.

She eased away from him. "You need to leave now. You're only making me confused. Making my life confused."

He got to his feet, his smile widening. "A certain amount of confusion can occasionally be beneficial. But I'll go. I'll see you at work tomorrow."

She followed him to the door, thankful he didn't try to kiss her again. Giving in to a relationship with Cade would be easy, but eventually she'd have to come clean with him about Dylan. She needed to, even if it would be the hardest thing she ever did.

Of course, when she told him, whatever this was between them would simply come apart. This was one lie he'd never forgive her for, and it was one lie she couldn't risk telling him. Not yet. She needed to see that he really wasn't going to be ruled by the guilt of what he thought he owed his parents, or by the money.

Shutting the door, she leaned against it, her eyelids closing reflexively. The Wheelers would dominate Dylan's life. They had money and Mrs. Wheeler was used to getting what she wanted. She might not think Dylan worthy of their family, but if she did want the child, there'd be no stopping her. Cade wouldn't be very interested in taking Brijette's side when he found out she'd lied to him and had continued to lie, even when she realized he hadn't known his mother had offered her money to have an abortion.

She pressed her fingertips to her forehead, beginning to feel a bit Scarlett O'Hara-ish in her need to think about it tomorrow. Sleep. She needed to sleep on it and everything would be better.

She opened her eyes and went cold from head to toe. Dylan stood in the hall, her face wrinkled into an angry mask. She'd obviously been there for more than a few minutes.

"I hate you."

The words cut into Brijette like barbed wire. Words Dylan had never said to her before.

"You knew I liked Cade and you went and let him kiss you. Why do you want him to like you again? You aren't even trying to get him to stay here. What's wrong with you?"

She spun around, racing to her bedroom and slamming the door.

Brijette followed and sagged against Dylan's door, but didn't try to go inside. She didn't know how to explain it to herself, much less to her daughter.

"Dylan, please remember that Cade and I

are adults. He's even older than me. You're still a young girl. I'm not doing this to hurt you."

"I don't care."

No more words came from Dylan's room. Brijette tried to talk to her a little while longer, but didn't enter. It wasn't because she wanted to give the child privacy. It was pure cowardice. She was in uncharted territory and definitely too tired to deal with it tonight.

BRIJETTE LOADED the last box of supplies into her SUV with Cade's help. In the passenger seat, Dylan stoically refused to get out.

"You sure you'll be okay without Alicia?"

Brijette nodded. He hadn't mentioned last night and she was loath to broach the problem with Dylan, though she needed to. The girl still wouldn't speak to her this morning, but she'd made her come with her. Maybe if they were stuck together most of the day they could eventually get past this.

"Dylan." She didn't respond. Brijette wanted to yell at her but didn't. "Dylan, get the small box with the papers to sign the patients in. It's at Emma's desk."

Brijette slammed the rear door of the SUV. When Dylan didn't move, Cade gave her a questioning look.

"We have a problem."

He rested his shoulder against the car with a wicked grin that had always been able to melt her heart. Today was no different. "I figured you'd think that, but you'll find I've become quite adept at problem-solving."

It was her turn to grin. She led him away from the vehicle where Dylan was now fiddling with the radio. The thump, thump of music reached them even through the closed windows. "Well, here's a problem for you. My daughter seems to have seen what went on in my living room between the two of us and now she's furious with me."

Cade tilted his head, his brows drawing together. "But why? I thought she'd be glad. I thought she liked me."

She laughed at that and it made her heart feel lighter; what she faced with Dylan wasn't much to laugh at. "You really are dense. Of course she likes you. She *really* likes you." Cade remained perplexed and Brijette gave him a half frown. "Are you truly this blind? Dylan has a crush on you."

Cade's mouth rounded in astonishment and she couldn't believe he hadn't noticed. "Don't worry, I don't think you're a lecherous man. You showed her attention and she's not used to having a man around. She fell for you. I'm sure she knows she can't be your girlfriend."

"But other men you've dated, how did she treat them?"

She turned her head so she didn't have to see him. "I haven't brought anyone to my house, Cade. I haven't dated since you."

"Except Dylan's dad."

"Well, yes, of course, but I meant since that."

She hurried into the building, wanting to whack herself in the head. What a major mistake. Being around Cade was driving her nuts, and if she wasn't careful she'd make a huge mess of things.

"If you want, I'll talk to her."

She jumped at the sound of his voice, not realizing he'd followed her.

"Um...sure, if you have any idea what to say. Right now, I'm at a total loss as to how to handle the situation."

"Why don't you go get the paperwork you need from Emma and wait here until I come back."

Stunned, she watched him leave. She could definitely get used to having help with Dylan, especially as the boyfriend years approached. As she walked to Emma's desk, she tried not to think about what it would take to have Cade helping her with Dylan. It would require her to be completely honest with him. Suddenly she wanted to tell him the whole story, but she couldn't. Fear strangled her every time she contemplated it.

Ten minutes later, when Cade entered the hallway, the thought still paralyzed her brain.

"I don't know how it went, but I talked to her. She didn't say a word to me, though."

"It'll be all right."

Taking her keys out of her pocket, Brijette raced to the door, ignoring Cade's questioning glance. Needing to tell him the truth had incited a panic attack every time she was near him. "I'd better go. It will take me a while to get the boxes on the boat."

"I could come help you. We've only got a couple of patients scheduled. I could start late."

"No, you've got enough to do here. Dylan will help."

She shut the car door quickly, before her mouth could let loose the words that would start a whole new kind of trouble for her.

ANOTHER LONG DAY had finally ended. A day that had Brijette wondering, once again, where all these patients were coming from. She tilted her bottled water for another drink, then pressed the cool plastic against her damp forehead. She'd never expected to be this busy when she came to Willow Point. The need was much greater than she'd anticipated, and she wasn't sure how she could keep up with all the work. The steps on the front of the store creaked as A.G. sat down next to her.

"Stairs finally call it quits?" Brijette pointed her bottle in the direction of the new wooden braces, not bothering to ask why he hadn't ripped apart the whole set and started over. You didn't do things like that around here.

"Yep. 'Bout fell through myself the other day."

She sighed and rested against the tread behind her. A teenage boy who worked part-time with A.G. at the store was helping Dylan load the boat. The sweat and dust from working in the heat had dried on Brijette's skin, and she imagined she'd made mud on her forehead with the damp bottle, not that she cared.

"How's things up your way?"

"Fine, same as always. One of the docs in town moved and we've taken on most of his patients, so we're swamped at the clinic."

A.G. didn't acknowledge her answer, but continued to survey the dirt-and-gravel parking area. "Ain't had no trouble, have you?"

The unusual question caused her head to

swivel toward him, almost unconsciously. "What kind of trouble?"

"Any kind, bad kinds."

She tried to get a read on him, but he still hadn't looked at her and likely wouldn't. "No, not really."

"No drug problems 'round Cypress Landing?" He shifted on the hard wood step, squinting in the afternoon sun.

"Well, yeah, that's everywhere, but nothing unusual."

"You sure?"

She reached across and hit him on the arm with the water bottle. "Okay, enough, A.G. If you need to tell me something, lay it out there."

"I got nothing to tell, but I hear things, and your name got mentioned in passing by some folks in my store one evening. I didn't know 'em but they weren't the sorta folks I'm tryin' to be friendly with."

She squinted at him. "What did they say?"

"Didn't hear, only got your name. But you watch yourself. I'm thinking there's folks here doing things they ought not, and I don't want you to get caught in the middle of it."

The man cut a piece of tobacco from a small block and stuck it in his mouth. He'd said his piece on the subject and more questioning would get her nowhere. She couldn't imagine why a customer that A.G. didn't know would mention her, but the thought of the prescriptions appearing in the local pharmacies immediately came to mind.

"Saw the new doc the other day. Sunday afternoon, as a matter of fact."

Brijette leaned forward so she could see the old man's face better. "What new doc?"

"The one that works at the clinic with you, that Wheeler boy. He was here seein' to ole Ms. Fourchon, the widow down the road. She was too sick to go to the doctor and I reckon her daughter asked him to come check on her."

"You must be mistaken." No way Cade Wheeler had come here to see a patient, on a Sunday no less.

A.G. stared at her, then spat tobacco in the dirt close enough that she had to move her feet to keep from getting splattered.

"I ain't been mistaken in years. Took that truck of his across the ferry and drove here. He missed the road to her house and stopped by for directions. I rode there with him to make sure he found the place. I guess I know what I'm talkin' 'bout."

She took another swig of her water. "I've got to go."

A.G. didn't speak as she strode toward the dock, jumping on the boat, where Dylan waited. Easing toward the river, she racked her brain wondering what Cade could be doing visiting a patient at home. He hadn't mentioned making a house call, but she'd never have believed him if he'd told her. The Wheelers did not lower themselves to venture to this part of the world. Even Doc Arthur had kept his house calls confined to in and around Cypress Landing.

Entering the river, she throttled up the boat, the wind and water droplets spraying her face. Truth was, she didn't want to imagine Cade fitting in or becoming a part of this area. It was easier to consider him an interloper, a rich kid doing his uncle a favor, a man who'd never understand this place or her and her way of life. If he became anything else, everything she'd struggled to build would fall apart. Keeping Dylan from him hadn't bothered her when she believed he was as callous and calculating as his mother. But what if she'd been wrong?

Shaking her head to get rid of that thought, she steered the boat toward Cypress Landing. Being wrong about Cade could lead to giving in to those feelings of wanting and need she had every time he came around, or even every time she thought of him. She should've started dating a long time ago, but she never did. Had she been waiting to see if Cade would come back and prove her opinions of him were wrong?

THE TREES on the bank passed in a blur as Dylan staunchly refused to look at her mother and fought desperately to stay awake. She was tired after spending the day at Willow Point and having to load the boat.

Her mother and Cade were ganging up on her. After he'd kissed her mother it was as if Cade had decided to not be friends with her anymore. She liked Cade and she knew he couldn't be like a boyfriend, but she wanted him around and wanted him to be her friend. Now he was being like…like a stupid parent. She wiggled in her seat. That was something worth considering. She'd imagined it once but her mom and Cade didn't always get along so well, especially at first. Lately, though, they'd been much better together.

She glanced at her mom, capably maneuvering the boat. Would Cade be a good dad? Would her mother ever quit acting like she wanted him to leave as soon as possible and go back to

Texas? Maybe she could do something about it. The least her mother could do was marry Cade and keep him in the family. Her mom said Cade wasn't like them because he was rich and had grown up with lots of money. Was that a bad thing? Cade didn't act rich, not that she knew any really rich people, except maybe Mr. Robert who let her ride his horses whenever she wanted. But Cade wasn't anything like Mr. Robert, who was always distracted, worrying about his business, usually with a cell phone glued to his ear. She had to start making plans to get the three of them—okay, the two of them—together. She nodded slowly. This could work.

CHAPTER TWELVE

BRIJETTE STEERED her SUV into the clinic parking lot. She was a bit late since Dylan had decided not to get up. The situation with the drugs and the prescription pads had her worried. Sometimes she felt as if she was just waiting for the next catastrophe. Twice, she'd phoned Jackson to see if there were any new leads in the case, but each time he'd had nothing to tell her.

Shoving open the back door, she hoped they didn't have a waiting room full of patients. A body in a white jacket suddenly stepped from one of the rooms. She hadn't even been paying attention, and she was already at her top speed. The chart the man was holding went flying across the floor as she slammed into him.

"What the—" He spun around, grabbing her by the shoulder. "You wanna slow down there, sweetheart."

Brijette stumbled backward. A swath of

brown hair swept across the man's forehead, and ocean-blue eyes watched her. Okay, who'd let the movie star into the clinic? He adjusted the stethoscope around his neck, and she noticed again the white coat with embroidered letters on the chest. "Who are you?"

He smiled and held out his hand. "Andrew Scott Fitzgerald the Third. I'm the new doctor."

She shook his hand, then glanced up and down the hall. "Are you serious?"

"I'M GIVING YOU samples of this new medication for your blood pressure. That way you can try it for a few days and we'll see how it works before you have to buy any."

The woman nodded, stuffing the medication packets in her purse along with the piece of paper on which Cade had written the instructions for taking them. He knew she didn't have insurance, but she needed the medicine.

She started toward the door but stopped. "I might not be able to pay the whole bill for today."

"Don't worry. Do what you can. Emma will take care of you."

He'd have gotten a reprimand if he'd ever told a patient in his former clinic that they didn't have to pay the full bill. But here he only had to keep it from Brijette, who would likely decide he had an ulterior motive for doing it, which of course he did. It felt great. It felt right. But she'd never believe that. It was better if she didn't know.

The woman smiled at him as he walked her to the door.

In the hall, Brijette stood next to Andy, looking every bit as stunned as he'd hoped.

"I see you've met our new doctor."

"Cade Wheeler, what are you talking about?"

"This is Andy. He used to work with me in Dallas. He's come to help at the clinic. And don't let his ridiculously long name put you off. Even he doesn't know what his parents were thinking."

Andy laughed and Brijette grinned, too. "How long are you staying?"

Andy's brows furrowed and he glanced at Cade. "I'm...um...I'm not going anywhere. I'll be staying on after Cade leaves."

She gave Cade a questioning look. "How did you get your uncle to agree to this?"

Cade laughed. "I didn't really give him a lot of choice."

"I can't believe you didn't tell her I was coming," Andy said.

"Yeah," Brijette joined in. "Why didn't you tell me he was coming?"

"It slipped my mind."

"Slipped your mind?" Both of them spoke in the same breath.

"See, you two are working together already."

He strolled up the hall where he had a patient waiting in the exam room. "Let's get to work. With Andy here, we might even get finished early."

Brijette and Andy were still standing in the hall when he went into the next patient room. Of course he hadn't forgotten to tell Brijette that Andy was coming. He'd wanted to surprise her, to prove to her he had the best interest of the clinic at heart and that he could get this done without her intervening to help convince his uncle. Not to mention he'd been a bit afraid she'd protest having another man in the office who had the same background as himself, that she'd think he couldn't understand the patients. Andy might struggle a bit at first but he wanted to be here more than he wanted to throw money around in Dallas, and he was a good doctor. Maybe Brijette would soon realize that being born into money didn't automatically make you an insensitive, immoral ass.

"WHEN DID YOU AGREE for Cade's friend to come and work at the clinic?" Brijette straightened the stack of magazines she'd dropped off for Doc Arthur.

"I don't know. A few weeks ago, I guess. Andy's found a house he wants to buy. He'll be moving in this weekend."

"Buying a house? Moving in? Come on, Arthur, do you really think this guy is going to stay here? Did you see the car he was driving? And most importantly, why didn't you bother to tell me he was coming?"

The man squinted at her. "Is this twenty questions?"

"More like fifty."

Arthur chuckled. "Yes, he's staying. I actually got to drive that fancy car he has and I have to say I might consider getting one myself. But you'll need to ask Cade why he didn't mention Andy to you. Maybe he thought you'd have a bias against him because he has money?"

"Now that's ridiculous." She left her chair and crossed the kitchen to the refrigerator.

"Is it?"

She found a pitcher of lemonade and poured a glass. "It's not Cade's money I have a problem with. It's his and his family's use of it, and their morals related to life and money, that bother me."

Doc Wheeler twisted in his chair. "Fix me

one of those. You know, I never thought of Cade as immoral."

"I don't mean immoral, immoral."

"What other kind is there?"

She gritted her teeth as she poured Doc's lemonade. "His family doesn't think like I do. Especially that mother of his—she can be a pure monster."

"Lots of people don't think like you do. But I doubt if you really know how Cade's mother thinks."

She set his drink in front of him and settled into her chair. "Well, I honestly don't care right now. I only hope this guy doesn't decide to take off the minute Cade leaves."

"I don't suspect he will, and maybe we can convince Cade to stay. Then I could come in and work one or two days a week and sort of retire."

She paused with her lemonade halfway to her mouth. "Would you want to do that?" Doc Arthur retire? It was an idea that had never crossed her mind.

"Sure, there are lots of things I'd like to do, like travel a bit."

Now she felt guilty. She'd been complaining and thinking only of herself when she should have been considering what was going on with the man who'd helped her build her career.

"If that's the case, we'll have to find Andy a wife so he'll be inclined to stay."

Doc Arthur slid his glass back and forth on the table. "You want to volunteer for the position?"

She almost choked. "Not me."

"Good. I'm afraid Cade wouldn't be too happy, otherwise."

"I don't think Cade cares what I do."

"You're wrong. He does care, and if you'd give him half a chance he'd do something about it."

"Well, I don't need Cade Wheeler in my life. I do fine on my own."

Doc tossed one magazine aside and picked up another. "You might be surprised how much better you'd do with him, and you're not on your own. In case you've forgotten, another person lives in that house with you, someone who might be more than happy for you to try to make a life with Cade, someone who you might owe that opportunity."

She wanted to run for the door but her body was frozen to the seat. He was saying that he knew the truth, and she didn't know how to respond. Then her survival instinct kicked in. Her mumbled, "I have to go" hung in the air, but she was long gone before Arthur Wheeler could comment.

At the end of the drive, a red truck veered into the grass to keep from hitting her head-on. She slammed on her brakes, spewing gravel.

The truck backed up and Brijette rolled down the window. "Sorry, Robert. I didn't mean to run you off the road."

He shook his head. "It's all right. Better slow that thing down when you get on the highway."

"I will. Hey, did you ever hear about your horse?"

Robert rubbed his forehead. "I'm pretty sure my nephew is involved, so I'm looking into it myself to try to give the boy a chance."

"That's good of you."

The man shrugged. "When are you bringing Dylan by to go riding? I still have horses left, you know. That wasn't my only one."

"We'll see. I'm sure she's ready."

"If I'm not there, you know where everything is."

She closed the window as Robert headed toward Doc Wheeler's place. Everyone in the neighborhood came to check on the doctor. He and Robert had been around Cypress Landing for as long as Brijette could remember. She hoped Robert wouldn't bail his nephew out of trouble every time. The boy needed to learn a lesson and possibly get help. Having plenty of money didn't keep one's family members from getting into trouble.

Brijette wondered if Cade would ever learn that lesson or would he, like a lot of others, always believe that his money could save his butt? She'd seen exactly what that could look like. Her parents had been killed by a drunk driver when she was even younger than Dylan. The nineteen-year-old kid who'd run into them head-on while he was driving on the wrong side of the road had walked away from the accident, uninjured, and he'd never stopped walking. He'd received a get-off-easy ticket that had been paid for with his very wealthy parents' money. These days drunk drivers didn't get off so easily, but back then a big name and cash went a long way.

Cade hadn't been touched by the incident with the drugs ten years ago, but rightly so, because he hadn't known a thing about it. The only problem she had with the whole thing was that no one ever even questioned him. Even though he and his mother acted as if Brijette had nearly gotten him thrown in jail, she'd never seen anything to indicate Cade was even close to being in trouble. He'd been whisked off like the prince of some foreign country whose name couldn't be associated with hers.

She hated that she actually wanted him to prove her wrong, but she did. In her mind she'd always had this idyllic vision of what life would have been like with Cade if… Of course, that thought held more ifs than she could list. Keeping this monstrous secret was…well, it was inexcusable. Brijette didn't like to think of herself being unjust or unfair. She promised herself, once Cade proved he had changed, that he wasn't going to teach Dylan to be a selfish person or one that deserted her friends when they needed her most, then she'd come clean. She'd tell him the truth. And let hell rain down, because that's exactly what it would be like. It wasn't just the wrath of Cade she feared but the total annihilation of her relationship with her daughter. She had to admit that Cade really didn't have much left to prove, but her fear of what the truth would mean for her and Dylan kept her quiet. She needed to find a way to tell Dylan and Cade that wouldn't ruin her relationship with both of them. At least until then, she and Dylan could both enjoy Cade's company.

NAVIGATING BRIJETTE'S driveway, Cade wondered what they would be doing today. Dylan had been quite specific about what he should wear—long pants, cool shirt, heavy shoes for hiking. Maybe she and her mother intended to drag him into the woods behind their house. When he stopped his truck next to Brijette's SUV, he got a bad feeling in the pit of his stomach. Standing atop a ladder, Brijette paused in the middle of lashing an ancient canoe to the top of her vehicle. Her confused expression made him fairly certain she had no idea he'd been invited on this trip. He slammed the heel of his hand on the steering wheel. He knew he should've called to talk to her.

Dylan came bounding from the house and threw open the passenger door of his truck. "Aren't you going to get out?"

"I can tell by your mom's face she didn't have any part in inviting me."

The girl shrugged. "Don't worry. She doesn't mind if you come. She just doesn't know she doesn't mind."

He snorted. "Is that how it is?"

Brijette climbed from the ladder, glancing between the two of them, not speaking.

"Cade's going with us."

"So I gathered when he came wheeling in here and you rushed to meet him. Why am I the last person to know?"

Cade began to feel a bit like an interloper. "I don't have to go if you'd rather spend the day alone with Dylan."

Her gaze traveled over him in a way that wasn't exactly angry. His muscles tightened. This was different.

"No, you should come. You'll either love it or hate it."

"Love or hate what?"

"Cat Island Refuge," Dylan chirped.

"What is that? An animal shelter for cats?"

Brijette shook her head. "It's a wildlife area. Dylan and I go there occasionally to practice tracking, have a picnic, mostly spend time together."

"A day with my two favorite ladies—sounds good to me."

Brijette stumbled as she moved to put the ladder away and Dylan giggled. Cade smiled at Brijette, giving her what he hoped was a sexy look. But she rolled her eyes, so he figured he might have missed the mark. That's what he got for studying so much during medical school and not practicing his flirting skills at the local bar with the rest of the students.

"I'm going to get the food." Dylan disappeared inside.

He turned to Brijette. "Are you sure it's okay if I go? I promise I wasn't aware that you didn't know Dylan had invited me. From now on I'll to speak to you personally."

She leaned against the car, crossing her arms in front of her, smiling. "It's fine. You'll get a taste of what Dylan and I do for fun. It's not exactly what you'd find in the city, but we'll see how you survive."

He didn't answer, realizing he might be about to take a test. He watched Dylan fly off the porch and toss a small cooler and a tote bag in the Tahoe. She mouthed the word "food" and rubbed her belly before climbing in the back seat and motioning for Cade to get in the front.

"I guess we're ready," Brijette said, climbing behind the wheel and starting the engine.

Dylan began to jabber, filling them in on what she'd done at her friend's house this week and how she'd gone to ride horses at Mr. Robert's. He turned in his seat so he could see the girl and noticed Brijette glance at Dylan in the mirror. A moment of sheer panic hit him. If this was a test, he hoped he'd pass with flying colors. He hadn't been this worried about getting a good grade since he'd taken his exams to get into medical school.

DYLAN SHOOK HER HEAD at him for what felt like the fiftieth time, and if Cade hadn't liked being with the two of them so much he'd probably have gone to the car. That is, of course, if he could have found the car, which he couldn't have.

When they'd arrived at the refuge he'd helped Brijette unload the canoe, which Dylan insisted on calling a pirogue, a name he only slightly recalled from his last stay in Cypress Landing. After an hour of paddling, they'd pulled their transportation ashore and plunged into the woods. He couldn't help that he had trouble staying quiet. He had questions, like what the heck did they see on the ground and how did it make sense to them?

Brijette waved him over to where she and Dylan were studying the ground. "See, Cade, this is a bear track. A black bear."

He looked around the thick forest. "Are you expecting him to put in an appearance?"

"Could be," Brijette whispered. "I can tell by this track we've only missed him by a few minutes."

He put a hand on Dylan's shoulder. "Which way did he go? Maybe we should leave."

Glancing at Brijette, he decided something wasn't right. Finally she burst out laughing.

Dylan snorted. "It's an old track, silly."

She pointed to the indentation on the ground with a stick and rambled off a long list of reasons she knew this track had been made before today and how the bear had stopped here, then ambled off that way, then heard or saw something and veered to the left to sprint through the trees.

"And you get all that from these prints?"

Brijette nodded, grasping his forearm and dragging him closer to the ground. The wind blew loose strands of her hair into his face. She pressed his finger against the dirt. "Feel the track. Really look at it, the way it's deeper here." She led him a few feet farther. "See how that's different from this one? See the change of the indentations and how the soil is bumped up here?"

Surprisingly, he did see. It must have taken years for Brijette to learn to track like this.

"That wasn't very funny about the bear track."

Brijette put her hand to her mouth to try to keep from laughing, but she couldn't, and even he had to smile.

"You really had me going for a minute."

"I know. Bear? Where? We need to go." She spun her head from side to side in a nice imitation of his panic when he thought he might be bear bait, then held out her hand to help him to his feet. He wrapped his arms around her, hugging her close. Her eyes darkened, but she continued to smile. He let her go and moved to study the next track.

Up ahead, Dylan stirred a stick in the edge of the water. He desperately wanted to get to know these two better. He once thought he knew Brijette very well. He'd been wrong. He'd only scratched the surface.

In the past, the thought of dating a woman with children had been an instant no-way. Could Brijette be so special to him that he even wanted to know her child?

Looking back at them, the girl announced she was hungry and ready to eat. Her blond ponytail bobbed as she skipped and her green eyes made him think of a mischievous cat. Mother and daughter were alike yet different. Brijette carried the dark mystery of the swamp in her eyes, on her skin, while Dylan was light, airy, sunny. She was like…him. The revelation reeled him onto his heels and he fell to the ground on his butt.

He struggled to his feet while the two of them were talking, but he didn't hear them. He tried to wipe the suspicion from his mind. It was his mother, what she'd said about Dylan being like him that had planted the possibility in his brain. The girl was born much too long after he'd left Cypress Landing. He and his mother had both seen the birth certificate, and it had appeared to be legitimate. But it didn't have to end there. She could be his, he and Brijette could share their lives and this child, maybe even have more children. That idea had him feeling things he'd rather not dwell on at the moment.

They hauled the nylon bag from the canoe and Dylan tossed a blanket on the ground. Cade couldn't remember having a picnic since… since he'd spent the summer in Cypress Landing and had them with Brijette.

After finishing her sandwich, Dylan curled up on the blanket and napped, or at least pretended to. Cade wasn't sure which. He noticed today that Dylan, rather than trying to compete with her mother for his attention, was doing everything she could to throw the two of them together. Several times, Brijette had to call her when she'd ambled off, leaving the two of them alone. He didn't know what her game plan was, but he figured he knew Dylan well enough to know she had one.

Brijette tossed a paper towel in the bag of leftovers. "Well, Doctor Wheeler of the City, what do you think of our backwoods?"

He stared across the rippling water to the

cypress trees rising from the shallow murkiness. The birds chirped, and even though his skin was damp with sweat from the early summer heat, he couldn't imagine a trendy restaurant or an air-conditioned clubhouse where he'd rather have been.

He caught her hand and brought it to his lips, kissing the backs of her fingers. "Thank you for today."

She closed her eyes and when she opened them again she looked at him, maybe for the first time since he'd been in Cypress Landing, without the resentment, or the accusations, or the hurt and anger of the past.

"You should come with us again," she whispered.

"I want to. I want…" He stopped himself because he wasn't completely sure what he wanted, but whatever it was Brijette surely wasn't ready to hear it. Not yet. "I'll come anytime."

"Good," a voice chimed from the other side of the blanket. "Next time we're going camping."

He tilted his head to one side. "Do you mean we're going to spend the night in a tent?"

Dylan stretched, though he knew she hadn't

slept a minute. "That's right, and if you're scared, you'll have to get over it."

"I think I can handle camping in a tent." He knew he could handle it, that and a lot more.

CHAPTER THIRTEEN

"THIS IS ONE HEALTHY baby." Brijette bounced Regina Broussard's child in her arms. "Oh, and I talked with the lady in charge of the GED classes. She said there'd be no problem getting you started. They'd even help you get financial aid for college, and the school has on-site daycare."

"Thanks so much, Ms. Dupre. With your and Dr. Wheeler's help, we're going to get to school much sooner than we thought."

Brijette handed the baby to the girl, frowning. "Do you mean the elder Dr. Wheeler? I didn't even know you'd met him."

"No, ma'am, the Dr. Wheeler that's here," Regina said.

"He helped us find a house," her husband added.

Brijette narrowed her eyes at him. "Are you sure?"

T.J. Broussard laughed. "I'm sure. He called

us maybe two days after we left here and gave us the agent's name and number. We got a nice little place right here in town and didn't even have to give a dime up front. Lights, water and everything was already on." He reached to take the baby from Regina, and Brijette noticed a cut on his upper arm.

"T.J., that arm of yours is infected."

He stopped without getting the baby. "I cut it at work and got it stitched at the emergency room."

"Look's like you haven't kept it clean and dry."

He shrugged. "Kind of hard when you work outside."

"That's true, but you need to let me clean it and get you antibiotics before you go." She rummaged in the cabinet for her supplies. In a few minutes, she had a fresh bandage on his arm and was handing him a bag of sample antibiotics.

"I guess I'll go to the front and check on our bill while you finish with the baby."

He left, carrying the fee sheet Brijette had set on the counter.

"I'm glad you two have moved to town."

Regina shifted the baby in her arms while Brijette finished making notes on the chart.

"Me, too. I'll be even happier when we get done with these courses and leave for school in Lafayette."

"You don't like it here?"

The girl frowned. "It's not that. I think T.J. might be hanging around the wrong people, and if we could get away from here he could start over."

Brijette continued writing, wondering if the alarm bells ringing in her head were audible. "Can we help?"

"No, y'all have done too much for us already. I don't want T.J. to get into trouble."

She put the papers aside and faced Regina. "Do you think he's involved in something illegal?"

The girl adjusted the blanket around the baby. "Oh, no, nothing like that, but things will be better away from here."

Brijette didn't respond and returned to her work. She didn't want Regina to think she was prying, and asking more questions would sound like an interrogation. She could only pray the young father would make the right decisions.

When the couple left, she searched for Cade and finally found him in the kitchen.

"Hey, Emma made cake." He held a cup of

coffee in one hand and a sizable piece of Emma's homemade sour-cream pound cake in the other.

"Why did you help T.J. and Regina find a house?"

He lowered his paper plate. "Heard that already, did you?"

"From the two of them a few minutes ago. I thought you didn't think they'd make it, that it was a waste of time to help them."

"I still think they'll have a tough time, but I never said I didn't think they deserved a good place to live."

"But you paid the first month's rent and had the utilities connected and paid the deposit."

Cade frowned as he adjusted his grip on his cup. "Did they tell you that?"

"I don't think they realize it. They think the real-estate agent had one ready to go and let them live in it with no deposit."

"I didn't want them to know I'd paid for them or they might feel like they owed me. From what I've seen, that boy is very proud and wants them to make it on their own, no handouts."

"You still haven't explained why you helped them."

He took a drink of his coffee before answering. "Is it that difficult to believe I have a decent bone in my body? That I care about the people around here, too?"

She crossed and uncrossed her arms, not wanting to answer because she didn't think she could lie to him. "I guess for me it is hard to believe."

"Why?" He set aside his coffee and cake, as he waited for her answer.

"Probably because for years I imagined you as someone who was only interested in himself and what was easiest in life."

"I know why you think that, but, like you, I made a bad decision. When you needed me to stand up for you, to support you and be there for you, I left. It was easier for me to walk away, so that's what I did." He caught her shoulders with his hands. "I've regretted it many times, but I didn't know how to fix it. That decision doesn't define who I am. I've made a dozen better ones since." He slipped his arms around her and hauled her closer to him.

"Cade, we're in the office."

"I know where we are. It's just that when I see Regina and T.J., I think that could be us. If I'd stuck around or you'd gotten pregnant and I'd married you, my family would have disowned me. We'd have needed a helping hand. But you know, I think that life, the one I missed, could have been really special."

He kissed her and she held on to him. He feathered kisses across her cheek and she turned her mouth toward his for another kiss.

"Now who's forgetting we're at work? You better be careful or… Brijette, are you crying?"

She was. She struggled away from him, scrubbing at her wet skin. "Sorry, I guess I'm a little emotional or hormonal or something today." She hurried from the room straight to the bathroom, where she grasped the sides of the sink and held on. What had she done? She'd denied her daughter her father and denied this man his child for years. She'd made a terrible decision. She'd always blamed Cade's leaving and the offer of money for an abortion on the fact that he and his family had different beliefs, different values than she did. Things she didn't want her daughter to learn. But since Cade had been here she'd found that he hadn't known about the money for the abortion, didn't even know she'd been pregnant and maybe, like her, he'd done things when he was younger that he realized were mistakes. How could she ever tell him the truth? He'd hate her. And Dylan… she'd really hate her. She splashed water on her face and patted it dry with a paper towel.

Sooner or later she'd have to find a way to tell them both. But it would have to be later, not now. The thought of ending what she'd only just begun with Cade scared her to death.

AT FOUR-THIRTY Jackson Cooper called Brijette at the clinic asking if she could come check out another house. She had no idea how long it would take and she hated to ask Norma to keep Dylan for an indefinite period of time. A patient folder landed on the counter next to her. She glanced up and Cade winked at her.

"What are you doing this afternoon?" she asked him.

"That depends. What do you have in mind?"

She shook her head. "That is such a man's answer."

He grinned. "Consider the source. Now, what do you want?"

"Could you possibly get Dylan and watch her for a while? Jackson called and they need me to track."

"Are you sure I don't need to go with you?"

"No, I'll be fine, but I really don't want to ask Norma to keep Dylan late again."

"I'll be glad to pick her up."

"You're sure?"

"Brijette, I said I'd do it."

"Thanks."

"You'll owe me." He gave her long ponytail a tug.

From the corner of her eye she could see Emma bent over her paperwork, smiling and pretending not to listen.

"I'll owe you what?"

"You'll have to owe me. I'll decide what later, but you could start by getting Mary Carson to lighten up with me. She's always frowning."

"Give her a break, Cade. She has a hard time with her son."

"What's wrong with her son?"

Brijette could see the woman in question down the hall and she waved a hand at Cade. "I'll tell you about it later."

"You still owe me." With that he strode down the hall and disappeared into a patient room.

She turned to Emma. "I guess I'll have to leave early."

"Good thing. If you stay around here much longer you might get indebted up to your… well, you might get pretty deep in debt. But, if you have to be in debt, that's one man I wouldn't mind repaying."

Brijette pushed a chart across the desk and tried not to smile. "It's not like that, Emma. He's a friend, and Dylan likes him."

"If it's not like that, you're not nearly as smart as I thought you were."

Brijette gathered her things and left the clinic. Could her life come full circle like this? At seventeen, she'd thought Cade would be the last man she'd ever love. Now, nearly ten years later, that still held true. Not because she'd planned it or tried to hold on to what she'd felt for him. All that had died when she'd suffered what she'd thought had been his betrayal. Or had it? The thought of him melted her insides. Maybe Cade was exactly what she needed.

THE SUN had started to sink below the trees when Brijette finished her appraisal of the tracks at the house by the river.

"What do you think, Brij?"

She took the sheets off her clipboard. "I made notes on all the prints that I mapped. Three of them match the ones at the other house. They must have moved here when you found the other place. There's one set that's nothing like the others. Those four are all over the property and continue along the trail to the river."

Jackson tugged at the radio on his belt. "Yeah, they keep conveniently picking these houses near the river, which tells us they're moving stuff that way."

"There's also another set of prints that I only found a few of. It's like this guy came by once or twice but wasn't here regularly. I found the same set at the other house. The imprint leaves a design that looks as if it's from an expensive kind of boot, and the person has a bit of an odd gait. Nothing major—you might not even notice it when he's walking but it's there, in the tracks."

Jackson took the papers from her hand and stuffed them in a folder.

"Rumor around town is that whoever's behind this is a community member, maybe even a prominent citizen who everybody knows and would never suspect."

Brijette snorted. "Oh, please. That's a small-town urban legend. Every time there's a major crime around here, people want to say it's someone we know who's leading a double life."

Jackson grinned. "Well, rumor is often based on fact."

"Let's hope this isn't one of those times. I'm through here. I'll be going, but call me if you need me."

Brijette left for her car. She had to pick up Dylan at Cade's house. It would be incredibly easy to get used to having help with her daughter. Too easy.

CADE GRABBED Brijette's arm as she hurried past him in the clinic. "What's up with Mary's son? She called in this morning to say he was sick and she had to stay home with him. He's grown, right?"

"Yes, he's grown."

"So why does she have to stay home with her grown son?"

"I don't know, Cade. But he's had a lot of drug problems over the years, been in and out of rehab."

He raked a hand through his hair. "Wait, did you say a nurse who works here has a son with a drug problem?"

Brijette wrinkled her forehead. "Yeah, I said that."

"Brij, come on, we're missing prescription pads. How hard is it to make the connection?"

"No, Cade. She's worked here since before I came. I can't believe she'd do something illegal."

"I'm not saying she has, but maybe her son."

"He never comes here."

A patient emerged from one of the exam rooms and walked to the front. "It's something we need to consider."

She nodded slowly. "You're right. It's not

something I want to think about, but we can't ignore the possibility."

He loosened his grip on her arm to take her hand. "That's all I'm asking. Hey, come to dinner at my house tonight."

Brijette appeared startled. "Dylan can't come tonight."

He stared at her pointedly. "I know."

"Oh. Okay."

He'd finally deciphered Dylan's game plan. She'd decided on a new approach to get him to stay in Cypress Landing—which was why she'd phoned him last night to say she'd be spending the night with a friend and would he have dinner with her mother? She didn't want her mom to be by herself. He was glad to do it, thrilled even. As Brijette entered an exam room to see a patient, he smiled to himself.

"You're such a pushover, Wheeler."

Andy had paused beside him in the hallway. "You think?"

"Absolutely, but since she's the only female I've ever seen you give more than a few minutes of your time, I guess that's okay."

Cade rubbed his forehead. "You're right. I never thought of that before."

"Maybe you should consider the fact that you haven't been seriously interested in any other woman but this one in the whole time I've known you. And I've known you since grade school."

Andy didn't leave, but waited quietly, as if expecting an answer, though Cade wasn't sure of the question. He did, however, have one important thing on his mind.

"What would you say if I told you I might stay on here at the clinic?"

The other man smiled. "I'd say it's the smartest thing I've heard come out of your mouth in a while. Not counting that invitation you just gave the woman you're in love with."

Cade nearly dropped his chart. "We're not… I mean, I'm not…" Was he?

Andy smacked him on the back. "Of course you are, and she is, too."

"Do you really think she feels that way?" He couldn't read Brijette well enough to see the signs that she loved him.

"I know she does. Everyone at this clinic knows, and I don't mind telling you we're all a bit tired of waiting for the two of you to get together. So would you do something about it?" He picked up a lab report for his next patient.

Andy walked away and Cade leaned against the wall. Falling in love with Brijette again hadn't been hard. He'd simply had to unloose that part inside of him that had never stopped loving her. Had she done the same thing? He pushed open the exam-room door to see his next patient.

A FEW HOURS LATER Cade sat in his kitchen, watching Brijette slice tomatoes. "The grill's hot. I'm going to the deck to start the steaks. Come out when you're ready."

"Okay," she called over her shoulder.

Before going outside, he slipped behind her and kissed the side of her neck. "I needed to do that."

"Get cooking. I'm starved." She pointed the knife at him threateningly.

He obeyed, wondering how long it would take him to convince her he was serious about staying in Cypress Landing, and serious about her and Dylan.

The question was still on his mind when she joined him on the deck.

"This is beautiful." She tipped her wineglass toward the backyard. "Do you miss the city?"

He opened the grill to check the steaks, then sat in a chair next to her. "You've got to be kidding. No, I don't miss it. How could anybody sit where we are and miss the streetlights and traffic?"

She swirled the wine in her glass. "Some people would."

He leaned farther back in the chair and stared up at the late-evening sky. "Not me."

"So, why don't you stay?"

He kept his gaze skyward. Why didn't he? Everything he wanted was right here.

"Cade, is the grill supposed to smoke like that?"

He jumped to his feet and flipped the lid on the grill to find flames licking at their supper. He scooped the steaks onto a platter and slammed the top down, twisting the knob on the grill to the off position, then waved the tray of near-burnt steaks in front of her. "They're done."

She bent forward in her chair, laughing, spilling wine on the wooden deck. He pulled her to her feet and into the house. The platter clinked on the granite countertop as he set it down to reach for the plates, only to be stopped by Brijette's hand on his arm.

"You never answered my question."

Her sooty black eyes held his and the thought of making an offhanded comment melted away. She wanted the truth, and damn if he didn't want to give it to her. His fingers tightened on the edge of the counter behind him.

"I'd like to stay. What would you think if I did?"

She took his hand so his palm rested flat on her chest, his fingertips brushing the base of her throat.

"I want you to stay here, Cade. I want it very much."

His hand slid from her chest to the nape of her neck and he brought her mouth to his in a rush. Their lips met with a force of passion unsatisfied for years. She grabbed his shoulders and his free arm went around her waist, while his other hand held her locked to him, their lips and tongues colliding with more hunger than he'd ever known. He started to move from the counter and they stumbled until Brijette's hips banged against the island in the middle of the kitchen. Her upper body bent toward the countertop and he crushed her against him. Her fingers found the buttons of his shirt, and for a moment he thought of picking her up and carrying her to his bedroom, but she shoved his arms from her and tugged his shirt over his head, dropping it to the floor. Her mouth inched along the side of his neck, then farther down across his chest. His body shivered and he held on to the counter with one hand, tangling the other in the midnight strands of her hair.

He hadn't wanted anyone like this in years, maybe never. At least not since he'd fallen in love with Brijette the first time. He slowly began to work loose the buttons of her shirt, slipping his hands inside to touch her warm skin. When she pulled him to her, his last sane thought was that this was going to happen right here, with no discussion, no conversation, just the two of them desperately rushing toward the fire that had been burning between them for too long.

CADE WASN'T SURE how long he'd been asleep, but moonlight through the wide window illuminated his bedroom. He patted his hand across the bed, searching for Brijette, but only met empty space. Turning his head slightly on the pillow, he saw her curled up on the window seat across the room. They'd finally left the kitchen and hauled their dinner to his room on a large tray. In the middle of his bed, they'd eaten the warmed-over steaks. He'd never had a night like this. When they were younger their moments had been stolen wherever they could.

He got up, taking the rumpled top sheet with him, and padded naked to the window. He sat behind Brijette, wrapping the sheet around both of them and tossing aside the light quilt she'd been covered with.

"What are you doing over here?"

She tried to look at him and he kissed her cheek. "I'm thinking that I need to go home. What if Dylan needs me early in the morning and I'm not there?"

He snuggled her closer to him. "I want you to stay. Bring your cell phone in here. If she can't get you at home, won't she call you?"

Brijette ran her hands over her arms. "Yes, she will."

"Besides, if she calls and can't find you, who do you think she'll call next?"

She elbowed him softly in the ribs. "You're right. How does it feel to know you've got my daughter completely wrapped around your finger?"

Cade pressed his lips against her neck. He'd never before considered what it would be like to have a child or have one love him. Dylan wasn't his, but he couldn't imagine loving her any more than he did. "It's like nothing I've ever known before, and I can't begin to describe it. Though it's completely mutual because she's got me totally wrapped around her finger, too. And she knows it."

Next to him Brijette went still. He combed his fingers through her hair, letting it fan across his shoulder. Whatever happened, he didn't want to spoil what was between them right now. A thousand more nights wouldn't be enough for him. Squeezing her tight against him, he decided he'd said enough. Everything else he needed to let her know would have to be done without words. A smile flitted across his lips. He liked that idea better.

BRIJETTE CAST THE FIRST and last vote for herself as the most horrible person in the world. She was cruel and selfish. Worst of all, she realized it and knew that she wasn't going to do a thing about it. Not tonight. It was time. Time to tell Cade the truth about Dylan. In her mind she could see him stalk angrily across the room. This night would end, and there'd be no more. She couldn't blame him if he never forgave her when he found out how she'd lied. Maybe right after Dylan was born and even when he first came here, she'd had a plausible excuse, but not now. The only excuse she had was to save herself from the hurt she knew would come. But if she could love Cade a bit longer, maybe he wouldn't take it so hard, maybe he'd understand why, even after she realized he hadn't wanted the child aborted, she'd still hesitated to tell him. Of course, they'd have to tell Dylan. The response from her was even too frightening to imagine. She could lose her daughter's trust forever. She ran her palms on top of Cade's arms, the hairs tickling her skin. Give her a day or two more of this perfect life—the three of them together, happy—then she'd ruin it. She'd have to.

"I'll stay," she whispered, staring at the silvery water of the creek as Cade kissed her shoulder.

CHAPTER FOURTEEN

"WHERE THE HECK did Cade run off to this afternoon?" Brijette shouted from the exam room where she was putting away supplies. She'd just seen the last patient for the day and she hadn't seen Cade since midmorning.

Andy poked his head in the door. "He had to go pick his mother up at the airport."

Brijette's hand paused midway to the cabinet and she took a deep breath.

"I imagine that's how he thought you'd feel, which is probably why he didn't tell you."

"I don't know what you're talking about."

Andy thumbed through a chart, shaking his head. "I saw you freeze up at the mention of his mother's name."

"I was just wondering why she flew. It's not that long of a drive."

Andy ignored her excuse. "Cade told me his mother isn't very happy that he's here working with you. Something from the past, he said."

Andy waited for her to fill him in, but she didn't. If Cade hadn't enlightened him, she certainly wasn't going to.

He shrugged when she didn't answer. "Well, if it makes you feel any better, she hasn't enjoyed getting the cold shoulder from the Dallas society crowd. She's much more used to giving it than being on the receiving end."

"Why's she been getting the cold shoulder?" Brijette asked, hoping she didn't appear too interested.

"You can imagine how the country club set acted after the clinic paid off that woman's family."

Brijette didn't have a clue what he was talking about, but she was afraid if she let on he wouldn't finish and she really wanted to know where this story was going. "You think they're treating Cade's mom unfairly?"

"I can talk about them because I grew up in that world. They're treating her how they'd treat anyone whose son had been in the middle of a scandal. I don't think it would have mattered if Cade had taken the case to court and proved he wasn't at fault in the woman's death, those people still would've cut his mother out of their circle. But when Cade and the clinic paid the family off, and the clinic asked Cade to leave, they might as well have hung a guilty sign over his head. I guess the saddest thing is his mother really thought those ladies were her friends. Too bad she had to find out that they don't know the meaning of the word."

She pushed past him as Andy rambled on about his parents and their so-called friends and how glad he was to have left all of that behind. Andy could go on for hours, which was probably why he was such a hit with the old men who gathered at Main Street Coffee Shop for breakfast or with the group who played dominoes every morning at Haney's store. He was so busy talking that he didn't notice she was rushing to get out the door.

"I've got to go now, Andy."

He nodded. "I'll lock up when I finish these charts."

In her car, Brijette turned on the ignition, then sat for a while. What had happened at the clinic in Dallas? Had Cade been responsible for someone's death, then used his and the clinic's money to avoid a lawsuit? Had the rich boy bailed himself out of trouble? She didn't want to believe it, but that's exactly how it sounded. Had everything been a lie?

The past three days since she'd spent the night with Cade had been better than she could ever have imagined her life being. Even Dylan was ecstatic at the way their relationship had evolved. But why hadn't he told her about this thing in Dallas?

Slowly her hands tightened on the steering wheel. Why hadn't she told him Dylan was his daughter? How could she be angry at Cade for not telling her something when she'd been withholding the truth from him? Every day she opened her mouth to do it, and every day she stopped herself, because she didn't want her happiness to end. She'd gone beyond selfish. Today was the day. She'd go to his house. He could tell her what happened in Dallas and she'd finally tell him about Dylan. It was the right thing to do, and wasn't that the way she'd been brought up? Hadn't she been trying to teach her daughter the same lessons?

She shifted the vehicle into Drive and started in the direction of Cade's house. On the outskirts of town she slowed. Cade had gone to pick up his mother, which meant either he wouldn't be home or she would be there. Just then her cell phone rang.

"Where are you?"

It was Cade on the other end, with no hello or anything.

"I'm actually on my way to your house if your mother isn't there."

"Good. Get over here right now. My mother won't be around when you get here. I've explained to her that this is something you and I need to discuss. And don't worry about Dylan. I've already called Norma and asked her to let Dylan stay late."

"Okay." She found herself talking to a dead phone. The woman had found something, she was certain of that. Any thoughts of confronting Cade about what happened in Dallas were gone.

In only a few minutes the phone rang again.

"Well, you've really done it this time." Cade's mother's voice was shrill in her ear.

"Mrs. Wheeler, I don't know what you've told Cade, but..."

"I've shown Cade, not just told him. But I want you to know that I didn't tell him about giving you the money for the abortion, which you so obviously didn't have. If he finds out about that, I promise I will do everything in my power to make sure Cade gets custody of that child."

"Mrs. Wheeler, I haven't done anything that would make the courts take my daughter from me."

"We'll see. You remember that when you're talking to Cade."

Brijette ended the call. In a matter of minutes, she arrived at Cade's house. Lights glared from the kitchen window and she wondered how things had gotten so messed up. Lies. That was it, of course, but she'd always felt she had a necessary reason for everything she'd done.

He must have been waiting at the door because her feet had barely touched the ground when Cade appeared on his front porch. She stopped at the bottom of the steps. She didn't have to hear him say it to know what his mother had found. Only one thing would put that much pure anger and disgust on his face. He knew about Dylan.

She hesitated on the top stair and, without a word, he grabbed her arm and dragged her inside. They'd made it no farther than the entry hall when he slammed a piece of paper onto the antique library table. The silver candlesticks and floral arrangement decorating the table rocked.

"What the hell is this?"

She fingered the edge of the document. "It's Dylan's birth certificate." As much as she wanted to look at him she couldn't bring herself to do it, so she stared at the smudged evidence under his hand. "How did you get it?"

"My mother got it and I don't want to guess how. She knew someone in the right place, I'm sure! I'm just wondering if you want to explain this date. It's not exactly the time frame you led me to believe that first night I asked you about Dylan."

She let her hand drop. "No, it's not. I had a fake birth certificate made up when Dylan was born."

His fingers dug into her arm. "Why would you do that?"

"Because I didn't want you and your family to one day decide you wanted her."

"Like I had a choice to not want her in the first place? How could you not tell me you were pregnant with my child? I don't for one minute believe that it's anyone else's."

Her hair fell in her face as she bent her head. "She's yours, but you don't know the whole story. Your mother doesn't want me to tell you this, and I'm sure she's going to make more trouble for me when she finds out I did, but you need to know."

His hold on her arm relaxed a bit and he shoved the birth certificate to the center of the table. "So tell me the story, not that I think it will make a difference."

"When I got caught with the drugs in my backpack, I'd just found out I was pregnant. I didn't know how to tell you, but I was going to. Then you left as soon as I got into trouble, and never said a word, but your mother came to see me."

"Because you had your lawyer call her."

She finally lifted her head. "That's not true, Cade, and you can go ask the man himself if you like. He's retired but he still lives here. She came on her own and offered me money to never see you again and to tell you I didn't care for you anymore if you tried to contact me. But I told her I couldn't, that I was going to have your baby. So she left, but the next day she came again." Brijette stopped to get her breath and shove her hair away from her face. Angry lights still danced in Cade's eyes.

"This time she said she had talked to you and that you had decided you couldn't raise a child, not while trying to go to medical school, so you thought I should get an abortion. I didn't want to believe her, but she was your mother. Then once you came back here, I began to see I had been right to doubt her. I know now she lied to both of us."

His hand dropped from her arm. "What? That's absurd. You're lying. My mother never did that."

"She may deny it, but you can go ask my lawyer. He knew what was happening. Your mother offered me much more money to have the abortion and stay away from you."

"How could you have agreed? How could you ever think I would say something like that? Hell, I loved you, Brijette."

She pressed the heel of her hand against her forehead. "What was I supposed to think, Cade? I was seventeen and locked up. You left town before I had the chance to see you. You never tried to contact me, then your mother came saying all this. Why would I have thought she was lying?"

"I didn't contact you because you'd asked my mother for a payoff to disappear from my life. It sounded to me like you were using our relationship, hell, using me, for money. You weren't someone I wanted to see again. Now you expect me to believe my mother made all that up? That you never asked for money? That she gave you money to abort a child when I didn't even know you were pregnant?"

"She did, Cade."

He spun away from her. "But you didn't have the abortion."

"Of course not, and I never intended to. My lawyer didn't tell me not to have the abortion but he made it pretty clear that if you and your mother were willing to do such a thing, then I shouldn't care if I didn't totally fulfill my end of the bargain, unless it was what I wanted. And it wasn't. Later, my aunt helped me find someone to make the fake birth certificate."

"So, from the beginning you thought I didn't want Dylan, that I wanted you to have an abortion."

Brijette struggled with the lump in her throat. "Until after you arrived and were angry at me for taking money to end our relationship, but never once mentioned telling me to get an abortion."

He faced her again, and this time the anger had dissipated, but this was worse because his hurt was evident and she had caused it. "But after everything…the last few weeks, you still didn't tell me."

She reached to take his hand but he avoided her. "I wanted to. I was going to, but I knew you'd be angry and I hated for things to change. Dylan…" She put her hands to her throat. "How will I ever tell her? I just didn't have the words for either of you."

He stiffened. "Well, you'd better start thinking of some. I can't believe you didn't call me, even after you'd had the baby, to see if I still felt the same."

"I was afraid you and your mother would change your minds once I'd had her and you'd try to take her away from me. You had money to swing the system in your favor."

"Damn it, Brijette, this isn't about having money. This is about you not trusting me enough, believing in me enough, to tell me I had a child. You sold your daughter into a single-parent family because of your own petty beliefs. My family has money—therefore I'm evil. You don't have money, so to my mother you're a gold digger and thus evil, also. You and my mother both make me sick."

He picked up the phone on the end table in the living room and punched in some numbers. "Uncle Arthur, it's Cade." He was quiet while his uncle talked. "That's right. But I need a favor. I want my mother to stay with you for the rest of her visit. She's not welcome in my house right now and I'm sure she knows why. She can come get her things in a bit. I'll be at Brijette's." He was quiet a moment longer then said goodbye.

"What are you doing?"

He picked up his keys. "You're going home to get your speech together. I'm going to get Dylan. We'll be at your house in ten minutes."

Panic clogged every nerve in her body. Panic

and fear. "God no, Cade. Give me a day or two. Let me figure out what to say so I can break it to her slowly."

He stopped in front of her, his feet spread and his fist tight around his keys. "I've missed out on being her father for nearly ten years. I'm putting a stop to that now."

"She'll hate me."

"You should've thought about that while you were spinning all these lies." He brushed past her and out the door.

Brijette ran to her car. She had no idea what words to say. She only knew that in the end it wouldn't matter. Dylan would be hurt, confused and most of all, angry. Her relationship with her daughter was about to change forever, and she wasn't prepared for it.

CADE COULD TELL Dylan knew something was up the instant she got into his truck.

"Where's my mom?" she asked while fastening her seat belt.

"She's at your house. We're on our way there."

She had no more questions, which told him how worried she was. Normally, Dylan would have pounded him with fifteen questions before they got out of Norma's drive. But tonight she stared through the window wordlessly. He hated to upset her life, but she needed a father. Hadn't she been doing everything she could to get him and her mother together? But he wouldn't marry Brijette, he might not even stay in Cypress Landing anymore. How many people knew the truth? How many people in this little town had been lying to him about his own daughter? He sucked his breath in between his teeth. Of course, Uncle Arthur knew. Damn them. He'd take his daughter and leave. At least he could tell when his country-club bunch was lying. Here, everyone acted oh-so nice just as long as it suited them.

He stopped the car in front of Brijette's house. She was standing in the doorway, but Dylan didn't move right away.

"Something bad is happening, isn't it?"

He reached over and smoothed his daughter's blond hair. "In a way it will be bad, but it's good, too."

She sat for a few seconds longer before pushing open the car door.

In the living room, Dylan took a seat on the couch and he sat beside her. Brijette perched on the small coffee table facing both of them.

Cade rubbed his hand up and down Dylan's thin spine. "Your mother has something to tell you." The girl's eyes glistened with tears already, and he felt awful. "It's going to be all right, I promise."

She nodded and turned to her mother. He kept his hand on her, wanting to hold her, to help her. She was about to find out he was her father, and it would be painful. It wasn't exactly how he'd dreamed of becoming a parent.

"I HATE YOU! You lied to me my whole life!" Dylan jumped up and scurried behind the couch. She couldn't be close to her mother. She didn't even know who that woman was. The mother she'd always known would never have made up stories about her father. She'd have told her the truth. She'd grown up wondering why she didn't have a dad and Cade had been there all along, in another city, not knowing she was his little girl. Her mother was mean. She'd tried to keep her away from her father.

"Dylan, please try to understand. I was young and confused."

Her mother pleaded with her, but Dylan didn't care. She looked at Cade, who had come to stand by her, and she saw a tear at the corner of his eye. Did men cry? Was Cade, her dad, crying? She didn't even try to stop the sob that came out. She threw her arms around his waist, knowing what she had to do. Pushing away from him, she went to her room and slammed the door.

In the living room they were still talking, but she couldn't hear what they were saying. Racing around her room, she threw open her dresser drawers. It only took about five minutes to get what she needed. She'd come back for more later. Wrenching the door open, she marched into the living room, suitcase in hand.

Then the tears came rolling, even though she'd promised herself she wouldn't cry. Except, her mother's face seemed to crumple like an empty candy wrapper, and her legs folded beneath her so she sat down in the middle of the floor. Dylan bit her lip. She wouldn't change her mind. She was killing her mother, she could see that, but she couldn't stay in the same house with her. Not right now, not after she'd lied to her. Cade was her dad, her real dad, and he'd never lied. As soon as he found out she was his daughter he'd come running to tell her. He wanted her, really wanted her to be his daughter. And she wanted him to be her dad.

"I want to go live with Cade."

No one said a word. Cade opened his arms and she raced to him. Her mother never moved from the floor. Her dad—she liked saying that even if it was just to herself—took her suitcase and led her out the door to his truck. They'd left the door open, and she could see through it into the living room where her mother still sat in the middle of the floor. Dylan put her fist to her mouth to block the sob, but it echoed off the insides of Cade's truck.

He placed a hand on her shoulder.

"Don't worry, Dylan. We're going to get through this, the three of us. Everything's going to be okay."

She didn't answer but she believed him. If her dad said things were going to be fine, then they were, 'cause a dad would know.

CHAPTER FIFTEEN

THE IDEA OF CALLING in and saying she wasn't coming to work tempted her, but Brijette's refusal to give in to misery kept her from doing it. After applying a few extra strokes of makeup that didn't begin to cover her swollen eyes, she managed to arrive at the clinic only ten minutes late.

Alicia met her as soon as she came in the staff door and caught her hand. "Cade called us all together this morning and told us about him and Dylan. He said he wanted us to know what was going on if things seemed a little strange the next few days. Are you okay?"

Brijette nodded. She was beginning to wonder how she ever thought she could get through this day.

"If you need to talk, let me know." Alicia gave her a quick hug. "And remember, you did what you thought was right at the time."

"I only hope Dylan will be able to see that one day."

"That girl is smarter than most twenty-year-olds. She's mad right now. Cade told us she's staying with him, but she'll get over it."

"I need to stay busy, or thinking will make me nuts."

Alicia snorted. "That won't be a problem. Every room is full and so is the lobby."

Brijette sighed, taking a chart from the rack next to the exam-room door. "At least some things never change."

Alicia grinned. "Hey, change can be good, no matter how difficult it is at first."

Brijette stepped into the first exam room and forced a smile. "Mrs. Willis, how's your blood sugar been?"

TWO HOURS AND several patients later, Brijette had to admit coming to work had been much better than sitting at home, brooding over what had happened. After all, this was her life, too. Cade walked past her and she grabbed him by the arm, pulling him into the kitchen.

"I need to talk to you."

Surprisingly, he wouldn't look at her. He hung his head, staring at the floor.

"What's the matter with you? Is Dylan all right?"

"She's fine. I… I hate what happened last night. At the time I felt like you deserved it and I guess I kind of still feel like that, but I know it was hard on you…and Dylan."

"You could have made her stay instead of taking her home to live with you."

"She's not living with me, only staying until she can get adjusted. You've had her for years. I wouldn't think you'd begrudge the two of us a little time now."

The feeling of being torn in half made Brijette want to scream. Part of her actually wanted to agree with Cade, that he and Dylan did deserve time together—but if it could only have been under different circumstances. A voice in her head that she would've preferred to ignore quietly reminded her that this situation was of her own making. She scrubbed a hand across her forehead, trying to gather her thoughts into a useful order.

"I wanted to talk to you about getting Dylan into counseling. I think with everything that's gone on, it would be good for her to have another person to talk to who will be unbiased and not tainted by emotions."

"For your information, I believe any advice

or guidance I've given her hasn't been 'tainted' with emotion. But I agree with you on the counseling. Where will we have to go for that?"

"Emalea Cooper, Jackson Cooper's wife, is a psychologist and she works with kids. If you want to set that up I'll be glad to see that she gets there." At the kitchen door he turned to her. "I wanted to tell you you've done a good job with her by yourself. She's a good kid, smart. But I'm still mad as hell at how you lied to the two of us."

With that, he was gone.

She leaned against the counter, trying not to cry. From here on she'd have to do better, make better decisions that weren't based on fear, but on what was best for her and, most of all, what would be best for Dylan. Flipping through the phonebook on the counter, she found Emalea Cooper's number.

"MORE TEA?"

Brijette shoved her glass across the table in response and finished peeling a shrimp.

"I had a good idea that girl was Cade's, even though you tried to hide it."

"Why didn't you say anything to him?"

Doc Wheeler bit into a spicy potato he'd cooked with the shrimp and chewed for a minute. "It wasn't my place," he said finally. "To be honest, I was angry at Cade and his mother when they left you here after you were arrested. I'd thought Cade would be different than my brother and his wife, but when he left here I felt like he had become them."

"What do you think now?"

"That he made a mistake when he was younger, like you. Right now, all of you are paying for those mistakes."

"If his mother would have stayed out of it, none of this would have happened."

"You made your own decisions, you can't blame her. Besides, I understand why she did what she did and why she is who she is."

"She did it because she loves money and thinks she's better than everyone else unless they have as much or more money than she does."

The older man wiped his hands and leaned back in his chair. "There's more to it than that. It's true she was born to a rich family—her mother's parents were wealthy. But her father died when she was young and her mother made very bad decisions. Her mother started going to nightclubs and meeting all sorts of men, and she drank a lot. She ended up marrying one of the most crooked ones because she claimed she'd fallen in love. The woman's family disowned her and tried to take Cade's mom, but her mother wouldn't hear of it. They both moved with this man to a small town in Texas in the middle of nowhere."

Brijette dropped the shrimp she'd been peeling. "So she really grew up in the country?"

"For a while. Her stepfather had been living in the town for a long time. Everyone knew he was a thief and always up to no good. People there treated her like she wasn't a bit better than him. She pleaded with her mother to leave, but she never would. Her mother always claimed that she loved this man and she couldn't leave him. Pretty soon her mother began helping her new husband steal things. That went on for three years, then her mother and stepfather were killed in a robbery, and Cade's mother was brought to live with her grandparents. I don't think she ever got over hating that small town or the fact that her mother had been consumed by a kind of love that was destructive to both of them." He tipped his chair forward and began eating again.

"How do you know all this?"

He remained quiet for a moment, staring at his plate. "There was a time when she and I were very close. I guess I'd have to say that my brother and I were both in love with her."

"You've got to be kidding." Brijette knew her face registered complete shock, but she couldn't help it.

"No, not at all. He and I both wanted to marry her. I was already setting up my clinic here and my brother was staying in Dallas, living the life our family always had. Making money, going to all the right parties, the country club, belonging to the right social clubs. She chose that life over one here in Cypress Landing. Can you see why, after all that, she and my brother would be upset that Cade would want to stay here or want to work with me?"

Brijette nodded. "I guess so. Is that also the reason you didn't keep in contact with Cade much after he left?"

The older man nodded. "I was afraid it would cause problems in the family and the boy had to grow and decide for himself what kind of life he wanted."

She crumpled the napkin in her fist. "I wish I knew what he wanted. He's going to be part of Dylan's life from now on. What if he decides to go back to Dallas?"

"He'll definitely be going back to Dallas."

Brijette jumped from her chair to see Mrs. Wheeler standing in the doorway.

"Now that you know my life history, I hope you'll be satisfied. I don't want my son or my granddaughter growing up in the conditions I grew up in."

"It's not like that in Cypress Landing and I'm no criminal."

"Your past seems to indicate that you are, and lying to everyone all these years about your daughter is criminal in itself. Did you actually think she'd be better off struggling along here with you than living with us, where she could attend the best schools and have everything she needed?"

Brijette's fingers knotted around the chair she'd grabbed for support. "She has everything she needs now. Remember, you were the one who didn't even want her to be born."

"I didn't want you to use the child to try and tie yourself to Cade. I wanted to protect my son first and foremost."

Brijette stood, picking up her plate. "He didn't need protecting from me."

"He could have ended up in jail with you if I hadn't intervened."

Brijette carried her dishes to the sink. "I'm leaving. There's no reasoning with this woman."

As she passed Mrs. Wheeler on her way to the door, she stopped, her hands balled into fists at her side.

"Don't think you're going to come in here and throw money around and take my daughter away from me."

The older woman tugged at the prim collar on her blouse and Brijette could see the nervousness in her gesture. "It won't be up to me. That will be for Cade and Dylan to decide."

"I worked my way out of the kind of life you were in for only a short while. You got out of that situation by the good fortune of being born to money. Does that make you a better person than me?" Brijette stalked away, not waiting for the answer she knew wouldn't come. She'd had enough of the whole Wheeler family. Unfortunately, her daughter was a Wheeler, which tied Brijette to them, like it or not.

CADE SMILED AS Dylan bounced into the car. Brijette had been right about Emalea Cooper being good with children. After only three or four visits he could see Dylan already becoming more at ease with this new situation.

"So, how did it go with Mrs. Cooper?"

"Okay."

"Anything you and I need to talk about?"

The girl shrugged.

"What does that mean?"

She shrugged again.

He sighed. How one child could be so talkative one minute and so completely closemouthed the next he'd never understand.

"You'll have to talk to me because I don't know what all that shoulder-wiggling means."

"Mom always did."

Now they were getting somewhere. "Well, your mom has known you longer, and she is your mom. I think they know stuff that other people can't figure out."

"Is that true?" Dylan twisted to look at him and he moved his shoulders up and down. She stared at him for a minute, then burst out laughing and he laughed with her.

They rode in silence for a few minutes and he saw her staring out the window as they passed Brijette's house.

"Would you like to go see your mom?"

She shrugged her shoulders.

"Dylan."

"I don't know, all right? I'm still mad, aren't you? What she did was wrong."

He pulled into his driveway, *their* driveway now, without answering. Inside his head multiple responses to that question battled for a chance to be heard. In the end, he had to go with his heart and what he knew was right. Shutting off the engine, he turned in the seat of the truck to face his daughter.

"Yes, in some ways I'm still mad. You and I can hang on to that for as long as we want. Months, years even. It's already been nearly two weeks now. Or, we can try to see your mom's side and try to understand why she kept that secret. What does Mrs. Cooper say?"

Dylan studied him closely. "She says about the same thing you did."

"We could call your mom and have her come over and make pizza with us."

She didn't answer right away but glanced at the groceries on the back seat of his truck. "Maybe she could come after we eat, for dessert or something."

"That sounds good. I'll call her."

Dylan got out and grabbed a few bags of groceries, then shuffled inside while he dialed Brijette's number on his cell phone. The girl was right. Pizza took a while to make and none of them might feel much like eating at the end of this.

THIS WAS HER TRIAL. Brijette knew it, and as she picked at the crust of the blueberry pie with her fork, she wondered what her sentence might be. They didn't really expect her to feel like eating, did they? So far she'd asked Dylan a few questions that the girl had answered with a few words.

"I need to call Andy and ask him something. I'm going to let you and your mother talk."

The look of panic on Dylan's face when Cade got up brought tears to her eyes. For years it had been the two of them and they'd faced everything together. Now the child didn't even want to be left alone with her. Cade disappeared inside the house and they sat in silence.

"Dylan, I'm sorry. I know I've said it before, but I mean it. I made a big mistake."

Her daughter spun her saucer around several times, then looked up. "You lied to me a lot. Why did you do that?"

Brijette hung her head. "I thought I was doing the right thing. It's complicated. I was young and I did fall in love with Cade. Then I got pregnant with you. Remember, we talked about how that happens back when your friend Katie's sister got pregnant and had a baby."

Dylan rolled her eyes. "I know where babies come from, Mom."

At last, a glimpse of normalcy. She'd never have thought she'd be glad to see Dylan giving her that particular look, but she was. Now things were going to get harder. Once again, the time had come that she'd either have to conceal the full truth from Dylan or tell her exactly how things had been. Only this time the truth didn't really have to be known. If she told Dylan her newly found grandmother had tried to pay Brijette to not have Dylan, it could ruin that relationship forever. Mrs. Wheeler had caused a lot of heartache for Brijette and for Cade. She deserved to never have a close relationship with her granddaughter.

"I was pregnant when I got in trouble for carrying the drugs in my backpack, but I hadn't told anyone, not even Cade. Mrs. Wheeler really wanted him to go to medical school and she was afraid if Cade and I stayed together he would never get to be a doctor. So she offered me money to stay away from him. Only she told me he wanted that, and she told him I wanted it. Does that make sense?"

"She tricked both of you."

Brijette nodded.

"But she thought she was doing what was best, huh?"

A bug landed on her pie but Brijette didn't care because she wasn't going to eat it, anyway. She watched it crawl around, then slowly looked at Dylan. "That's right. She was trying to protect Cade, just like I was trying to protect you. I took the money because I knew I'd need it to make a better life for you and me. She offered it because she knew Cade would be a great doctor and she wanted him to get the chance."

Dylan nodded but didn't say anything, and they sat in silence for a few minutes until Cade stepped back onto the patio. He sat in the chair and glanced between them.

"Would you like to go spend the night with your mom?"

Brijette's heart leaped to her throat, though she didn't miss the quick flash of panic in her daughter's eyes.

"Umm...I'm really tired. I think I'd rather go to bed now." She pushed back her chair, walking around the table to hug Cade.

Brijette held her breath. She tried to keep the disappointment from her face, tried not to expect anything right now. The first verdict was coming. Dylan paused, then came to her side and hugged her.

"Night, Mom."

"Night, Dyl." The words nearly stuck in her throat, then she was gone. Her daughter disappeared into the house and Brijette folded her arms and dropped her head onto them. Her shoulders shivered slightly with the tears she couldn't stop. Damn, this was hard. She deserved it, but she didn't want to have to get her just desserts this one time.

On the back of her head Cade's hand smoothed her hair and she felt a paper towel being rubbed against her arm. She raised up from the table but kept her head bowed.

"I'm sorry, Brijette. I really thought she'd go home with you."

Blotting her face with the paper towel, she glanced at him. "It's okay. At least she's speaking to me. Thank you for asking me over and giving us a chance to talk."

His hand covered hers and she straightened. "Eventually we'll be sharing custody of Dylan and it's important that we work together, don't you think?"

She nodded, but didn't really want to consider custody issues yet.

"And thank you for not telling Dylan the part about my mother paying you to not have her. That could make for a bad situation between them."

"You heard that?"

He nodded.

"I think we've all got enough problems as is."

"True, but you still could have ruined their relationship, possibly forever."

She stared at his hand on top of hers. "I've ruined enough relationships lately to last me a lifetime."

His hand tightened on hers. "They're not all ruined, Brij, just changing, evolving."

When she finally met his eyes she wasn't sure what she saw there—fear, regret, sadness? She certainly felt those things. Suddenly, he moved his hand and shifted in his chair as though uncomfortable. The visit was over.

"I'd better go." She got to her feet and he followed her to the door, saying nothing.

At the bottom of the steps he shouted after her, "She'll be ready for more soon."

Brijette glanced back at him, then kept moving toward her car. She prayed he was right and wondered if she and Cade would ever be able to get back what they'd shared before her lie had done its damage.

CHAPTER SIXTEEN

THE NEXT WEEK Brijette had dinner at Cade's house twice. The second visit she came over to help fix the meal, and they all laughed together. She tried not to be too elated or read too much into it, but the icy wall between her and Dylan seemed to be slowly melting. By her third visit she hit pay dirt.

They were cleaning up the kitchen and Cade had gone into the other room to answer the phone when it happened.

"I packed a bag today. I think I'll come home and sleep in my room tonight, if that's okay."

The plate Brijette held in her hand slipped and she set it on the counter before she dropped it.

"That's great. I mean, of course it's okay." She wanted to say more, to scream and jump up and down, but the ground on which they were treading remained unsteady. They had to face this calmly, although she wasn't the least bit calm.

Later, back at the home they'd shared for the

past three years, Dylan hurried to her room, then stuck her head out the door.

"Hey, you cleaned up my room."

Brijette stopped in the open doorway. "I only cleaned what was out here. I didn't go in the closet, or your drawers, so those are like they always were."

Dylan nodded, then completely changed course. "Do you have any chocolate ice cream?"

"Of course."

"Good. Can we have some and watch this new movie Dad bought for me? I haven't watched it yet."

For reasons she couldn't explain, hearing Dylan call Cade "Dad" stole her breath every time. She'd done it a few times at his house. She'd have thought it would upset her, but it didn't. The feeling was different and, at the moment, completely unexplainable.

"That sounds like fun." Brijette started toward the kitchen and Dylan followed her.

Her daughter watched as she scooped ice cream into the first bowl.

"Do you think Cade will ever forgive you for lying to him?"

The spoon clattered against the bowl. Boy, Dylan knew how to start off with the hard questions.

"I can't answer that, honey. I hope he will, but I'll understand if he can't completely forgive me. This has been very hard for him, too."

She kept filling the bowls and neither of them spoke until she was finished. As she pressed the top onto the ice-cream container, she looked at Dylan. "Do you think you'll ever forgive me for lying to you about your father?"

"And about the drug thing, don't forget about that."

"Right. The drug thing, too."

Her daughter was quiet. "It hurt my heart."

Brijette's throat knotted and the backs of her eyes burned. She stared out the window, unable to face her own child.

"I know, but I didn't mean for it to. I was hoping to protect you from that. But it hurts my heart, too, that this had to happen to us."

"To me and you? Or to you and Cade?"

Finally she turned to Dylan, who was so serious but not upset, as she'd been that first night. "Mostly it hurts my heart for me and you, but I hate that I did this to the three of us."

"Dad says it'll be all right."

"Do you believe him?"

Dylan nodded, then stuck her spoon in her

ice cream and picked up the bowl. "I'm not so mad anymore, but I still don't like it."

Brijette nodded. "I can understand that. But I hope you'll give me a chance to prove to you that I'm not going to hide anything from you ever again."

"Do you think maybe I could go back to Willow Point with you one day soon? Rick was going to show me and Ellen an old haunted cabin near the store."

"Sure, I'd love for you to come with me. I know Ellen is A.G.'s granddaughter, but who's Rick?"

"The boy who helped me load the boat the last time I was there with you."

Brijette picked up her own bowl and followed Dylan to the living room, where she slid the movie into the player, then began to eat her ice cream as Dylan launched into a tale of ghosts and goblins found at Willow Point.

And so they began. She'd dreaded having to redefine her relationship with her daughter when she was this young. But here they were feeling each other out, almost like strangers. It wasn't what she would have wished for, but it was probably more than she deserved. She smiled at something Dylan said and thought to herself how wrong she'd been to believe that lying was the greatest form of protection.

BRIJETTE'S CLOTHES were soaked with sweat by the time she, Alicia and Dylan had loaded the last boxes onto the boat. It was hard to believe the sun had not even begun to pink the sky yet. The store would be sweltering and she didn't relish another day of drowning in her own perspiration. At least she had Dylan with her today. Thank goodness she and Cade had agreed to send Dylan to see Emalea Cooper, the town's psychologist, because Dylan seemed to be recovering from the shock of learning Cade was her father. She was still wary of Brijette, which was heartbreaking, but she knew that winning her daughter's trust would take time.

"Mom, are you ready?"

Dylan and Alicia stood waiting for her on the boat. She untied the line and jumped on deck.

They'd just left the river behind when Brijette noticed a boat heading toward them from the tree-lined canal to her left. She hoped the other boat would change direction or slow down, otherwise they'd ram into them. Alicia grabbed her shoulder as the boat neared. At the last moment, it veered sharply to one side, grazing the side of Doc's boat.

"Sit down and hold on," she shouted at Dylan, who had been kneeling in the seat, watching the boat wheel around behind them.

"Mom!" Dylan yelled back. "They were wearing ski masks. Did you see?"

Brijette didn't answer but glanced at Alicia, who nodded. She'd noticed the masks, too. Brijette had been trying to convince herself that she'd imagined it, but they couldn't have dreamed the same thing.

The throttle vibrated under her grip as she pushed hard to get more acceleration from the boat. Behind them, the other boat closed in, its engines roaring above the hum of their own. Doc's boat wasn't designed for speed, but they'd never needed to make a getaway before now.

When the boat pulled alongside them, Brijette had to swallow her heart to speak.

"Dylan, get on the floor!"

The girl had barely landed on her stomach when one of the men fired a shot across the bow and motioned for Brijette to stop. She yanked on the throttle until the engine sputtered and the boat rocked in the water. Two of the men grabbed the railing on Doc's boat and sprang onboard.

Without a word, one of them grabbed Alicia and tossed her over the side. For a minute she didn't come up and Brijette prayed she hadn't hit her head. Then, she bobbed to the surface and began treading water.

The other man caught Brijette's shirtfront and pressed a cold metal pistol against her forehead. Dylan screamed, and at the edge of her field of vision Brijette could see her daughter fighting against the man who'd thrown Alicia out.

"Take what you want, just let us go."

In front of her, black eyes sparked with laughter. "Don't worry, my boss is letting you off easy. But if you don't quit helping the sheriff you won't be this lucky next time. You or your daughter."

She felt the boat rail press against her legs, then he pushed and she tumbled backward into the water, fear gripping her as she realized that Dylan was now alone on the boat with the two monsters.

Her head above water, she gasped for air and clawed the side of the boat. Above her, she heard a thud and Dylan cried out in pain, then the girl flew through the air, landing with a splash in the lukewarm, murky water. Brijette swam toward her as fast as she could. Alicia also swam to her from the other direction. Brijette prayed they wouldn't be hit by one of the boats but she also wondered what they would do. She and Alicia weren't wearing life vests and the canal that led to A.G.'s was surrounded by brush and reeds they couldn't possibly walk through. The boat engines roared and a smaller man who'd never left the attackers' boat stared at them, while the guy who'd threatened Brijette spun Doc's boat around and headed toward the river. Suddenly, the smaller man opened a compartment at his feet and threw a life vest toward them. He reached for another, but his boat's driver saw him and left the wheel, knocking him to the deck.

The driver didn't return to retrieve the vest floating in the water and Brijette had seen all she'd needed to see. When the smaller man had thrown them the vest, the sleeve of his T-shirt had ridden up his arm, revealing a scar that appeared to have recently had stitches removed. It was a long and crooked cut, one she wasn't likely to forget—especially since she'd only recently treated it for an infection. T.J. Broussard had helped two men steal Doc's boat. Regina had been right. He was in trouble. Big trouble.

Alicia swam over to her with the life jacket. She grabbed it with one hand and caught hold of Dylan's life vest with the other. Pulling her daughter to her, she wiped Dylan's wet hair away from her teary face.

"Are you hurt, Dylan?"

"My arm hurts bad." She sniffled, rubbing her eyes and holding her other arm above the water. Nausea welled in Brijette's stomach at the sight of the child's misshapen arm.

"What's wrong with it, Mom?"

"Hold it next to you and keep it really still, Dylan. I think it's broken. Try not to move it around."

Through Dylan's grimace of pain, she managed to look hopeful. "Will I get a cast?"

Brijette studied her daughter. "I imagine so."

"If I do, can I get people to sign it?"

Brijette nodded. At least the idea of the cast was distracting her for a minute.

"Do we swim for the river?" Alicia asked.

"No, we should head for A.G.'s store."

Alicia groaned. "That's a long way."

"It's farther but there's not much current. I think it's the safer option."

Dylan was already some distance ahead of them, floating on her back, her vest keeping her well above water. She balanced her injured arm across her chest and kicked with her feet, periodically glancing around to be sure she didn't run aground.

For nearly ten minutes they paddled in silence with Brijette keeping watch on the edges of the waterway, though she didn't know what she'd do if she saw a snake or alligator slip into the water.

"I hear a boat."

Brijette strained to hear what Alicia did, and then she, too, could hear it. An engine humming in the distance.

"Let's pray they're friendly."

A boat appeared in the distance and Dylan spun around to watch its approach. "It's Mr. A.G."

The old man stopped next to Dylan and grabbed her life vest, hoisting her into his boat. "Watch my arm," she said. "It's broke."

He flipped a rope ladder over the side and Brijette and Alicia climbed aboard. "Where's ya boat?" he asked, scratching his chin.

"Some men with guns took it." Dylan proceeded to give A.G. the details of the story, complete with a few sound effects.

When she finished, he arched a brow at Brijette. "Didn't cause the child no trauma, I'd say."

"We need to get to the sheriff and report this. It may not seem serious to hear her tell it, but it was."

A.G. nodded. "When you didn't show, I started worryin', then this fella came by and said he thought he heard a gunshot. I knew nobody hunts near this canal, so I came to check on you."

"It's a good thing you did." Alicia sighed, sitting on one of the seats. "Can we please go now, before another criminal comes along and takes this boat?"

A.G. switched on the engine and steered toward the river. Brijette racked her brain for a clue to what she'd stumbled across while tracking that would get her into this much trouble. This hadn't been a random attack. They'd been waiting for her. The man had threatened her; his "boss" had threatened her. They thought she knew more than she did. But how could she protect herself when she couldn't see the missing piece they believed she had?

"YOU'RE SURE you know the guy."

"I'm one-hundred-percent positive, Jackson. I just worked on his wound a week ago."

"Did they say what they wanted?"

"They took the boat. I guess they wanted it and maybe whatever drugs might be onboard."

He studied her briefly. "Were there drugs on the boat?"

"A few, for emergencies."

"And prescription pads?"

She pulled at the hem of her wet scrub top. "Well, yeah, I occasionally write prescriptions for the folks in Willow Point who have a way to get to town."

"What else happened that I need to know?"

"He said if I didn't quit helping the sheriff with his cases, next time would be worse for me…and for Dylan."

Jackson let his hands drop to his sides. "What have you not told me?"

She rubbed the heel of her hand against her forehead. "That's the problem, I can't think of anything I've come across that would incriminate one person in particular."

"Somebody thinks you've found something."

She sighed. "I wish I had. I'd tell you, and this whole mess would end."

Jackson stuck his notepad in his pocket and rolled his pen between his fingers. "You let me know if you think of anything else." He stared at her for an instant longer, then walked away.

She let out a slow breath and collapsed against the wall. He thought she was lying, thought she knew more. Admittedly, she had an idea, was tying a few things together, but none of it made sense to her yet, so it certainly wouldn't make sense to Jackson. The sensation in her gut was like the one she often got when she was tracking—as though she was right on the verge of seeing something important. Maybe the reason she couldn't see it was that she knew she wouldn't like what she found.

The air-conditioning in the hospital waiting area made her wet clothes feel icy against her skin. She glanced at the room where one of the ER doctors was taking care of Dylan. The sound of the electronic doors opening at the end of the hall caused her to look up, and she was filled with dread.

She hadn't stopped to call Cade to tell him what had happened. At the dock, A.G. had notified the sheriff and Jackson had met them at the emergency room. There'd been no time to talk to Cade. She wiped her hands across her wet scrubs. Truthfully, she could have tried harder, but she hadn't been in a hurry to face him. He'd be angry that she'd taken Dylan. He hadn't been certain it was a good idea, even though the child had accompanied her to Willow Point on many previous occasions. His mother had naturally thought it was the worst thing on earth. Now they'd think they were right and they'd deem her a terrible mother. She felt bad enough already. But Cade's expression told her she'd be spared nothing.

CHAPTER SEVENTEEN

"ARE YOU ALL RIGHT?" Cade knew he held Brijette's arm a bit tighter than he should. He nearly pulled her close, but he remembered at the last minute that this was the woman who'd for years failed to let him know he had a daughter. Worse, she'd now taken his girl off and gotten her injured, then not bothered to let him know.

"I'm fine, but Dylan's arm is broken."

"Where is she?"

"They're working on it right now."

"You should have called me."

"I was going to call you but Jackson met us here and I had to give him a report. He just left."

"You should have phoned me from the dock. Thankfully, Emma had to speak with the clerk in the emergency room about a patient. The clerk mentioned to her that you had to bring Dylan here or I probably still wouldn't know."

"That's not true. I was about to get in touch with you."

He didn't really believe her, but the tears were starting to fill her eyes and he hadn't come here to make her cry.

"I told you she shouldn't go with you. But you wouldn't listen."

"She's been with me countless times before and we were fine. Why would I have thought this time would be different?"

"Because we were already having these problems with the prescription drugs."

"I had no reason to think that anyone would come after us."

He dropped her arm. "That's the problem, isn't it? You don't think."

"You're being unfair, Cade."

He leaned in closer to her as a nurse hurried past. "You should know everything there is about being unfair. You've practiced it so well for the past nine years."

"I'm not going to stand in this hall and argue with you. It won't help Dylan. I'm going to get a cup of coffee."

She left and for the first time he noticed her wet clothes. Lately, he had to keep reminding himself that he was still angry at her, that he couldn't trust her. He had to admit that he'd felt something, a special connection with her, but that was before he'd learned the truth. If he were honest, he'd also admit that he'd found himself in love with Brijette again. Was love like that? Could it go away when he realized she'd done things she shouldn't have, lied to him? That wasn't how he'd imagined love would be. At the moment, distrust overrode everything else. If she'd lied and hid this from him, what else could she be hiding? He rubbed his hand across his eyes.

Hearing footsteps, he looked up to see Dr. Lowe, the emergency-room physician, approaching.

"Hi, Cade. Is Brijette around?"

"She went for coffee. Is Dylan okay?"

The other doctor glanced past Cade's shoulder. "She'll be fine. I need to talk to Brijette about what we're going to do with that arm."

"You can talk to me. She's my daughter and I'll be seeing that she gets the medical care she needs."

Cade had to admit Dr. Lowe did a good job of hiding his shock. It didn't work, but he tried.

"Uh, okay." He paused and appeared relieved as Brijette appeared at Cade's side. Cade imagined he didn't want to give the information in front of him even if he did claim to be

Dylan's father. Dr. Lowe barely knew Cade, who was still considered a stranger in Cypress Landing. The whole situation made him crazy. Brijette lied and when everyone found out, they still stood behind her.

"I'm referring Dylan to an orthopedist in Baton Rouge. He does a lot of work with kids who have broken bones. I don't think she needs surgery, but I've put an air cast on it and I'd like for him to see it and decide on further treatment. The nurse is making the appointment right now, but it should be for first thing in the morning."

Beside him, Brijette nodded as Dr. Lowe left.

She turned to him. "I'll have to take the day off from the clinic tomorrow to take Dylan to Baton Rouge."

Cade gritted his teeth. "I'm taking her."

He should've known that would spark her anger. Her hands knotted into fists and he thought briefly that she might actually hit him.

"No matter what you think, I'm still her mother, and as of this second you don't have a legal claim on her. So, I'll be taking *my* daughter to the doctor."

"You'd better believe I'm going to change that as soon as possible. I'm talking with a lawyer right now to get custody of *my* daughter." That was a lie. His mother had been urging him to do it but he kept putting her off.

Brijette stared at the floor and pinched the bridge of her nose, shaking her head. "We're crazy to argue like this. We should both take her. It's what she would want."

"But, how will they function at the clinic?" The question was automatic, though he couldn't have cared less if they had to close for the day.

"Doc Arthur can come in and help. He told me the other day he was ready to start seeing patients, and Andy will have to make do. We'll cancel what appointments we can."

He hated to agree with her, but she was right. Dylan would be pleased if they both went. Since the girl had started to forgive her mother for keeping his identity secret, she'd been on track again, trying to get the two of them together. But she was no doubt beginning to realize it wasn't going to be as easy as it was before.

CADE RUBBED HIS FINGER along the windowsill, watching the drive. Brijette was due to arrive any minute.

"I don't know why you let her keep the girl

overnight after what happened. You're the doctor. She should have been with you."

Cade frowned, going to the kitchen table where his mother sat with a cup of coffee. Dylan wasn't the only one with a mother who'd lied. Finding forgiveness for his mother wasn't easy and he hadn't done it completely, but he had invited her to stay at his house again.

"She was hurt and wanted to stay with her mother. It's only natural."

"Her mother's the reason she got hurt in the first place. I can't believe you'd let her go off in that boat to the middle of nowhere. It's obviously a haven for criminals. But we already knew that because that's where *she's* from."

"That's enough." Cade wasn't sure why he was coming to Brijette's defense. "I especially don't want to hear you talking like that around Dylan. Brijette is still her mother."

"I hope you'll have sense enough now to sue for custody. I'm sure when a judge hears about this incident he'll give it to you."

He played with his cup on the table without speaking.

"Well, what are you thinking?"

His fingers tightened around the warm ceramic. "It's strange to me that you're so determined I should get custody of a child you originally thought shouldn't be born. And don't say it's a lie and that Brijette fabricated the whole thing. I talked to the lawyer who arranged the paperwork. Would it have been so wrong for us to marry and have a child?"

His mother had the decency to look ashamed before she spoke. "You know what happened to my mother, how she got involved with that terrible man when I was young. It was a sick kind of love that killed her in the end."

"That has nothing to do with Brijette and me."

"Doesn't it? You were crazy about her. There she was sitting in jail, arrested for drug possession, but you still claimed to love her and wanted to be with her. At least my telling you she asked for money to stay away from you brought you to your senses. At the time I had to think of you first, not the child she was carrying. For all I knew, it wasn't even yours."

"Is that how you justify your lie? By saying that it brought me to my senses? You do realize that, in reality, you used a lie to get me to do what you wanted. Now that it's clear Dylan is mine, I've got to do what's right for the two of us."

"I agree, and you need to do whatever it takes to get full custody and bring her to Dallas with us."

Cade shook his head. "What's so great about Dallas? After everything that's happened, I can't believe you'd want to stay there. Those people you call friends don't even speak to you now."

"That's not true. They're busy. Besides, it's the only life I know. I'm comfortable there."

Cade sighed. He didn't know what was best for Dylan or for him, but he didn't think dragging her hours away from her mother would make the child happy. He wasn't sure it would make him happy.

He could see the Tahoe approaching. He only knew that today the three of them would be going to the doctor. They'd be like a real family. He felt good, and he almost hated to admit the fact.

"I'll see you later." He could feel his mother's gaze boring into him.

"Don't let her trick you into falling in love again."

He glared at her. "I think you have my life confused with yours. My relationship with Brijette is nothing like the one your mother had with your stepfather. You're so involved in the lifestyle you and your so-called friends lead. Why can't you see there are a whole lot of people in Cypress Landing enjoying life and friends, and it has absolutely nothing to do with money?" His footsteps on the wood floor carried the sound of finality, even to him. He could have said more, but what was the point? She wasn't likely to listen and he had more important things on his mind.

DYLAN JUMPED FROM the car the minute it stopped rolling. Behind her, Mrs. Wheeler shouted for her to wait. She couldn't yet call her dad's mother grandmother, though Mrs. Wheeler had asked her to. Her dad said she didn't have to until she felt like it, and if she never felt like it that was okay, too. She was all right for a grandmother and she liked to buy her stuff. Today, she'd picked Dylan up at Norma's and wanted to take her to town. It was early and Dylan hadn't had breakfast, so she'd insisted they stop at Haney's. As she waited for Mrs. Wheeler at the top of the steps, she giggled. The woman slowly picked her way across the rocky parking lot, staring at the ancient gas tanks sitting out front. Cade's mom was used to the city, and life in Cypress Landing seemed to be like life on another planet to her. She had a hunch the woman would be upset when she realized the real reason Dylan had insisted they have breakfast here.

Mrs. Wheeler finally made it to the top step and the young girl pushed open the door to the store.

"Dylan!" Four different voices called her name. She ran to the small table and made her way around, giving her best grandpa hugs to the four old men playing dominoes. She might not have grown up with a real grandparent before now but that didn't mean she didn't have any.

From the front counter, Janie waved at her. "What do you mean going to hug those old farts before you give me one?"

Dylan laughed and squeezed past the potato-chip rack to get to Janie. "I had to make sure who's winning so I can sit by the right one."

The gray-haired woman winked at her. Finally, her grandmother appeared in front of the counter with a not-so-happy look on her face. She frowned even more as she watched Janie pile eggs and grits onto the plate she passed to Dylan.

"This is Cade's mother," Dylan said. "He's my dad, you know, so that makes her my grandmother."

"I'm Janie." The store clerk reached across the counter and Dylan thought for a second her grandmother would refuse Janie's slightly greasy hand, but finally, she gave it a shake.

"Aren't you going to tell her your name?" she asked.

"Well, you told her I was Cade's mother, so I'm sure she can figure out that I'm Mrs. Wheeler."

"No, I mean your first name."

Janie squeezed her shoulder. "Dylan, not everybody likes to go by first names when they meet."

"Ellen. Ellen Wheeler," her grandmother replied, though Dylan thought she didn't seem pleased at being forced to share that information.

Dylan smiled at her as she trotted around the counter to the domino table. Grady Redding had a chair positioned next to his.

She watched her grandmother, who was still waiting in front of the counter, as if Dylan might actually be ready to go. Was she in for a surprise. "Get breakfast and sit there." She pointed to the table across from where she and the men were playing. Her grandmother didn't get food, but took a seat at the table Dylan had pointed to.

"This is Ellen Wheeler. She's Cade's mother," Dylan announced. She'd decided not to waste time waiting for her grandmother to introduce herself. She wondered if everybody in the city was this unfriendly with strangers.

"You've got yourself a mighty fine granddaughter, here," the man sitting nearest her grandmother informed her.

The woman nodded her agreement. As Dylan helped Grady play his turn, the four gentlemen pelted her grandmother with questions. Two of the men weren't married, and Dylan nearly snickered as she imagined they might be flirting with her grandmother. If she realized it, the woman would die. Dylan could tell Ellen Wheeler didn't really like Cypress Landing or the people who lived here. But Dylan was determined to make her get to know them. Most adults thought kids were deaf and dumb and couldn't see what was going on. But Dylan knew her grandmother wanted Cade to go live in Dallas, and she wanted Dylan to go with them. But where did that leave her mom? Besides, she liked Cypress Landing, even though the city might be fun for a while.

After they left Haney's, Dylan let her grandmother think they were going to wander around and shop, but she had one more destination in mind. Dragging the woman into the children's clothing store, she didn't stop until they were standing next to a group of women gathered around a quilting frame.

"Hey, y'all, this is my grandmother."

She didn't miss the pleased glance her grandmother gave her, and she felt a bit guilty for purposely saying it like that. But she had to do whatever she could to try to get the woman to see this town wasn't so bad.

Her grandmother hesitantly started asking questions about the quilt. One of the ladies pointed to a chair, telling her to pull it up to the table and join them.

Her grandmother sat down in the chair.

"I'm going next door to Mrs. Cecile's to paint." Dylan plunged through the clothing racks, escaping before her grandmother had a chance to stop her. She heard the ladies laughing as she pushed through the door and onto the sidewalk. Her grandmother hadn't been nearly as difficult as she'd expected. Her mother and Cade were going to take much more work.

CADE STARED at his mother as she went into great detail about the intricate workings of quilt-making. He glanced at his uncle, who wore an interested expression, but Cade didn't miss the glint of amusement in his eye. He took a bite of his jambalaya and chewed to hide his own smile. Whatever had gotten into his mother had her suddenly excited about something that in her regular circle of friends would have been completely foreign. Dylan had a hand in this, no doubt. He was amazed that a nine-year-old could figure out exactly what would get his mother to connect with small-town life when he hadn't been able to figure it out himself.

“Did you hear me, Cade?”

“No, sorry. I was thinking about my schedule at the clinic tomorrow.”

“I’ve decided to stay here another week. The ladies are trying to get some quilts ready for a competition, and they’d like me to help.”

She glanced at her watch and took a most unladylike gulp of her tea. “I’ve got to go. Ilene Brinson is going to get me started on some squares so I can have them ready for tomorrow afternoon.”

She gave them both a huge smile that Cade hadn’t seen in…well, he couldn’t remember. Then, she hurried away.

He and his uncle sat staring at each other in silence. Slowly, Arthur smiled and soon they were both laughing.

“I can’t believe my mother is going to help make a quilt. Her friends in Dallas would be horrified.”

“I told you, Cade. There’s a different side to your mother that hasn’t seen the light of day in a long time.”

“Well, I hope she keeps that side out for a while. I think I might actually like it.”

His uncle broke off a piece of bread and nodded. “I think we would all like it, including her.”

CHAPTER EIGHTEEN

"THE BOY DOESN'T KNOW anything that's of much use. He'd been trying to make some quick and easy money."

Jackson rested his big frame against the post on the front porch of Haney's store. Brijette sighed, thinking about the trouble T.J. had gotten himself into. She glanced through the window where she could see Dylan inside playing dominoes with the men the girl always called her grandpas, even though she'd been here last week with her real grandmother. It was Thursday, and although the sheriff's department had recovered Doc Arthur's boat, they hadn't released it yet, so she'd decided to take the day off and spend it with Dylan.

She turned her attention back to Jackson. "What had T.J. been doing with them? He has a young wife and a baby at home."

"Just running packages on the river from different pick-up and drop-off points. He doesn't know for sure what was in the packages, or if he does, he isn't saying. He sure doesn't know who the boss is, or else he should be an actor, but I think he'll give us the names of the other men on the boat soon enough. He swears he didn't know they were going to attack you. Are you sure you haven't noticed something you're not telling me?"

She stuck her fists into the pockets of her shorts. "There is one thing. You know how I told you I found that one set of prints at both sites and how the prints looked a bit odd?" She shifted her weight from one foot to the other. "I only realized it recently—I had a feeling but couldn't pin it down. Then I remembered. I've seen that track before, but in a different place. It was at Jody Mills's house the night he died. I saw them before I found him. The shape and the stride were unusual and that's why I noticed them, but when I found Jody, well, I never thought of it again, until now."

The big man crossed his arms in front of his chest. "And you knew this for how long?"

"A day or two. I would have come to you sooner, but honestly, I wasn't sure if I was being paranoid or not."

"You think this person might have killed Jody?"

She shook her head. "I don't know. I don't know how many other tracks were there or how old they were. I didn't work the case."

Jackson scratched the stubble on his chin. "We might've benefited from your help, but you and I both know after you were the first one on the scene and found the body, it was better for you not to have anything to do with the investigation."

She nodded, not wanting to recall the time when her friend had died.

Jackson raked a hand through his hair. "I've got to tell you something you won't like. I've already been to the clinic and broken the news to them."

Brijette's stomach tightened. She didn't like the sound of this.

"We arrested one of the nurses at your clinic and her son last night. The Carson lady."

"What?"

"We'd been watching the son for a while, and when the time was right for the arrest we got him and his mother."

"Why didn't you tell me you'd been watching my coworker's son?"

Jackson's face hardened. "You don't get to know everything, Brijette. But I guess that explains a lot of the prescriptions from your office."

She tried to collect her thoughts. "Do you think Mrs. Carson and her son are involved with the people who took the boat?"

"You're asking the same questions we've been asking, but we don't have an answer. If I had to guess, I'd say yes, it's all related. But we don't have enough information to say for certain, not yet."

Dylan came bouncing through the door and onto the porch. "Hey, Mr. Jackson, you wanna sign my cast?" She offered the injured extremity and the permanent marker she always seemed to have ready.

"Sure." Jackson squeezed his name in among the others and passed the marker back to Dylan. He opened the door and looked back at Brijette. "If you remember more, I hope you'll let me know immediately." He disappeared into the store without waiting for her response.

"What's wrong, Mom?"

She pulled Dylan's ponytail and smiled. "Nothing, we're only talking."

"About what happened on the boat?"

"Yes, but don't worry. We're not in danger."

"That man said if you didn't stop helping the sheriff, we'd be in a lot of danger."

"I hate that you had to hear that. But what do you think I should do?"

Dylan scratched a spot on her T-shirt and frowned. "You don't listen to a dumb crook. You should keep helping the sheriff so he can catch the bad people and get them out of Cypress Landing so everybody will be okay. I'm not scared of him."

Brijette threw her arm around the girl's shoulder as they walked down the steps. "Good, because there's nothing to be afraid of. The sheriff and his deputies will help protect us."

CADE STUCK THE LAST chart for the day into the basket on Emma's desk. Everyone else had gone home. The thought of leaving Cypress Landing had taken a back seat in his mind since he'd learned Dylan was his, but lately the idea of going back to a city clinic made him depressed.

He liked the pace here, but he'd promised his father he'd stay in Dallas with his mother, and he'd already made a mess of her life with what happened at his previous job. He really should go back to Dallas and try to make things better for her. He'd never done much else his dad wanted. He probably owed it to him. But at what price?

Voices filtered into his thoughts and he went to the hall, peering toward the kitchen from where the sound emanated. He wasn't the only one here. Brijette and Andy seemed to be having a heated discussion. A muscle deep in his gut twitched. He shouldn't have cared that Andy and Brijette were staying late and arguing, but the idea of the two of them together sent hot sparks along his nerves. Women practically fell at Andy's feet. In an ugly film that played in his mind he suddenly pictured them in each other's arms, and he tore down the hall.

"You're crazy, Brijette."

Andy's voice tapered off as Cade burst into the room.

Brijette took a half step back. "Are you all right?"

He tried to imagine how he must look, barging in like a wild bull. What had he been thinking?

"I—I thought everyone had gone. I heard voices and was afraid we might have had a break-in."

Brijette nodded but Andy's mouth quirked and Cade knew he hadn't fooled his friend.

"I'm glad you're here." Andy tipped his soda can in Brijette's direction. "This woman has gone completely insane."

"I haven't. You don't understand, Andy,

because you're not from here. You don't realize what it means for patients to really need you."

Andy snorted. "Cade may buy that line you keep trying to sell about how we can't understand these people's needs, or care about them because we're not from here, but let me tell you, you don't have to grow up dirt poor in a small town to care about people."

Brijette didn't have a response for that and Cade wished he'd said it himself. The truth was, he had started to believe it when Brijette kept saying over and over how different they were because of their backgrounds. Andy was right. They weren't that different. Andy had left behind a lot to come here, but it was what he'd wanted, what made him happy.

"Are you going to tell her she can't do it?"

Cade glanced at Andy, who was staring at him. "Can't do what?"

"I haven't mentioned it to him yet." Brijette wrung her hands together.

"You're going to love this, Cade. She's gotten her boat back from the sheriff and plans to load it Thursday and take off to that clinic of hers."

"No!" He hadn't intended to shout, but when he did Brijette's eyes widened and she took another step away, distancing herself from him.

"It's too dangerous for you—or have you forgotten what happened before? If you're not concerned for yourself, think of Alicia and Dylan. You do have a daughter to raise."

"I don't think those men would take such a risk again. And Alicia won't be going with me. I'll go alone. As for Dylan, why do you think I'm doing this? I want my daughter to learn that doing what's good for others is important."

Cade stuck his hands in the pockets of his lab jacket. "I think it would be a lot better for her if you were around two years from now instead of six feet under."

"That's funny, I would've imagined you'd find that prospect rather attractive. Then you and your mother could have Dylan to yourselves." Brijette's voice was cold and bitter. He wouldn't have thought she had any words left that could hurt him again, but apparently she did.

"I've never said I wanted to take Dylan away from you." The anger had left his voice without his meaning for it to. He figured he sounded the way he felt, tired and a little lost.

"But you do want her."

Andy made a move to slip past Cade and out the door, but Cade caught his arm.

"Come on, man, this conversation is beginning to get personal. The two of you can take it from here."

Cade held on. "You'll have to run this place on Thursday by yourself unless Arthur can come in to help."

"What?" Brijette squawked across the room, but he ignored her, speaking to Andy instead.

"I'm going with her to the clinic. I won't let her go alone."

He waited for Andy to argue but his friend only smiled.

"Now that's a better idea."

"Wait a minute. We can't leave Andy here by himself. He'll be swamped." Brijette turned to Andy.

He shrugged. "I'm not scared of having to work hard. I'm going home so the two of you can finish this battle alone."

Cade let Andy pass him but Brijette didn't move. They stared at each other until the outside door slammed behind Andy.

"Why are you doing this, Cade?"

"To protect my daughter's mother's stupid neck."

"The people there might not even let you see them as a physician. They don't know you."

"I've treated a patient out there before."

"That was one person."

"Fine, I'll be your assistant and try to make sure nothing happens to you on the trip." He paused for a moment but couldn't stop the next words from rushing past his lips. "I can't believe you think I would want something to happen to you."

She kept her gaze on the floor. "It would make your life easier."

"I'm not sure how losing the mother of my daughter would make my life easier. Besides, I've had it pretty easy for most of my life. I don't mind a bit of difficulty. It makes you more appreciative of the good times."

"I thought all you ever wanted were the 'good times.'"

He crossed the room to stand in front of her, maybe closer than he should have. "A lot of the things you think about me aren't true."

She still wouldn't meet his eyes and he tilted her chin, forcing her to look at him. "I still care about you."

He didn't know what he expected from her, maybe a cynical retort. But slowly tears began to trickle down her face.

"I don't know why you would," she whispered.

"Neither do I. I'm not saying I can forgive the lies. I really don't know what I'm saying."

With a shove, she pushed past him, the plastic soles of her shoes slapping the hardwood floor as she hurried away. He didn't follow her. Why should he? He had no idea what to do next, except show up Thursday to load the boat.

CHAPTER NINETEEN

THE WAVES from the moving boat rippled across to the edges of the reeds and bounced around the base of the huge cypress tree that filtered the last rays of summer sun. Brijette rested in the seat of the boat and tried not to sigh. That would be like saying she actually enjoyed this, and she didn't want to enjoy these trips with Cade.

This made the fourth time they'd been to Willow Point together, and she knew after four weeks without incident she should insist he stay at the clinic in town. But she hadn't yet. He'd fit in so easily the first day that it had been a shock. Fortunately, Cade hadn't pointed out how wrong she'd been. Brijette had believed the river people would see him as a stranger and, thus, untrustworthy. But they'd lined up to get a peek at the new doctor. She'd brought a "divider screen" and fashioned a second exam table so they could both see patients, without any help from a nurse. He'd fumbled a bit in the beginning with having to administer the shots and dress the wounds on his own, but by the second visit he had everything down pat…and she'd fallen in love with him again.

It was a useless feeling considering the gap she'd so successfully created between them. He'd never forgive her, never trust her again. He'd get weekend custody of Dylan and likely drive to get her every other weekend or have Brijette put her on a plane to Dallas, but he'd go back to his other life soon. Better that she stop this now. The longer he kept visiting the clinic, the more the patients became attached to him and the more she became attached. The wind blew her hair in her face and she slipped off her ponytail holder, smoothing the loose strands together again and refastening the band tightly.

At the wheel of the boat Cade smiled at her.

She stood, holding on to the rail.

"You can stop coming with me, you know," she shouted above the hum of the engine. "I think whatever danger there was is past. I'm sure I'll be safe from now on."

He still hadn't met her eyes, his attention focused on the waterway ahead of them. She tried again.

"I know they need one of us at the Cypress Landing clinic. Doc isn't able to help Andy much with the load. Andy isn't one to complain, but I'm sure he's got to be feeling overwhelmed."

Brijette tightened her grip on the rail as the boat rocked, the engine slowing to a low idle before going silent. When he'd completely stopped the boat, he looked at her.

"What are you trying to say, Brijette?"

"That you don't have to come and help me anymore."

"Am I doing a bad job? Do you think the people there don't like me?"

"No, that's not it at all. They've taken to you very well and I haven't seen them take to many people, even Alicia. Of course you do a fantastic job. You're an amazing doctor."

One side of his mouth tilted upward. "Amazing, huh? I know people in Dallas who wouldn't agree with you."

She hadn't forgotten what Andy had said that day about Cade and the lawsuit in Dallas, but she'd decided to let it go. It would be like trying to find something wrong with him after he'd found out she'd lied. It hadn't seemed right to bring it up before now.

"Andy mentioned a lawsuit one day, but he didn't say what happened."

Cade sat and gazed off toward the trees.

"An older woman came in one day and said she'd been having trouble sleeping after her husband had died several months before. He was the head of a big oil company that his family had founded years ago—" He glanced at her and lifted an eyebrow. "Old money, the kind our clinic catered to. My nurse took her history and I questioned her further. Her regular physician had moved and she'd decided to use us. She said she hadn't been prescribed a medication before now to help her sleep. Based on what she told me, I wrote her a prescription for a sleeping aid, a mild dosage. But before she went to her pharmacist, she changed the dosage I had ordered to the maximum amount for that medication. Not only that but she had gotten pills from another doctor. She swallowed most of them that night and died. The woman had a history of depression and attempted suicide. She hadn't given us an accurate medical history, but the family insisted I should've called the other doctor."

"That's not standard, especially if the guy had moved. I mean, you would have gotten her records later, but if you wanted to help her that day you only had her word to go on."

"I wanted to go to court. I felt I had followed

procedure, but the clinic didn't want the negative publicity and the family was very well known. They could have destroyed the clinic simply by telling lies to their friends. I happened to be the most expendable."

She covered his hand with hers. "I'm sorry that happened. Is that why Andy said your mother's friends gave her the cold shoulder?"

He nodded. "As soon as they heard what had happened, we became social pariahs. I didn't really care since I never went to the country club or hung around with those people. But it really killed my mother. She wants me to go back there and prove myself to be a good doctor. She thinks everything will return to normal if I do. But I doubt that will happen soon."

Brijette slid her palm along the stainless-steel rail while her other hand still rested on Cade's.

"Hauling yourself out to this clinic isn't going to fix that. It's hot and miserable and you could be back in town with air-conditioning right now. There's no sense in your coming with me until you leave for Dallas. Why don't you quit and go help Andy?"

He turned to her, flipping over his hand to hold hers. "I can't."

"What do you mean, you can't? Of course you can. Next week, don't come to the dock before daylight."

With his free hand he brushed his damp hair away from his brow. "I don't want that. Working out here with you in the backroom of the old store has been the best thing that ever happened to me. For the first time since I finished medical school I feel as if I'm doing what I had envisioned when I originally decided to become a doctor."

She frowned. "What, helping the have-nots? Is that what you dreamed of when you were a young rich kid roaring around in your sports car?"

"That's not how it was and you know it. You think I'm the one with a problem, but you have a prejudice toward me and anyone who comes from a well-off family. That's no different than the prejudice you accuse me of. You keep saying because I—and even Andy—was born to money, we think those who don't have it are lesser human beings than we are. I don't think that. There are plenty of people I've met these last few weeks who are much better than me."

"They are good people. I just never expected you to recognize that."

His fingers tightened on hers and he closed

the distance between them. "Why not? I recognized it in you."

That's when she let go, of herself and everything she'd been holding back from him. She kissed him—on the mouth, not safely on the cheek or forehead. He kissed her back, pulling her toward him until she had to put her knee on his seat to keep from falling. His hands slipped under her scrub top and moved up her back. He held her closer, then bent to lay her down on the seat across from them. The boat rocked and they fell the last few inches onto the cushion. He lifted himself to shove her top upward, his mouth pressing against the thin fabric stretched across her breast. She cried out and he immediately captured her mouth again. She didn't want it to end, ever, but she knew it had to.

"We can't do this," she whispered against his mouth.

"Sure we can, we already have a child together."

"No, it'll only confuse us. You don't need to stay here because of me or because of Dylan but because you believe it's where you belong."

He pulled back and sat in the seat behind the wheel, staring at her, his chest heaving.

"You can't come here with me again."

The muscles of his jaw tightened and his

lips thinned. He turned, taking hold of the key, then faced her once more.

"I don't think you heard me, but I'll make it really clear. I won't kiss you and I won't try to get close to you, but I will come to this clinic again for as long as I'm in Cypress Landing, because I do know it's where I belong."

He started the engine, jamming the throttle lever until the bow of the boat reared from the water. He didn't speak to her again, which was good. Brijette didn't want him to say another word or she'd likely drag him down to the bottom of the boat. He amazed her every day and she wanted that to keep happening, maybe for the rest of her life. She didn't know what it would take to earn Cade's trust, but she decided making that happen had become the most important thing in her life next to Dylan.

THE SUN HAD NEARLY SET when Brijette parked her Tahoe near Robert's barn. Her first stop had been at Norma's where she'd been informed that Dylan had seen Robert in town and he'd invited her to come riding when the heat of the sun eased. Straight ahead, she could see Dylan grooming the horse, Robert beside her.

"Hey, you two."

Dylan dropped the brush in a plastic carrier and motioned for her to join them. “Isn’t this horse beautiful? Mr. Robert bought her and he says I can come ride her whenever I want, like she was my own.”

“That’s very nice of him, but you’ll still have to be sure to get permission first.” She smiled at Robert. “I don’t want her worrying you to death.”

“That won’t happen.” He patted the horse. “Go ahead and put her in the stall, Dylan. You know, the one that opens onto the little paddock.”

Dylan nodded and led the horse into the barn.

“I haven’t seen you since you had that trouble on the river. They ever catch who did it?”

She shook her head. “Just the one guy who I recognized from the clinic.”

Robert picked up the plastic container full of brushes and combs for the horses. “That’s a shame. Maybe they’ll still catch them.”

Dylan returned and Brijette put her hand on the girl’s shoulder. “We’d better get going now.”

“Thanks for letting me ride, Mr. Robert.”

The man smiled and waved as they walked away, then he disappeared into the barn.

In the car, Dylan buckled her seat belt. "Did Mr. Robert ask you about the guys throwing us off the boat?"

Brijette glanced at her daughter. "Yeah, he did."

The girl wiggled in the seat. "Good. I told him you'd remember more than I did."

Brijette stuck the key in the ignition. "What do you mean? What did he ask you?"

"About a million questions. I finally told him I couldn't remember much because my arm hurt bad, which wasn't really true, but heck, I don't know what the guys sounded like or if I've heard their voices before."

Brijette stopped with the ignition key half-turned. "Why did he ask you all that?"

Dylan shrugged. "I guess he wanted to know. Hey, wait—" she looked around the car "—I left my tote bag with my stuff in it. It's got my shorts I had on this morning and the book I'm reading." She unhooked her seat belt but Brijette stopped her.

"Tell me where it is and I'll go get it."

"It's by the feed room."

Brijette threw the door open and hurried toward the barn. She didn't want Robert quizzing Dylan about what happened that day on the river, and she'd tell him if he were still here. But what bothered her most was why was he asking those questions at all.

Shadows filled the barn as horses stamped in their stalls. Halfway down the hall she could see the bag and she hurried toward it. A dim light shone from beneath the feed room door and she wondered if Robert was still there or if he'd gone and forgotten to turn it off. She bent to reach for the bag, and that was when she saw it. Her heart beating fast, she scooted a little way farther into the hall, her fingers exploring the ground. She lifted a clump of dirt and rubbed it between her fingers until it became dust and drifted to the ground. She traced the edges of the footprint one more time.

The door to the feed room swung open, the light blinding her, and a figure appeared. She knew it was Robert but her heart sailed into her throat. His face was hidden in the shadows, his body outlined by the light behind him. She would be okay. He wouldn't know why she was poking around in the dirt, would he?

"Brijette, what are you doing down there?"

"I came to get Dylan's bag and I…it…fell and I stumbled when I bent to get it." She laughed, but it sounded forced, even to her.

Robert stepped into the hallway. He smiled, but his brows were drawn together.

"Be careful, and bring Dylan back soon."

She gripped the bag's straps and sprinted for the car.

Sliding into the seat, she tossed Dylan the bag and started the car.

"Did Mr. Robert tell you his leg was hurting?"

"What?"

"He said he had an injury that hurts him a lot. He told me his leg always hurts before it rains. Did you know he almost got killed in a car wreck when he was young?"

Brijette knew Robert had an injured leg. She simply hadn't thought of it in years, probably not since she learned of it when he'd come in to get Doc Arthur to renew his prescription for pain medication. He was one of Doc's oldest friends. Maybe that's why she hadn't recognized that the footprint she'd been studying these past few weeks—the one she'd seen a year ago when she'd scrambled onto Jodi's front porch—was Robert's.

CHAPTER TWENTY

"JACKSON'S GONE to Lafayette until tomorrow. Do you want to leave a message?"

"No, that's okay." Brijette put the phone on its base and got a bottle of water from the refrigerator. In the hall, Cade gave Alicia instructions for what he wanted done with the patient he'd just seen. Her fingers tightened around the cold damp plastic. She'd have to wait even though the hair on her scalp felt perpetually on end. Revealing her suspicions to anyone would make them think she'd completely lost her mind. She still wasn't totally convinced herself.

When Jackson came back she'd get the papers she'd given him with the drawings of the prints she'd made at the last house. She'd take them to Robert's barn when he wasn't there and compare the drawings with his tracks. That would be proof that Robert had actually been present at all the places they'd found the drugs and even at Jodi's house on the day he died, an idea she'd rather not consider.

"Hey, I've got two rooms ready for you with patients waiting."

"Oh, okay, I'm coming," she called to Alicia.

Before she could make it to the kitchen door, Cade intercepted her. "You sick this morning? You've been awfully quiet."

She shook her head. "A little tired, that's all."

"Why don't you come eat with Dylan and me tonight? You can go home early and rest."

She nodded. "Okay."

"Try to reign in that excitement if you can, or I'll think you really like the idea."

Brijette smiled. "Sorry, I've got a lot on my mind."

"Need to talk about it?"

Yes, she wanted to say, but she couldn't, not until she knew for sure Robert was the one. Claiming that a local businessman could be involved in major drug dealing wasn't going to earn her popularity points in this town. Not unless she could conclusively prove it was true. For that she needed the help of the sheriff's department, since they already had an ongoing investigation. Until then, her suspicions were better kept to herself.

"No, it's just day-to-day stuff."

"You're not worrying because of the custody proceeding, are you?"

How could she possibly have forgotten that? Cade had been working with a lawyer to establish legal custody of Dylan, while his mother had decided to stay in Cypress Landing until the proceedings were complete. It was only right he share in their child's life, and she realized that now. Brijette certainly wasn't trying to fight his bid for joint custody because she'd seen how wrong she'd been to keep them apart. Slight nuances of Dylan's personality were now so obviously Cade's. He was being very generous in the custody proceedings and hadn't once mentioned leaving for Dallas. The possibility that he wouldn't made her happier than she cared to admit. He'd been angry with her that day on the boat when she'd stopped him from kissing her. But he seemed to have forgotten that lately. He hadn't tried to kiss her again, but she could tell he wanted to and she didn't plan on stopping him next time.

He squeezed her shoulder and she remembered he was still standing there watching her. "Everything's going to be fine."

He tugged her, gently at first, then roughly, pulling her against him, a place she hadn't been since she'd kissed him that evening on the boat.

She'd missed being there, even though she'd tried briefly to convince herself it wasn't true. Finally, she quit resisting. She wrapped her arms around his waist and rested her head on his chest, his heart thumping next to her ear. She almost believed him when he said the words. The image of the three of them, maybe even more than three of them, as a family, wavered in the part of her mind where she kept the dreams she wasn't sure she could make happen.

"Brijette, I want you to know that I've learned to love it here in Cypress Landing and I…"

"Hey, Cade. Can you come see what you think—"

Andy stopped short, in the doorway to the kitchen, his shoes squeaking on the wood floor. "Sorry, you two, but you could at least get a room."

Cade ignored him. "Later," he whispered, and untangled himself from her, following Andy into the hall.

What was it he'd been about to say? She could think of several different possibilities. "I'm going to stay here." "I wish I could stay but I made a commitment to my father before he died"—that would be the dutiful Cade. Or had he been about to tell her that he'd chosen a different path than his family had imagined for him, by ending his sentence with "and I love you"? Rubbing her forehead, she tried to push the thought from her mind. At the moment, planning her future was giving her a monumental headache.

BRIJETTE STUDIED HER watch after replacing the phone in the clinic's kitchen for the second day in a row without talking to Jackson. Ten-thirty in the morning and the lead investigator was already on a call. The dispatcher who took non-emergency incoming calls hesitated slightly before telling Brijette she wasn't sure where he was at that moment or when he would return. It made the back of her neck itch. Did the girl really not know, or was she not telling? Maybe they'd made a big break in the prescription drug case but were keeping everything under wraps until they caught whoever they were after. She wondered if they'd found evidence on Robert. What if they were arresting the wrong person or a low-level assistant who would never give them Robert's name for risk of his family being hurt?

Slamming the chart onto the counter, she tried to stop her errant thinking. This was her neighbor Robert, not an underworld criminal. He wouldn't hurt people like that, would he? She scribbled some notes on the chart, slipping the pen into her pocket when she finished. The truth was, she might not even know her neighbor, not really.

In the front she heard voices. They were indecipherable at first, then Cade's boomed loudly above the rest. "This can't be right."

She started across the room, hoping he wasn't talking to a patient. As she rounded the door into the hall, she saw Jackson Cooper striding toward her. "Jackson, thank goodness, I've been trying to reach you for two days and…" Her voice faltered as she noticed his grim expression.

He clasped her upper arm. His features became pained when the silver in his hand flashed in front of her. "I'm sorry, Brijette."

"Jackson, what is this?"

He gripped her tightly as he fastened the cuff to her wrist. Nausea hit her as the metal band clicked. She couldn't breathe and the edges of her vision began to darken.

Almost as if from a world away, Jackson's voice floated into her consciousness. "Brijette Dupre, you are being arrested…"

The words passed over her as she crumpled

to the floor with Jackson trying to hold her by the arm. Past Jackson's leg it seemed the entire staff had gathered in the hall. Cade's face was as white as the lab coat he wore. In his eyes she saw it, what she'd seen years ago, disbelief and distrust. History was repeating itself and she could see all her hopes and dreams draining away. Only this time it wasn't just Cade she'd be losing, it would be Dylan, too.

CADE SIGNED THE CHECK, handing it across the counter, and like that, Brijette was free on bail. Not exactly a phrase he expected to use in reference to the mother of his child. He wouldn't see her today, though. She was meeting with a lawyer and he had to get Dylan out of town. Brijette's voice begged him through her tears to please take the girl to his mother's house in Texas until she could clear her name. She claimed she was innocent. He hadn't known what to believe the last time she was arrested and he wasn't sure this time, either. The evidence was completely convincing. A shadow fell across the counter and he glanced up.

"Sheriff Wright." Cade didn't know what to expect from the man who had stood quietly watching during Brijette's arrest.

"You understand she didn't do this, don't you?"

Cade frowned. "Why did you arrest her, then?"

He walked to the far side of the room and motioned for Cade to follow.

"There's plenty of evidence to prove she was behind the prescription drug ring. We found records, drugs, prescriptions, you name it. When we finally got information out of T.J. Broussard, the father of that baby Brijette delivered, we were able to pick up one of the guys on the boat. Everything we found at his place led us straight to her. Once we picked her up and searched her house, the rest of the evidence was there."

"Sounds pretty conclusive to me."

Matt nodded. "That's what bothers me. It's too tight, too perfect, lying there waiting for us to find. Besides, I've known Brijette a long time and I don't think for a minute she'd do this."

"Even though she was involved in a similar incident when she was younger?" Cade stuffed his checkbook in his pocket.

"I don't believe the past has any bearing on the present. She learned a hard lesson. She's honest and upright, and you know it."

"Do I? She's lied and hidden my child from me for years."

The sheriff eyed the sunglasses in his hand. "We both know there was more to it than that. Why should she have told you when she didn't think you wanted the child?"

Cade didn't have a response because Matt had a point. In his heart he didn't believe Brijette had done wrong this time; even when she was younger it had just been a case of bad judgment. Before, it had been easier to believe she was guilty and go on with his life, never going against his parents. But this was the mother of his child. Not only that, she was the woman he loved. He couldn't run now, not again.

He pushed his hair away from his forehead. "Who would do this? Who would want to make her look guilty?"

"She says she knows who it might be, but honestly, it's so unbelievable it's going to be next to impossible to prove."

The door swung open and several people entered the room.

"We'll have to discuss it later. Are you waiting here for Brijette?"

"No, she doesn't want me to. I've brought her car here and my mother and I are going to take Dylan to Dallas. She'll stay there with my mother until we know what's going to happen. Brijette didn't want her to deal with the gossip."

Matt sighed. "I hope we can find something. My getting on the stand saying I don't believe she did it won't make much difference with the evidence we've got."

Cade pushed through the door into the thick summer air. Uncle Arthur and Andy could manage a while at the clinic by themselves. He only prayed that when he went back to help them, Brijette would be with him.

BRIJETTE LEANED against the hot metal of her car door. "I did not do this, Jackson. It's pure insanity." Behind the investigator waves of heat reflected off the asphalt parking lot.

"Hell, Brij, I know that. But what are we supposed to do? Your house looked like drug dealer central."

"Like I'd be stupid enough to have that stuff at my house."

"It doesn't have to make sense, as long as it's there."

"I keep trying to tell you, Robert is involved with this. I found his tracks at several of the scenes we went to."

"And I'm telling you, we have less than nothing on him. It's not like there's a plaster cast of those footprints in my office. All I've got is you saying that the imprint of his foot in the dirt matches tracks you saw at a crime scene. Tracks that are long gone by now, I might add. If we start asking questions he'll pack everything up and we'll never catch him. Then guess who's left?"

"I'll have to find more evidence myself."

Jackson shook his head. "Now you're being stupid. If he is doing this you could end up floating downriver. You have a daughter at home. I suggest you leave this to us."

"What, and hope I get released from jail in time to watch her graduate? You said yourself you've got nothing to go on. It could be years before you find who did this. While you're investigating, I'll be sitting on my butt in jail."

"It won't take that long, I promise."

She jerked the car door open. "It better not, Jackson, because I'm beginning to think I don't have time to spare."

She drove off, leaving the county jail and courthouse behind. At seventeen she'd spent time in a youth detention facility for ignoring what her good sense told her. This time she was older, and, unlike before, she'd done nothing to put herself in this situation. That is, nothing but find who was orchestrating the drug ring in Cypress Landing.

All these years Robert had been a neighbor and friend. Her daughter had spent hours at his barn riding horses. If he'd been able to hide his involvement for this long, the sheriff's department wouldn't be able to catch him that easily. She could go to jail. The thought made her nauseous and she tilted one of the air-conditioning vents toward her face. That kind of thinking would only slow her down. There was a way to solve this and she was going to find it. Robert would see. She wouldn't go to jail quietly.

Her house was a wreck as a result of the deputies stripping it in their search for evidence. Brijette stood in the entrance, staring at the contents of drawers that had been emptied onto the floor and the furniture that had been left at odd angles. Before she set foot inside, she heard tires crunching the gravel. She recognized the car immediately, although she hadn't expected Mrs. Wheeler to agree to Brijette's seeing Dylan before they left for Dallas. But Dylan scrambled from the car and raced toward her. Brijette stopped her at the front steps, not wanting her to go inside to see the mess the sheriff's people had made in their house.

Dylan threw her arms around her. "Mom, what's happening?"

Brijette hung on to her, trying to will her tears away, but they spilled over onto her cheeks.

"Don't worry. It's a mistake and I'm going to set everything straight. I did not do this."

"You promise. You're telling the truth."

She put her palms on either side of Dylan's face, holding her so the girl would have to meet her eyes. "I told you before that I would always tell the truth from now on because I trust you to be able to handle whatever it is you and I have to face."

Between her hands Dylan's head moved up and down.

"But Cade says I have to go with them to Dallas."

"You do need to go. I'll be very busy working with Mr. Cooper and Sheriff Wright to find out who did this to me, so it's a great time for you to see your grandmother's house. I'll bet it's very nice."

"I want to stay here and help you."

Brijette shook her head. "You can't, not this time."

She glanced up to see Mrs. Wheeler standing at the bottom of the steps. If Brijette hadn't thought her incapable she'd have sworn the woman had tears in her eyes.

"Now, you go with your grandmother and we'll be together again soon."

Dylan squeezed Brijette's waist before letting go and running down the steps and back to the car. Brijette followed her until she was near enough to smell Cade's mother's spicy perfume.

"Thank you for bringing her. I know you probably didn't want to."

Mrs. Wheeler fingered the hem of her blouse. "She needed to see you."

"I'm not guilty of this, I swear. Someone's setting me up and I know who it is. I'll prove it, too."

Brijette started back up the steps.

"She's a good girl. You've done a good job raising her by yourself."

At first she didn't think her mouth would function, she was so shocked. Cade's mother was giving her a compliment? "I… Thank you. It's been easy. She's got a big heart."

"She comes from fine stock."

Naturally, the woman thought Dylan's Wheeler blood automatically made her a wonderful child. Brijette began to climb the stairs again and she almost missed the woman's next words.

"On both sides."

This time when Brijette turned back to look

at Mrs. Wheeler, she was hurrying to the car. Not that it mattered because Brijette had absolutely nothing to say to that.

She went inside, bypassing the mess, digging for a pen and an old notebook of Dylan's. Grabbing a chair that had been shoved across the room, she pulled it to the kitchen table and began to write. Everything had to be timed perfectly. She'd watch and wait, and when she had her chance she'd make her move. She scribbled in the notebook: *9:00 p.m. Be on the hill by the tire distribution center.*

Robert's business was the ideal place from which to run a drug operation, with truckloads of tires being shipped every day. Couldn't the sheriff see that? She imagined Matt Wright saw it clearly, but being able to do something about it was another matter. This was her only option.

She put pen to paper again: *12:00 midnight. Check the doors and windows.* Her problems had begun here at Robert's business when she was seventeen. The drugs in her backpack made perfect sense. The truck driver who'd given them to her hadn't done it for himself; he'd done it for Robert. And the guy hadn't vanished by himself, either. The police had never found him. How could she not have realized before what Robert was doing? She doodled on the paper, finally writing: *4:00 a.m. Robert's house for his morning routine.* He wouldn't get off this time and she wasn't going to jail for him.

CHAPTER TWENTY-ONE

CADE THREW ONE LAST T-shirt in his suitcase and zipped it shut as he heard his mother and Dylan clatter through the front door.

He met them in the guest room which had become Dylan's when they arrived in Dallas three days ago. He figured it would take many visits with Emalea Cooper to help Dylan if Brijette actually went to jail. He paused, realizing the thought of Dylan seeing a psychologist in Dallas had never crossed his mind. He guessed his subconscious knew he'd be going back to Cypress Landing to stay. He'd made a promise to his father, but that was before he'd found out he had a daughter. And what was best for her had to come before promises he made to anyone.

"Where are you going?" His mother stared at him from the doorway.

"I'm going back to Cypress Landing. You don't think I can stay in Dallas with everything that's going on back there, do you?"

Mrs. Wheeler glanced at Dylan and her lips thinned. "You can't do a thing to help Brijette. She got herself into this and put Dylan in danger. She'll have to pay the price."

Cade sighed, pushing his hair back from his forehead. "Mother, you know she didn't do this."

"I don't know that."

"Stop it!" Dylan shouted, and threw a shopping bag across the room.

She spun around to face him. "You're going to help my mom and I'm going with you." She turned around to Cade's mother and put her hands on her hips in a manner that was all Brijette. "Grandma, stop acting like my mom is guilty. She's not."

She rushed to Cade, burying her face in his shirt, quickly soaking the front. She sobbed and he smoothed the thick blond hair so much like his own.

"You'll help my mom, won't you?" She looked at him, tears streaming down her cheeks.

He nodded. "Of course I will. But you've got to stay here. If you go back to Cypress Landing, whoever is trying to make your mom look guilty might try to use you to stop her. It's not safe for you there."

Watery green eyes watched him before she

bobbed her head once. She squeezed his waist, her gaze never wavering. "You love her, don't you? You love my mom."

He blotted the wet spots on her cheeks with his hand. "Yes, I do, Dylan, very much. When this is finished I'm going to live in Cypress Landing and the three of us can be together."

From across the room he heard his mother inhale sharply, but he didn't care. She'd been pampered for too long. He needed to take care of two other very important women in his life.

"Can you make my mom love you, too?"

He grinned. "Now, that I can't answer for sure, but I'm going to try extra hard."

He held on to her, hoping that when he saw her next she wouldn't have reason to cry again. He glanced across the room at his mother, whose face was slightly pale.

"Just remember, Mother, the other side of the tracks becomes your side, once you step across."

LATE EVENING SHADOWS were beginning to creep across her front porch when Brijette heard a car in the driveway. She stuffed her notebook in a kitchen drawer and walked to the window to see if the sheriff's office had managed to find a deputy who hadn't yet been by her house.

Since she'd left the court the other day,

there had been a steady stream of officers coming by to check up on her. She'd finally asked Jackson if they considered her a flight risk, but he'd only frowned, then mumbled how he didn't want anything to happen to her. That's when she realized they thought whoever had set her up might not wait for her to be sent to jail. They might be more interested in making sure she couldn't implicate them, just like they had with Jody.

The thought of what had happened to Jody had lingered in her brain since she'd realized she'd seen the same footprints at his house. Rumors had circulated back then that she might have been involved, especially when she'd found the body. She knew who to hold responsible for Jody's death, but she didn't know exactly what role Robert had played or why. Nor could she be certain to what lengths he'd go to keep his name clear. Fear twisted her insides when she saw a truck, not a police cruiser, pulling up to the house. But, in the next instant, she recognized the vehicle and hurried to the front.

Cade had one foot on the porch when she ran out to him.

"Where's Dylan? What's wrong?"

He gripped her shoulders and drew her to his

chest. "She's fine, still in Dallas with my mom. I'm just glad you're here and in one piece."

She backed away even though she felt safer in his arms.

"Why are you here?"

"I'm not letting you deal with this alone. Don't argue with me. Let's go inside and see what needs to be done."

She tried to smile, but found herself too tired, and only half her mouth curved.

After leading Cade to the kitchen, she pulled the notebook from the drawer. The look on his face as he surveyed the room would have made her laugh except she knew that eventually she'd have to clean the mess up.

"Well, I can see you haven't been busy cleaning house these last few days."

"Not even close. The sheriff's people tore the place apart and I haven't had the heart or the time to fix it. But if you're here to help me with a plan, you're a little late. Let me show you what I've been doing."

She dropped into the chair next to Cade and flipped open the notebook. Her goal was to get the book, plus hopefully, some solid evidence to the sheriff after tonight. Soon she'd have everything she needed to give Robert a taste of being behind bars.

"I CAN'T BELIEVE this is what you've been doing. Do you have a death wish?"

Brijette slammed the notebook shut. "No, but if I wait for the police, I'll be sitting in jail for the next several years."

She tried to stand but he blocked her with his arm. "We're going to get past this together, like a family."

Brijette hadn't cried since she got home from jail, but the tears pooled and threatened to overflow. Hearing Cade say out loud that they were a family shattered her restraint. She rested her head in her hands and let the tears run onto her hands and arms. She felt a dish towel press against her arm and she grabbed it, mopping at the liquid.

Cade placed his hands on her knees and she forced herself to meet those green eyes. "Everything's going to be fine, Brijette. We're going to be fine."

She rolled the towel in her hand. "You have to understand that my plan will work. I know the evidence we need is in Robert's building."

"Let the police get it."

"They can't search there without good reason, and unfortunately, because I say so isn't reason enough."

Cade took the notebook and skimmed the

first page. "Well, you'd better fill me in on what to do tonight, because I'm going with you."

"Fine. This is what you need to do."

He pushed the paper aside, squinting at her. "Wait a minute. No arguments? You're not going to say you don't want me to go?"

She reached for the pen on the table and yanked the notebook back in front of her. "Of course not, I need your help and I think we'll be fine. I know Robert's schedule as well as my own."

BRIJETTE'S PLAN called for them to start their search shortly after midnight. A tree limb that she let go smacked Cade in the chest. Clouds chased across the sky, frequently obscuring the half moon and leaving Cade to pray that he wouldn't get separated from Brijette. They were slinking along to Robert's business through the woods, and if the mosquitoes didn't suck them dry they'd probably be fine.

Ahead of him, he could barely see Brijette's silhouette as she crouched among the brush. He squatted beside her.

The underbrush stopped a few feet in front of them and in the clearing stood the tire factory. "What now?" He tried hard to discern her features in the dim light.

"I go inside and find what I need. You wait here and call me on my cell if you see someone coming."

He shook his head, and the leaves on the bush beside him rattled. "Let's try this. You stay here and call me while I go in and look around."

"No way. You don't know the building, nor do you know what you're looking for. Remember, I worked here that summer ten years ago and I was here again giving flu shots this past fall."

"I still don't like it. But what if I at least go check the warehouse while you check in the offices? Between the two of us surely we'll be able to find what Robert's hiding."

She remained quiet and he knew she didn't want her plan changed, but his idea was the better one. They'd cover more ground searching if they were both inside.

"You're right. Just set your phone on vibrate and add me onto your speed dial. I've already got you on mine. Plus, we can text message back and forth if we need to."

He nodded. "What about security guards? Alarms? Cameras?"

"There are no guards or cameras. There is an alarm, but I've got that taken care of."

"How?"

Her teeth flashed as she grinned. "Oh, it's just a little something I learned in jail."

TEN MINUTES LATER, alone with his tiny penlight and the thick smell of rubber, Cade was making his way through the stacks of tires in the warehouse. He hoped to find some evidence that would incriminate Robert, but he wondered how Brijette was going to pass on any information they found. The sheriff would automatically know she'd broken in. Near the bay doors, tires appeared ready to be shipped first thing in the morning, and at tire number three on this rack he hit the jackpot. He tugged at a black plastic bag taped securely to the inside of the tire, and it ripped loose. Digging his finger inside a small opening, he made a hole in the bag and poured a handful of pills into his palm—exactly what they needed to at least get the sheriff in here to do a search. He reached for his phone and across the room a door squeaked. He froze.

Squatting among the tires, Cade turned off his penlight and held on to his phone, afraid to make a sound, but desperately trying to hit Brijette's speed dial number while keeping the glow of the phone concealed. He raised himself to see above the tires and the flourescent bulbs in the ceiling flashed on. He hunkered down again, trying to warn Brijette, then he thought he heard a man's voice say "damned alarm" after which the warehouse grew quiet. Glancing over the top of the tires again, he found the room empty. Brijette had headed for Robert's office and he had no idea where that could be, but whoever was just there probably knew. Cade ran across the concrete floor, dialing Brijette's number.

Brijette laid another file on the desktop. Robert hadn't been nearly as secretive as she'd expected. She found what she needed in a small filing cabinet, nearly unnoticeable in a hollow in the office wall and half hidden by a bookshelf. She'd finally managed to move the bookshelf and pound the lock off the filing cabinet with a hammer she'd found. She fingered the notes and financial statements, figuring there was enough there to warrant further investigation, though she'd been hoping to find lots of cash that couldn't be traced to the business or even the drugs themselves. Maybe Cade had had better luck. The click of the door made her jump and she smiled, still studying the papers.

"I'm glad you're here. I think I've found what we need."

"And I bet you were expecting someone else."

The phone vibrated in her pocket. Robert was right. And Cade's phone call was a bit too late.

HEADLIGHTS GLARED in the window of the warehouse and Cade raced for the nearest door in the hope of getting a call to the sheriff from somewhere outside the building.

Crossing the paved drive, Cade crashed past the weeds and up a small slope. He cursed the moon, he cursed the country, and he cursed the cell phone company that chose this minute to have technical difficulties. Cell phone service in the backwoods was always sketchy but damn, why now, when he needed it most? He wanted to tear through the factory and find Robert's office, find Brijette, but he had no idea where to begin. He scrambled along the edge of the trees where he could see who had driven into the parking area. He wished it would be the sheriff, but, of course, he'd never been very lucky.

The car sat in the gravel lot for several minutes. A cloud that had been masking the moonlight moved aside and Cade noted a Mercedes emblem on the car's hood as the men exited. He couldn't see their faces, but he also didn't know a soul in Cypress Landing who drove the latest full-size sedan on the market. The four men entered the building and he hurried around to the back of the factory. He had to find another entry and he had to find Brijette. In his ear, static from the phone crackled and the dispatcher at the sheriff's office came on the line.

"Give me Sheriff Wright or Jackson Cooper. Hell, give me anybody you can get fast."

SHE COULDN'T BELIEVE that Robert had held a gun to her and put her in this chair. He'd walked in the door a few minutes ago and now she was his prisoner.

"I wish things didn't have to be like this, Brijette." Robert squatted beside the chair and tightened the ropes around her legs.

"You're responsible for what happened to me ten years ago, aren't you?"

Robert stood and shook his head. "I never intended for that to happen, but the guy we were delivering to got caught and he gave your name to the police. I couldn't let my driver who gave you the package get caught, too, because eventually the sheriff might have sniffed his way back to me. So, I helped him escape. I hate that you didn't get off, but you only spent a few months in youth lockup. It could've been worse."

"Yeah, it could have been like this."

"Oh, come on, Brijette, nothing bad will happen to you. I'm getting the money you didn't find—" he pulled a metal box from a hidden compartment in one of the filing cabinets "—and I'm leaving the country. Things are getting a bit too tight around here for me." He tugged at the collar of his shirt and grinned.

"Why would you do this, Robert? Why are you selling drugs? You've got a great business."

"And a terrible gambling habit. Or at least I did for a long time. I owed a guy money and I agreed to ship some drugs for him. I only planned to do it for a while, but the more I did it, the more money he and I both made. He didn't want me to quit."

"Is your nephew who took the horse involved, too?"

Robert snorted. "I don't have a nephew involved. When I told the man I've been moving the drugs for that I wanted it to end he refused to allow me to stop. Said he needed me. He took the horse just to be sure I knew he meant it. Once I realized what had happened, I made up the story about a nephew to get the sheriff off the case. I started doing these prescription drugs on the side a lot more the last few months, thanks to you and especially to Doc Wheeler and his absentmindedness with his prescription pad. I needed the extra money to help me leave the country." He waved a stack of green bills in front of her before stuffing it in a nylon bag. "Now I'm gone."

"Just like that. What about me? Are you going to kill me like you killed Jody?"

Robert paused. "I did not kill that boy." He kept his head down, slowly packing the last of the money into the bag.

"I went by to talk to him but he wouldn't keep quiet. He held a gun on me and told me to call the sheriff. We struggled. The gun went off and he got killed."

"How convenient for you. Will my death be that easy?"

He pushed the rolling chair she was in toward a small storeroom.

"You'll be fine in here until midmorning tomorrow when my secretary will come in to check to see what needs doing. It might be a little uncomfortable, but you'll survive."

He stuck a dusty rag in her mouth and tied it at the back of her head. She struggled against the ropes at her wrists.

"You stay still while I go find your friend, who I'll assume is the young Dr. Wheeler, because no one else is dumb enough to come here with you and do this."

From the storage room she heard voices in Robert's office. She struggled harder and he grabbed her throat. "Stop it. That's not him." She could see the fear in Robert's eyes, even in the dim light, and she stilled.

"I don't intend to kill you, but those people you hear will kill you if they find you. So do what I say if you want to live." He stepped back and shut the closet door.

Brijette could hear Robert speaking with the others on the other side of the wall. The words were muffled but he hadn't been lying. Cade wasn't there.

There was a lot of angry shouting and then a gunshot exploded, followed by another. No more loud voices rattled the walls, even though she kept hoping to hear Matt's or Jackson's voice. If the police were doing the shooting, she'd be a lot less worried.

Filing cabinets banged open and shut while Robert's associates discussed money. Obviously, they had yet to open Robert's bag. She pushed her feet against the floor, wheeling the chair farther into the closet, then stopped for fear that she'd bang into something, bringing attention to herself. In the back of the dark closet, she could hear the thump of hard-soled shoes against the linoleum. Her breath hung in her throat. The knob clicked and caught. Thank God Robert had locked her in here. A shout from the office caused the movement at her door to still and footsteps faded away from her.

Leaning forward against the ropes, she sucked air into her nose, trying not to choke on the rag. Tears of frustration, anger and fear dripped onto the cloth and she bit back a sob for fear she'd suck the material farther into her throat. She had to be quiet and maybe they'd leave. Had they shot Robert? Everything in her said they had. Cade must be in the building or at the edge of the woods. She prayed this new group of outlaws hadn't found him first.

The banging in the office halted and in the ensuing silence she strained for a signal that help had arrived. But the sound she could hear was a whispering that wasn't human. The worst fear she'd ever known engulfed her as the first whiff of smoke swirled into her nostrils. She fought to get free, the rope digging into her wrists and ankles. Her skin tore, but the ropes stayed secure.

No, no, no. Images flashed in her brain. Cade young and gorgeous beyond belief. Dylan newly born and crying. Dylan and Cade together, laughing at a silly joke. Writhing in the chair, she pushed against the floor again with her feet, sending the chair hurtling into the door. No way she'd end her life like this, not with everything unfinished between her and Cade. They had a child to raise and maybe even a life to live together with more children. She hammered her shoulder against the door as the smoke crept into her dark cell.

THE MERCEDES PULLED AWAY as Cade raced to the door. He'd been in the woods on the far side of the warehouse when he'd heard the shot inside the building. He ran hard, scared to death of what he would find. Once inside, he followed the swirl of smoke, screaming for Brijette at the top of his lungs.

Sooty clouds billowed from a door ahead and he grabbed a fire extinguisher from the wall. Spraying the doorway, he could see Robert on the floor beside his desk as flames danced across the rug toward him. He made a grab for the man, even though he could tell from the amount of blood around him that he had to be dead. After he dragged him into the hall, Cade covered his mouth and nose with the neck of his T-shirt, holding the fire extinguisher in his other hand, and stepped into the office again.

At the other end of the room, he spotted movement in a small hallway and he pushed forward into the smoke-filled space. He could see Brijette's head and shoulders protruding from the bottom half of a door. He jerked it open, finding her tied to a chair with a cloth in her mouth. He pulled the cloth loose and she burst into a fit of coughing. Tugging at the ropes holding her to the chair, he cursed and nearly lost his breath in the smoke. He reached his arms around her, grasping the bottom of the chair, and lifted her off the ground, stumbling back from where he'd come.

At the entrance, he tripped over the body he'd left lying there and fell to the ground. The metal chair clattered onto its side and Brijette's head made a wicked thumping sound as it hit the floor. Cade struggled to his feet, righting Brijette and the chair. Rather than try to carry her, he pushed her toward the tire storage area, the bent chair zigzagging from side to side and occasionally bumping the wall like an insane pinball. They entered the warehouse, and he fell to his knees when he heard the sound of sirens growing in the distance.

"You called the sheriff." Brijette's whispered words made him straighten and start untangling the knotted rope.

"Yeah, I did."

"You called me too late."

His fingers paused. He'd almost failed her worse than ever before. In his throat, a huge lump welled as he tried to put on a brave front so she wouldn't know how scared he'd been. "I know, damned cell phones. Never work when you need them to." His voice cracked.

Her breath rasped a few more times and she coughed.

"Cade."

He stopped, forcing himself to meet her eyes. "What?"

"In case something worse happens in the next few minutes, I have to tell you that I love you. You know it, right? I mean, you already know I've always loved you."

He put a hand on each side of her face and pressed a kiss on her slightly sooty lips. "I know. And you know I still love you and always will. But if this situation gets worse in the next few minutes I'm going to find a gun and start shooting because this is ridiculous."

She grunted, then snorted and started laughing until she choked.

"None of this was in my plan," she whispered when she caught her breath.

He hugged her to him, chair and all since he couldn't seem to get the ropes loose. "Some things never are," he murmured against her hair.

EPILOGUE

BRIJETTE WATCHED Cade put steaks on the grill as a light breeze pushed a puff of smoke in her direction. The long-sleeved shirt she wore felt good in the barely cool fall air. Across the yard the newly added gazebo cast shadows on the lawn and she could hardly believe she and Cade had been married there a few months ago. Cade had purchased the old house he'd been renting from Robert's extended family who'd yet to finalize what exactly they would do with his business.

"When's Dylan coming home?"

She glanced at Cade, who'd taken a seat across from her. "Not until tomorrow. She's spending the night with your mother. They're working on that quilt they're entering in the competition tomorrow."

Cade snorted. "I can't get over the fact that she bought a house here."

Brijette shrugged but before she could

comment she heard the sound of voices from the front of the house. "That must be Jackson and Emalea, right on time."

Cade got to his feet. "Jackson's always on time."

"I know one night you thought he was late."

"Yeah, but that was my fault."

He waved the couple to the patio as they rounded the corner of the house. Jackson went to the grill and lifted the lid. "My favorite."

Emalea laughed. "Everything is his favorite."

"Can't help it if I like to eat." Jackson and Emalea sat across from Cade and Brijette.

"Any word on Robert's killers?"

Jackson looked at Brijette for a minute, then sighed. "No, there's not. I wish I had better news. The investigation is still open but it's been several months and we haven't been able to tie anyone to that night. We never found the Mercedes or any clues to their identity."

"I wish I'd seen more so I could help."

Jackson shook his head. "It's a good thing you didn't. This way those people have no idea you or Cade were anywhere near there."

Cade's hand squeezed her leg. "He's right about that, Brijette. We wouldn't want to be constantly looking over our shoulders, wondering if somebody's going to come after us."

She nodded. "At least you and I can go to the clinic at Willow Point in peace now."

The sound of the phone ringing brought Brijette to her feet and she hurried inside to answer. Five minutes later, she was still standing in the kitchen listening to Dylan ramble on about her and Mrs. Wheeler's busy evening and even busier day to follow. When Dylan ran out of steam, Mrs. Wheeler took over with as much energy as the young girl.

Cade came in the room as she was hanging up. "I was beginning to worry about you."

She rolled her eyes. "I've just been through an entire lesson on quilt-making. It would seem your mother has become the queen bee of the quilting society in Cypress Landing."

He laughed. "She always has to be the queen of something."

"This is good for her, though."

"Do think she's changed?"

"I think she's finally learned how to be herself and enjoy it without trying to run everybody else's life."

Cade pulled her against him, his hand warming a spot low on her abdomen. "How much longer should we wait before we tell them?"

"A few more weeks, just to make sure everything's going well."

Cade nodded. “I hope you know this is killing me. I can’t wait to shout to the whole world that I’m going to be a dad again.”

“I’ll remember that one morning about 3:00 a.m. when this baby gets here.”

He kissed her on the cheek. “I guess I’d better get back to our guests before they think we’ve abandoned them.”

“I’m going to check the potatoes, then I’ll be right there.”

She opened the oven, touching the foil-wrapped potatoes, then closed it again. With a sigh, she tossed her oven mitt on the gleaming countertop. This was a long way from the wooden shack where she’d spent her early years. Somehow, dreams she’d kept hidden for most of her life had managed to come true. When she’d escaped the backwater she hadn’t expected someone like Cade to meet her back there. But he had. They’d both finally found what they’d been looking for when they first fell in love that summer in Cypress Landing.

* * * * *

Design Tip of the Day

> Ambience is everything. Imagine eating a foie gras at a luncheonette counter or a side of coleslaw at Le Cirque. It's not a matter of food but one of atmosphere. Remember that when planning your dining room design.
>
> —Tips from *Teddi.com*

"Now that's the kind of man you should be looking for," my mother, the self-appointed keeper of my shelf-life stamp, says. She points with her fork at a man in the corner of the Steak-Out Restaurant, a dive I've just been hired to redecorate. Making this restaurant look four-star will be hard, but not half as hard as getting through lunch without strangling the woman across the table from me. "*He* would make a good husband."

"Oh, you can tell that from across the room?" I ask, wondering how it is she can forget that when we had trouble getting rid of my last husband, she shot him. "Besides being ten minutes away from death if he actually eats all that steak, he's twenty years too old for me and—shallow woman that I am—twenty pounds too heavy. Besides, I am *so* not looking for another husband here. I'm looking to design a new image for this place, looking for some sense of ambience, some feeling, something I can build a proposal on for them."

My mother studies the man in the corner, tilting her head, the better to gauge his age, I suppose. I think she's grimacing, but with all the Botox and Restylane injected into that face, it's hard to tell. She takes another bite of her steak salad, chews slowly so that I don't miss the fact that the steak is a poor cut and tougher than it should be. "You're concentrating on the wrong kind of proposal," she says finally. "Just look at this place, Teddi. It's a dive. There are hardly any other diners. What does *that* tell you about the food?"

"That they cater to a dinner crowd and it's lunchtime," I tell her.

I don't know what I was thinking bringing her here with me. I suppose I thought it would be better than eating alone. There really are days when my common sense goes on vacation. Clearly, this is one of them. I mean, really, did I not resolve less than three weeks ago that I would not let my mother get to me anymore?

What good are New Year's resolutions, anyway?

Mario approaches the man's table and my mother studies him while they converse. Eventually Mario leaves the table with a huff, after which the diner glances up and meets my mother's gaze. I think she's smiling at him. That or she's got indigestion. They size each other up.

I concentrate on making sketches in my notebook and try to ignore the fact that my mother is flirting. At nearly seventy, she's developed an unhealthy interest in members of the opposite sex to whom she isn't married.

According to my father, who has broken the TMI rule and given me Too Much Information, she has no interest in sex with him. Better, I suppose, to be clued in on what they aren't doing in the bedroom than have to hear what they might be doing.

"He's not so old," my mother says, noticing

that I have barely touched the Chinese chicken salad she warned me not to get. "He's got about as many years on you as you have on your little cop friend."

She does this to make me crazy. I know it, but it works all the same. "Drew Scoones is not my little 'friend.' He's a detective with whom I—"

"Screwed around," my mother says. I must look shocked, because my mother laughs at me and asks if I think she doesn't know the "lingo."

What I thought she didn't know was that Drew and I actually tangled in the sheets. And, since it's possible she's just fishing, I sidestep the issue and tell her that Drew is just a couple of years younger than me and that I don't need reminding. I dig into my salad with renewed vigor, determined to show my mother that Chinese chicken salad in a steak place was not the stupid choice it's proving to be.

After a few more minutes of my picking at the wilted leaves on my plate, the man my mother has me nearly engaged to pays his bill and heads past us toward the back of the restaurant. I watch my mother take in his shoes, his suit and the diamond pinkie ring that seems to be cutting off the circulation in his little finger.

"Such nice hands," she says after the man is out of sight. "Manicured." She and I both stare at my hands. I have two popped acrylics that are being held on at weird angles by bandages. My cuticles are ragged and there's marker decorating my right hand from measuring carelessly when I did a drawing for a customer.

Twenty minutes later she's disappointed that he managed to leave the restaurant without our noticing. He will join the list of the ones I let get away. I will hear about him twenty years from now when—according to my mother—my children will be grown and I will still be single, living pathetically alone with several dogs and cats.

After my ex, that sounds good to me.

The waitress tells us that our meal has been taken care of by the management and, after thanking Mario, the owner, complimenting him on the wonderful meal and assuring him that once I have redecorated his place people will be flocking here in droves (I actually use those words and ignore my mother when she rolls her eyes), my mother and I head for the restroom.

My father—unfortunately not with us today—has the patience of a saint. He got it over the years of living with my mother. She, perhaps as a result, figures he has the patience for both of them, and feels justified having none. For her, no rules apply, and a little thing like a picture of a man on the door to a public restroom is certainly no barrier to using the john. In all fairness, it does seem silly to stand and wait for the ladies' room if no one is using the men's room.

Still, it's the idea that rules don't apply to her, signs don't apply to her, conventions don't apply to her. She knocks on the door to the men's room. When no one answers she gestures to me to go in ahead. I tell her that I can certainly wait for the ladies' room to be free and she shrugs and goes in herself.

Not a minute later there is a bloodcurdling scream from behind the men's room door.

"Mom!" I yell. "Are you all right?"

Mario comes running over, the waitress on his heels. Two customers head our way while my mother continues to scream.

I try the door, but it is locked. I yell for her to open it and she fumbles with the knob. When she finally manages to unlock and open it, she is white behind her two streaks of blush, but she is on her feet and appears shaken but not stirred.

"What happened?" I ask her. So do Mario and the waitress and the few customers who have migrated to the back of the place.

She points toward the bathroom and I go in, thinking it serves her right for using the men's room. But I see nothing amiss.

She gestures toward the stall, and, like any self-respecting and suspicious woman, I poke the door open with one finger, expecting the worst.

What I find is worse than the worst.

The husband my mother picked out for me is sitting on the toilet. His pants are puddled around his ankles, his hands are hanging at his sides. Pinned to his chest is some sort of Health Department certificate.

Oh, and there is a large, round, bloodless bullet hole between his eyes.

Four Nassau County police officers are securing the area, waiting for the detectives and crime scene personnel to show up. They are trying, though not very hard, to comfort my mother, who in another era would be considered to be suffering from the vapors. Less tactful in the twenty-first century, I'd say she was losing it. That is, if I didn't know her better, know she was milking it for everything it was worth.

My mother loves attention. As it begins to flag, she swoons and claims to feel faint. Despite four No Smoking signs, my mother insists it's all right for her to light up because, after all, she's in shock. Not to mention that signs, as we know, don't apply to her.

When asked not to smoke, she collapses mournfully in a chair and lets her head loll to the side, all without mussing her hair.

Eventually, the detectives show up to find the four patrolmen all circled around her, debating whether to administer CPR, smelling salts or simply call the paramedics. I, however, know just what will snap her to attention.

"Detective Scoones," I say loudly. My mother parts the sea of cops.

"We have to stop meeting like this," he says lightly to me, but I can feel him checking me over with his eyes, making sure I'm all right while pretending not to care.

"What have you got in those pants?" my mother asks him, coming to her feet and staring at his crotch accusingly. "*Baydar?* Everywhere we Bayers are, you turn up. You don't expect me to buy that this is a coincidence, I hope."

Drew tells my mother that it's nice to see her, too, and asks if it's his fault that her daughter seems to attract disasters.

Charming to be made to feel like the bearer of a plague.

He asks how I am.

"Just peachy," I tell him. "I seem to be making a habit of finding dead bodies, my mother is driving me crazy and the catering hall I booked two freakin' years ago for Dana's bat mitzvah has just been shut down by the Board of Health!"

"Glad to see your luck's finally changing," he says, giving me a quick squeeze around the shoulders before turning his attention to the patrolmen, asking what they've got, whether they've taken any statements, moved anything, all the sort of stuff you see on TV, without any of the drama. That is, if you don't count my mother's threats to faint every few minutes when she senses no one's paying attention to her.

Mario tells his waitstaff to bring everyone espresso, which I decline because I'm wired enough. Drew pulls him aside and a minute later I'm handed a cup of coffee that smells divinely of Kahlúa.

The man knows me well. Too well.

His partner, whom I've met once or twice, says he'll interview the kitchen staff. Drew asks Mario if he minds if he takes statements from the patrons first and gets to him and the waitstaff afterward.

"No, no," Mario tells him. "Do the patrons first." Drew raises his eyebrow at me like he wants to know if I get the double entendre. I try to look bored.

"What is it with you and murder victims?" he asks me when we sit down at a table in the corner.

I search them out so that I can see you again, I almost say, but I'm afraid it will sound desperate instead of sarcastic.

My mother, lighting up and daring him with a look to tell her not to, reminds him that *she* was the one to find the body.

Drew asks what happened *this time.* My mother tells him how the man in the john was "taken" with me, couldn't take his eyes off me and blatantly flirted with both of us. To his credit, Drew doesn't laugh, but his smirk is undeniable to the trained eye. And I've had my eye trained on him for nearly a year now.

"While he was noticing you," he asks me, "did *you* notice anything about him? Was he waiting for anyone? Watching for anything?"

I tell him that he didn't appear to be waiting or watching. That he made no phone calls, was fairly intent on eating and did, indeed, flirt with my mother. This last bit Drew takes with a grain of salt, which was the way it was intended.

"And he had a short conversation with Mario," I tell him. "I think he might have been unhappy with the food, though he didn't send it back."

Drew asks what makes me think he was dissatisfied, and I tell him that the discussion seemed acrimonious and that Mario looked distressed when he left the table. Drew makes a note and says he'll look into it and asks about anyone else in the restaurant. Did I see anyone who didn't seem to belong, anyone who was watching the victim, anyone looking suspicious?

"Besides my mother?" I ask him, and Mom huffs and blows her cigarette smoke in my direction.

I tell him that there were several deliveries, the kitchen staff going in and out the back door to grab a smoke. He stops me and asks what I was doing checking out the back door of the restaurant.

Proudly—because, while he was off forgetting me, dropping by only once in a while to say hi to Jesse, my son, or drop something by for one of my daughters that he thought they might like, I was getting on with my life—I tell him that I'm decorating the place.

He looks genuinely impressed. "Commercial customers? That's great," he says. Okay, that's what he *ought* to say. What he actually says is "Whatever pays the bills."

"Howard Rosen, the famous restaurant critic, got her the job," my mother says. "You met him—the good-looking, distinguished gentleman with the *real* job, something to be proud of. I guess you've never read his reviews in *Newsday*."

Drew, without missing a beat, tells her that Howard's reviews are on the top of his list, as soon as he learns how to read.

"I only meant—" my mother starts, but both of us assure her that we know just what she meant.

"So," Drew says. "Deliveries?"

I tell him that Mario would know better than I, but that I saw vegetables come in, maybe fish and linens.

"This is the second restaurant job Howard's got her," my mother tells Drew.

"At least she's getting *something* out of the relationship," he says.

"If he were here," my mother says, ignoring the insinuation, "he'd be comforting her instead of interrogating her. He'd be making sure we're both all right after such an ordeal."

"I'm sure he would," Drew agrees, then

looks me in the eyes as if he's measuring my tolerance for shock. Quietly he adds, "But then maybe he doesn't know just what strong stuff your daughter's made of."

It's the closest thing to a tender moment I can expect from Drew Scoones. My mother breaks the spell. "She gets that from me," she says.

Both Drew and I take a minute, probably to pray that's all I inherited from her.

"I'm just trying to save you some time and effort," my mother tells him. "My money's on Howard."

Drew withers her with a look and mutters something that sounds suspiciously like "fool's gold." Then he excuses himself to go back to work.

I catch his sleeve and ask if it's all right for us to leave. He says sure, he knows where we live. I say goodbye to Mario. I assure him that I will have some sketches for him in a few days, all the while hoping that this murder doesn't cancel his redecorating plans. I need the money desperately, the alternative being borrowing from my parents and being strangled by the strings.

My mother is strangely quiet all the way to her house. She doesn't tell me what a loser Drew Scoones is—despite his good looks—and how I was obviously drooling over him.

She doesn't ask me where Howard is taking me tonight or warn me not to tell my father about what happened because he will worry about us both and no doubt insist we see our respective psychiatrists.

She fidgets nervously, opening and closing her purse over and over again.

"You okay?" I ask her. After all, she's just found a dead man on the toilet, and tough as she is that's got to be upsetting.

When she doesn't answer me I pull over to the side of the road.

"Mom?" She refuses to meet my eyes. "You want me to take you to see Dr. Cohen?"

She looks out the window as if she's just realized we're on Broadway in Woodmere. "Aren't we near Marvin's Jewelers?" she asks, pulling something out of her purse.

"What have you got, Mother?" I ask, prying open her fingers to find the murdered man's ring.

"It was on the sink," she says in answer to my dropped jaw. "I was going to get his name and address and have you return it to him so that he could ask you out. I thought it was a sign that the two of you were meant to be together."

"He's dead, Mom. You understand that, right?" I ask. You never can tell when my mother is fine and when she's in la-la land.

"Well, I didn't know that," she shouts at me. "Not at the time."

I ask why she didn't give it to Drew, realize that she wouldn't give Drew the time in a clock shop and add, "...or one of the other policemen?"

"For heaven's sake," she tells me. "The man is dead, Teddi, and I took his ring. How would that look?"

Before I can tell her it looks just the way it is, she pulls out a cigarette and threatens to light it.

"I mean, really," she says, shaking her head like it's my brains that are loose. "What does he need with it now?"

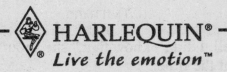

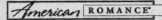

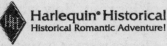

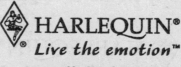

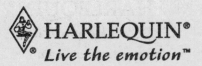

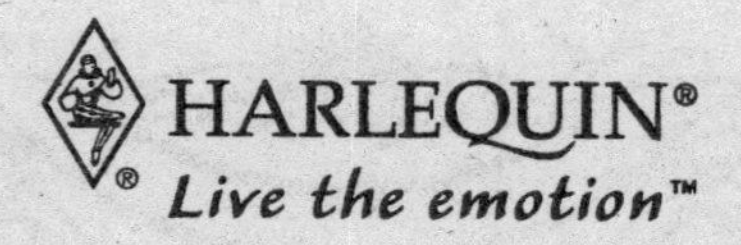
HARLEQUIN®
Live the emotion™

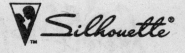